ACCIDENTAL ASSASSIN

ACCIDENTAL ASSASSIN

The Multi-Cultural Adventures of
Nshila Ileloka

Chris Elgood

Book Guild Publishing
Sussex, England

First published in Great Britain in 2006 by
Book Guild Publishing
25 High Street
Lewes, East Sussex
BN7 2LU

Typesetting in Baskerville by
Keyboard Services, Luton, Bedfordshire

Printed in Great Britain by
Antony Rowe Ltd, Chippenham, Wiltshire

A catalogue record for this book is available from
The British Library

ISBN 1 84624 001 8

FOR DELISE

A bit from here and a bit from there:
People and places snatched out of air.
A bit from then and a bit from now:
Composite characters taking a bow.
Traits that are fiction and traits that are true:
Mixed to conceal those traits that are you.

Contents

Prologue

Men Gazing

There's an alcove between the lift and the stairs in the foyer of the Galaxy Hotel. Three young men sat there. It was Friday evening, and the hotel was a place favoured by smart women. The trio liked watching the show.

'Have we finished fantasising, then? Geoff rates the baby-faced one with long blonde hair over in the corner. David goes for the statuesque black-haired receptionist. I like the one with the long legs and the mini-skirt who was bending forward to read from the menu stand just now.'

'That was the score till sixty seconds ago, Gary. Do you see the one who has just come in? She's talking to the Head Porter.'

'You mean the black girl?'

'Yes. Surely she's got to be Number One?'

'Don't agree. She looks unresponsive. I like them with some of the old "come hither" in their attitude. A bit inviting.'

'It's about taste, isn't it? For me that hint of aloofness is a turn-on. And how many women does the Head Porter here treat with real respect? Sure, he greets them all and makes polite comments, but those two have been talking for more than a minute.'

'All right, David. Let's do an inventory. About five foot

1

ten. Slender. Expensive clothes. Can't judge her legs because she's wearing knee-high boots. A three-inch heel on them. Upright carriage. Leather gloves. What else?'

'Very black skin colour, but more Arab than Bantu so far as her face goes. Straight hair, too, piled on her head. Makes her look a bit taller. Impressive, I agree. And now I look more closely I see what you mean about the expensive clothes. Modest size of handbag, too. Not one of those coal sack things most women carry around with them.'

'Yes, the colours, too. All black, except for that bright yellow blouse. The image fits together. It sort of makes a statement, doesn't it? Like "I can get everything right, all the time". Is that what you mean?'

'More or less. She's at the desk now. In a moment she'll probably walk down to the bar.'

The three men watched as the black girl covered the twenty paces or so between the reception desk and the bar. They noticed that the eyes of other men followed her, too. When she was sitting on a bar stool with her back to them, David spoke again.

'Anything more to say?'

'There's something special in how she walks. Most beautiful women walk self-consciously. It's as if they were saying "You really are looking at me, aren't you?" She seems quite unaware of watching eyes. Sort of not giving a damn either way. Totally confident.'

'She certainly has style. But I find her a bit scary.'

'Smart of you, Gary. She is. Very pleasant and polite in normal circumstances, but you always feel something powerful, almost animal, under the surface.'

'Do you know her, then, David?'

'Not well. But she's friendly with Mike Fanshawe who works with me in the city. She once came with him to a party and he introduced us. We didn't talk long and I

2

don't suppose she remembered me. But there was an incident. It was a party for youngish people in the financial services industry and there was a lot of boasting about salaries and bonuses. Somebody said something more than usually stupid and she really cut him to pieces.'

'Where does she come from?'

'Mike told me it was somewhere in Central Africa. There's some connection with witchdoctors and rain-making and magic.'

'She must have had an interesting journey from a mud hut out there to walking around the Galaxy Hotel as if she owned it!'

Chapter One

How it Began

Mike Fanshawe has told me several times that his friends like speculating about me. I don't remember that scene in the Galaxy Hotel, but obviously I was doing my Witch Queen act. I drop into it naturally when I am feeling good about myself, but I have other images, too. Everybody does, depending on what they are doing and the people they are with. Some of mine are very much down-market and more Oxfam than Harrods. The first image of all was the near-naked little girl playing in the dirt outside my mother's hut. That's a long way from the Galaxy Hotel.

Where do I start my story? Well, first of all I will make sure you get my name right. I don't want you mispronouncing it in your mind or showing your ignorance if you speak it aloud. It begins with the N-sound that you make by putting your tongue just behind your upper front teeth. If you do that firmly you will get a faint tingling in your nose. Then the 'SHILA' is just like the girl's Christian name in English. So we have 'N – shila'. The surname is four separate syllables – 'EE – LAY – LOW – KA'. Try it a few times and you will find Nshila Ileloka coming readily on your tongue. As to the beginning of my story, I am going for the day that old Kwaname lost his apprentice. Amos and Job were on the river in a canoe. Somewhere or other they had heard about

Europeans having boat races and they were experimenting with a time trial. Job had sold some cow hides to the trading post and bought an alarm clock with the pittance the trader gave him. Out on the river, they tried to get from one point to another in ten minutes. Their furious paddling made the canoe unstable, and then they hit a floating log. Both of them went into the water. Job survived but the crocodiles got Amos. It hit old Kwaname hard.

Kwaname had been our witchdoctor long before I was born. Some villagers must have known him when he was young, and watched him grow into the role, but people don't talk much about the witchdoctor in case he should hear them and take offence. They certainly don't talk about him to children, except to scare them. That works well, and caused me nightmares when I knew I had done wrong. What was he really like?

You have to picture a tall thin black man with a lot of fuzzy white hair. He was reputed to have considerable wealth hidden away in charm-defended locations, mainly in European currencies. Wealth in our tribe usually came from cattle and was flaunted by being fat. Kwaname was not so. In fact his ribs showed clearly through his skin. Maybe he was not rich after all, but everybody believed it, and the children told each other stories about places where he had been seen and where his hoard might be buried. His hair was striking. Europeans are sometimes surprised by the fact that African men get grey-headed with age just like whites. Perhaps this is because life expectancy amongst the tribes is lower, and fewer people get to be really old. Kwaname's hair was white and plentiful.

Kwaname did not work: not in the ordinary way. He never grew crops and never hunted or fished and never built a hut. His food was provided for him by the villagers, as was the limited amount of clothing you need in that climate and huge quantities of cheap tobacco for his pipe.

He spent the better part of the day sitting at the door of his hut under the baobab tree, watching the life of the village and smoking the pipe and dozing. He normally looked rather dirty, and he always smelt of the terrible substances used in his witchcraft. His expression was harsh and forbidding: children ran away from him and adults passed quickly with downcast eyes. Yet on some special days he looked different. Years ago somebody had stolen, or been given, a white uniform designed for a colonial administrator. This had found its way to Kwaname's hut, and when the mood took him he would parade around in all-white splendour. On those days he was far more approachable and would offer a spontaneous greeting to those he passed. Nobody knew when or why such days would happen. Attached to the sleeve of the jacket was a small square of yellow cloth with special marks on it. We all thought this was a charm of great power given to Kwaname by the spirits. Much later in life I realised that it was a laundry tag, suggesting that the uniform, had not been worn by its owner since cleaning, but had been liberated on its way back from the city. When the needs of the tribe demanded it, or Kwaname had some special purpose, he would appear in council in full witchdoctor's regalia: animal skins, a huge beehive-shaped hat, a necklace of bones and a fierce mask. Not much of his body was visible, but you could tell it was Kwaname himself by his feet. Years ago he had dropped something heavy on his right big toe. It was bent upwards in an extraordinary manner.

When not sitting immobile in front of his hut, or masquerading as a white colonialist, he would walk away from the village in one direction and return to it in the evening from another. Sometimes people would come upon him during the day, talking to himself in a strange language. All reports of such sightings described him as

7

sitting down: none described him as walking. There were two explanations: either he flew between different points or else it was not Kwaname who had been seen at all, but his ghost. If it was his ghost, then the real Kwaname was doing magical business elsewhere.

What were his thoughts on the day Amos died? In the years that followed I came to know him well enough to make a guess. He would have been sitting inside the door of his hut, just beyond the fall of the sunlight, scowling at the outer world. He would probably have been muttering to himself: engaging in one of those long soliloquies from which I later learnt so much.

'Bad. Bad. Bad! Why do people bother me with stupid talking when I have lost Amos? That idiot pair Nehanda and Mudiwa have asked me for a pregnancy charm. Another day I might have helped them. Right now I am so mad that I promised them a difficult birth, only successful if they gave up eating mangoes. They love mangoes. They are going to be miserable: and their husbands, too. Ha!'

'Amos. Amos. Why does it bug me so? I don't really need an apprentice. I have ten years left in me and I can do the job on my own. And in ten years' time the world will have so changed that nobody wants a witchdoctor any more! Already people go to the mission station to watch the television – and even believe what it tells them. I am an endangered species, that's what I am. I don't like it. My father Bwalya, his father Kasote, his father Mateti, and his father Kaunda, back as far as tribal memory goes. All of us skilled witchdoctors, rain-makers and so on. Why must I be the last?'

Kwaname would not move much during the soliloquy. But at intervals he would take his pipe from his mouth,

8

clear his throat and spit vigorously out of the door. 'Amos. I liked the lad. That's the truth. Why did I like him? He was learning: he really was. He wanted to know why things happen and what a craftsman can to do make them happen in the right way. He asked smart questions, but he was ready to do what I told him. And he was useful. I could send him on errands and he would get it right. He would find the right thing, or speak the right words, or find out how things really were rather than accept what the first person told him. His questions often made me remember things I had forgotten.

'Stomach cramp. That's the answer. Really nasty stomach cramp for that idiot Job who was in the canoe with Amos. I can't kill him. We would lose two able-bodied young men instead of one. And the thing was a mistake anyway, not deliberate. Two boastful young men messing around on the water. I can't kill him. But three weeks of watching him in agony will make me feel better.

'But it won't bring Amos back. What am I going to do? I don't need an apprentice, but I have grown used to it. Most old witchdoctors have one. I don't like being lonely. I don't like thinking of all the knowledge that will die with me. But a new one would just remind me of Amos. I liked him. I really did. I must be getting old. I need a mug of beer.'

I was years 9 years old at that time: the only daughter of the chief's youngest wife. My status in the household was almost zero, though in the tribe generally I was respected because of my father. He had three sons by his first wife, no children by his second and just me by his third. It was not a happy family. As the mother of three sons the first wife had a lot of power, but she was getting old and bad-tempered. The second wife lived in a state

9

of perpetual misery because she had no children. She had, I was told, been extremely harsh to my mother when the chief married her, though the relationship had improved by the time I became aware of it. She clearly felt that my mother, having only a daughter, had not done much better than she had. Of the children by the senior wife, Masuko, the eldest, was away at a secondary school in the city. The second and third sons were four and three years older than me and had no time for girls at all. Their names were Ndoro and Shumba.

All over the world a younger sister is an annoyance to growing boys, especially if she has no playmates of her own.

'Can I come with you?'

'No. You'll only get in the way. And girls can't do the things we are going to do.'

'What is it you are going to do? I bet I can do it. I'll try really hard.'

'Just shut up. We don't want you. Go and play at cooking mealies.'

'I know where you are off to. You're going to hide in the bushes and throw stones at the cattle so that poor old Chipako gets worn out chasing after them. That's really mean. You're not allowed to do it.'

'Shut up, Nshila. And don't try following us and don't tell tales about us.'

When the boys turn her away, the younger sister sometimes turns to her mother for support. If the mother really wants the girl out of her hair she says: 'You must take her with you, and look after her.' That's a double whammy for the boys: if they look after her, they can't do anything dangerous or exciting. If they do those anyway, they risk the girl telling on them. She is a drag or a security risk, or both.

It was worse for me, because I was an unusual child.

I was precocious and articulate and already the signs of psychic gifts were showing. I saw things. They were only the briefest flashes and disappeared when I shook my head. I quickly forgot them, presumably because they frightened me. But later on the adults might be talking about something and I would make a comment, quite without thinking, which made them wonder where my words came from. Here's an example. They were talking about two places at the river where canoes were normally beached. Somebody said. 'Mine is at the place where the blue gums come down to the river.' I said, 'A branch has fallen from the biggest one.' Dead silence. A branch had indeed fallen from the biggest one, but only that day. How could I possibly have known? I was unable to explain, and I had not been outside the village for any substantial time that day. I could not have seen it. The obvious answer was that Ndoro and Shumba had told me. They were asked if they had been to the place. They denied it. They were not believed. They were punished for lying. They found ways to take it out on me.

Knowledge sometimes came to me in this way, but much more came from the ordinary human actions of watching and listening and thinking. I noticed things. I noticed who went off in which direction, and when they came back, and in what mood they came back and what, if anything, they brought with them. It was not hard to figure out that Mutale was the best hunter amongst us. It was no more difficult to deduce that Shalo was dead lazy, going off to the fields in a determined manner, stopping beside a tree to pick up his hidden tins of beer, and staggering back with glazed eyes just after noon.

Naturally, I spent a lot of time with the women, doing the simple tasks that were assigned to me like fetching water and sweeping the hut and pounding mealie meal – very feebly, and only until my mother took over. All

11

the time, I listened to the gossip and fitted it together with bits and pieces from other sources. I realised early on that most of the things men believe to be secret are well known to their wives.

Because of their nastiness to me, I watched Ndoro and Shumba carefully. I listened to their talk. I pieced together what they were doing and – since they were normal healthy boys – much of it was forbidden. It was not quite blackmail, for I could not have said, 'If you don't do what I want I shall tell father.' I seldom got near enough to father to tell him anything, and if I had he would have seen me as a worse evil-doer than the boys. But I fixed things so that he found out.

The boys knew, of course, and it did not help too much. Their response varied between the punishment of quite heavy violence and the reward of being used as a look-out and early warning. As far as other children were concerned, being friends with the daughter of the chief was something to be undertaken with care. If those children sought friendship, that was OK, but if I made advances towards them, these were met with suspicion. I made little attempt to build such relationships because I never felt I had much to offer.

So perhaps I was not a very likeable child. Intelligent, watchful, secretive and sometimes sneaky. The only person for whom I felt genuine friendship was the eldest son, Masuko. I owe him a great deal. He now teaches science at a fee-paying school in Margate and I visit him whenever I can face that dreary train journey to the extremes of East Kent. He liked me. Why? Maybe because he was clever and determined and he saw the same qualities in me. Maybe, also, he was just coming to realise how far such qualities could take one in the world now opening up. Maybe, also, he found me a welcome contrast to his two brothers whom he thought of as ignorant thugs. A significant part of his school holidays was given up to study, and at 9 years old – doing well at our primary school and especially good at English – I was just old enough to help him. For instance, I knew what a play was and I knew about learning lines and I could read adequately.

'Nshila, will you help me with my lines? We are doing some scenes from Macbeth at a drama competition next term and I am going to be Banquo. Here's the book. Read me the bit where Macbeth can't figure out why the witches are calling him Thane of Cawdor, and even king.'

I stumbled through to '. . . such prophetic greeting? Speak, I charge you'.

Masuko looked all round him in surprise and came out with: 'The earth hath bubbles, as the water has, and these are of them: whither are they vanished?'

That bit lost me completely. I had to ask what he was doing. (In fact Masuko often spent as much time answering my questions as reciting his lines.)

'Why all the business of looking around you?'

'Read the stage directions, Nshila. If the book says "Witches vanish" I've got to look surprised, and wonder where they have gone to.'

'Oh. Yes.'

At the time of this play-reading practice I had just begun my acquaintanceship with Kwaname and people who vanished were intriguing. I was also very interested in 'the insane root that takes the reason prisoner' a few lines later. Masuko found it hard to satisfy my curiosity. And I was sometimes inadequate as well as over-curious. Plenty of times I had to say 'I can't read this word. It looks like so-and-so. What does it mean?' But I was certainly the best helper he could find in the village, and he used me again and again for the play, and for other subjects he had to fix in his memory. I think the challenge of explaining things to another person helped him to get a better grasp of them in his own mind. I learnt a great deal from him. Much of it stuck in my memory. It brought me little reward at the time, but my excellent memory is a big asset today.

One day I said something that made Ndoro lose his temper with me in a big way. He had been at his nastiest all day and to score a point for myself I showed that I knew where he had been the afternoon before – spying lustfully on the twin daughters of Gilbert Chilufya. I was lucky to be a hundred yards away from him when I called the names over my shoulder, for he came after me fast and I felt really, really scared. I was quite quick at that age (I still am – I have run in the London Marathon for the past three years) but an angry 13-year-old boy can quickly overhaul a 9-year-old girl.

Where to seek refuge? The area round an African village is not like an English town. It has no side streets or alleyways: no dark doorways where you can hide: no buses you can jump on at the last minute: no taxis appearing conveniently with their flags up. Nothing except scrub. I ran, but I ran in fear.

Was I right to be afraid? Certainly. Ndoro in a temper would hurt me badly. He did not have steel-toed boots like an English thug but he would probably grab a stick from a nearby bush and hit hard enough to break something.

Help! Where to go? It's desperate! He's gaining! And then I realised I was near the baobab tree under which was Kwaname's hut. It had been there from the moment I started running, but I had never thought about it because nobody, nobody at all, went to Kwaname's hut without proper ceremony. And no child could possibly go there at any time. Well, I did not have time to speculate on what Kwaname might or might not do to me, and whatever

14

it might be, there would be a small delay. If Ndoro caught me it was instant, certain, severe pain.

I dived through the door, fell on my face and gasped something like 'Help me, sir!'

Things got very confused. Kwaname was facing away from the entrance and studying his appearance in a big broken mirror. The hut was dark, but I could see that much from my position on the floor because the mirror was opposite the open door. I don't think Kwaname saw me straight away, being startled by the noise of the door and the bright light beyond it. Evidently, he thought the cause of the disturbance was outside the hut and he rushed out to confront it.

I had just seen this tall figure looking in a mirror. What I did not know was why he had been so engrossed. In fact he had just made some improvements to one of his devil masks and was studying the effect. So when he rushed out of the hut, Ndoro got the full blast of an angry witchdoctor in full regalia. He ran. Fast. He also tripped over a fallen branch and landed face-down in some cow dung.

So when Kwaname re-entered the hut he was in good humour. He took off the devil mask, which restricted his vision, and saw me grovelling on the floor. He realised what had happened, and since I had unwittingly provided him with a satisfying experience he treated me kindly. He gave me something to drink – it tasted foul but I dared not refuse it – and talked to me a bit about what I had been doing to get into trouble. It went on from that, covering what sort of life I had and the relationships that existed in the Chief's hut. I can see now that he was pumping me for information, but at the time my relief at survival was so great that I noticed nothing else.

*   *   *

15

'Gutsy little kid, that!' Perhaps that's how Kwaname saw it. 'Seeking refuge in my hut was either very brave or very stupid. Everybody else – man or woman – would have preferred a serious beating to crossing my threshold. But she did not seem stupid: didn't cry or scream or cringe in the corner. Answered my questions quite intelligently, too. Knows a lot about what is going on around her. Observes things.'

My adventure was known soon enough. Before I got home, Ndoro had told the story and been beaten by my father for his part in my presumed death or transformation. I suppose they were pleased to see me, but they showed it by harsh words and punishments. That was fortunate, because by the time they had cooled down enough to let me explain, I had thought out what to say. It did not seem wise to suggest I had enjoyed the experience in any way. I told them I had been so terrified that I remembered little except his shouts and screams and the chanting of a spell. That left them worried, but uncertain. The consensus seemed to be 'Take no action, but watch her carefully and hope she does not fall sick'.

I faked a few complaints over the next few days, mainly to get sympathy and identity myself as a victim. In fact I felt perfectly well and as the days went by I became inwardly excited by my unique position. Few people had been into that hut and suffered no harm. Perhaps there was something special about me.

Chapter Two

The Hut under the Baobab Tree

I could not resign myself to doing nothing at all. A month later I began to pass closer than usual to the hut, and even linger a bit on my way, much as a girl does when she wants to attract a man's attention. It worked. There came a day when he was sitting in the doorway of his hut, and he crooked a finger at me. It was one single gesture, no part of his body or his face moving at all – only that one finger beckoning – once. But it was firm and obvious enough. I walked slowly towards him. He was immobile till I was a few feet in front of him and bowed my head. 'Nshila,' he said, and motioned me to sit behind him, just inside his hut.

After that nothing. Absolutely nothing for forty minutes with the tension building up inside me. Did I speak to him? Did I cough to gain his attention? Did I run away? Was he even awake? Was he in a trance? Was he communing with the spirits? Then, suddenly, he was pointing and asking, 'Where's he going?' It was Kapepwe, passing down behind the blue gums towards the low creek. 'He's going to spend an hour mending his canoe,' I said. 'He's supposed to be looking after the cattle, but he's sneaking off to the derelict canoe he hopes to repair. He can't get the loan of his father's canoe and he wants one so badly that he's got this secret project. He hopes that nobody

17

else knows about it. I know, but he doesn't know that I know.'

I went to the hut at irregular intervals after that, being careful that nobody saw me. Each time, I now realise, Kwaname was using me as a source of information. How did he see the relationship?

'No, of course not. Not an apprentice!' He would have scorned that idea. 'Who ever heard of a girl being taken on? But she's sharp and she's useful. I really like somebody who has brains and imagination. And apart from me, she is not scared of anybody. They all like to puff themselves up and show how strong and brave and clever they are, but she sees their failings as well as their strengths. There's no harm in letting her call, and talking to her.'

The relationship developed, as the papers in this country say. It got about that I sometimes visited him, and people eventually got used to it. After all, I was the Chief's daughter, and I was an odd girl anyway, and a girl could never be a danger to anyone, could she? Old Kwaname never used the word 'apprentice', but over the span of two years I picked up far more than an official apprentice might have done. I was smart and I was interested, and I watched and I listened. Probably I learnt more than Kwaname consciously taught me. And I did not make any stupid mistakes like that boy in the tale called 'The Sorcerer's Apprentice'. I never showed off my knowledge, because boastful girls were quickly punished in the tribe. Also, I never wanted to harm anybody. My interest was academic, if you can use that word of a child still at primary school. I simply liked to work out how one thing caused another. I still do.

I was unconsciously deceiving Kwaname about the knowledge I was picking up. Or perhaps I was letting him deceive himself. But he was also deceiving me, and using me. He got lots of useful information through me, and at times he used me to leak his own ideas into the tribe. I frequently had vivid dreams, and Kwaname encouraged me to describe them because he thought they might reveal things from my subconscious. At times he would suggest that the dream had a meaning, and more than once he was right. One dream had included a man lying at the door of a hut screaming. In my dream the man had no identity, but Kwaname said, 'That sounds very much like Nkumbula.' He skilfully wove a story around my dream and had me believing that something nasty was going to happen to Nkumbula. 'Perhaps you should tell somebody about that dream,' he said. 'Nkumbula ought to be warned in some way.'

I did what he suggested. The person I told was Nkomo: harmless enough himself, but he spoke to others and soon the message was everywhere. And if something bad was going to happen to Nkumbula, where was it likely to come from? From the witchdoctor, of course. All over the world a close group like a tribe will have a rumour-mill. Things got exaggerated. Somebody remembered that Nkumbula had been very rude to Kwaname two years ago when the rains were poor. Somebody else had seen Kwaname digging clay from the banks of the old creek. Within two weeks everybody knew that Kwaname had made a clay model of Nkumbula and stuck pins in it. Nkumbula would be seriously ill.

Kwaname had! Nkumbula was! I did not know it at the time and I never faced the full reality till I was in one of those late-night arguments at university where you solve the problems of the world and the universe and everything. Kwaname had practised 'similarity magic' in which an event is acted out in ritual play and the corresponding real-life event happens to a living person. It is all psychological, of course. The person being attacked has to know that the attack is coming and has to believe that its success is inevitable. He then gets so worried and upset that he really does fall ill. But he has to know about the attack. If Kwaname had made an image and stuck pins in it and nobody had known what he had done, then Nkumbula would have felt nothing. Kwaname used me to make sure that people knew. There is a perfect parallel with the way government ministers in this country leak rumours to the media in order to manipulate public opinion. I don't suppose the Rt. Hon. Sir Edward Whotsit, Secretary of State for Whatever, thinks of himself as close kin to old Kwaname in the hut under the baobab tree; but he is so!

You must remember that I had an imperfect understanding of what was going on. I was at school, certainly, but primary school in those days in the remote African bush was not very sophisticated. I learnt to speak English and I learnt to read and write, and I learnt arithmetic and I knew stories from the Christian Bible, but all this was 'foreign knowledge' – quite different from what I absorbed from the tribal environment. In that environment illness and death were no big deal. They were never much of a surprise. They were cause for weeping and wailing, of course, but if they appeared natural then that was the end of it and life went on. So if old Kwaname caused a few deaths I was quite able to tell myself that maybe it was not really he that did it, or that the victim was not much use to the tribe anyway, or that it was an adult matter and if it was serious one of the adults would have taken action.

That's why I can't ever be sure whether Nshila Ileloka, the child, really killed Samuel Shonga. Kwaname was not the most skilled model-maker, and when he made a clay image it really could have been anybody of the appropriate sex. (He usually got that right.) So when Kwaname called to me to put my hand on a knife, then put his hand over mine and united us in skewering a rather ugly male image, I did not resist. As the knife went in I did hear the words 'So pass, Samuel, son of Kotane!' By that time the deed was done. I do know for certain that Samuel Shonga was stabbed to death by his wife three weeks later. Is that when my career started?

Chapter Three

Zach Kawero Reports

Nshila had told me to report to her in the Galaxy at 7 p.m. I got there about ten minutes past and saw her sitting at the bar, handing out polite put-downs to a city type on the next stool. She was clearly in Witch Queen mode, which is usually bad news. It makes her critical and bitchy. As I scrambled onto a stool and muttered an apology, the city type faded.

'You're late, Zach!'

'I'm sorry, Nshila. I had trouble parking the car.'

'You should have come by tube. You know it takes ages to park that tank your father gave you.'

'Yes, Nshila. I'm sorry.' It was not the moment to point out that her scarlet BMW is just as hard to park as my Mercedes.

'You know I hate sitting alone and having to fend off creatures like that.' She jerked her head to indicate her recent companion.

I thought that was pretty harsh on the poor unknown. He had looked quite presentable. Instead of him, she was side by side with me. I am often described as a tall black nerd with glasses. Sometimes they make it 'a tall, scruffy black nerd with glasses'. I don't think I do much for her image.

'Anyway, what have you got for me?'

I got my notes from my brief case. 'You asked for research on a man named Brad Pullinger. You wanted to know whether he was a fine upstanding citizen or not. The answer's clear. He is evil.'

'Give me the evidence then.'

'He is a top-flight con-artist who has caused a huge amount of suffering and distress. I have turned up four examples.' I gave her the first.

'Pullinger's first scam involved computing equipment. His targets were middle-aged people, trying to gain competence in a strange field. Pullinger bought stocks of unsold but outdated items. He re-packaged them and described them as having a higher capability than they possessed. Users found that they had to purchase numerous up-dates and modifications before the equipment could cope with present day demands.'

'That's nothing special,' said Nshila. 'I could name six computer firms that do much the same thing and call it "legitimate commercial practice".'

At that moment I dropped my briefcase, and papers spilled over the floor. I grubbed around to pick them up, murmuring apologies to the occupants of other bar stools. Nshila did nothing to help. When everything had been gathered up, including a packet of headache tablets and another of toothpicks, I addressed her again.

'Perhaps you're right, Nshila. My second case may be more convincing. Pullinger started selling dodgy electronic equipment into the medical field. This was not in Europe, but in third world countries where checks are less rigorous and you can often become an 'approved supplier' by bribery. People died because the equipment was out of action or malfunctioned. The wrong diagnosis was made, or the wrong quantity of drugs was given because the equipment's measuring devices were wrong.'

'Does that make him a high class evil-doer, Zach? Maybe

24

his customers were better off with his dodgy equipment that with none at all. You must do better.'

'Yes, Nshila.'

Are you getting the idea that I am scared of Nshila? Do you think I am wimpish? Well, you're right about being scared and you're wrong about wimpish. Anybody out of our dark continent is scared of witchcraft, and quite rightly so. I won't be able to convince any pig-ignorant European, but if you are Africa-born you will know what I mean. Witchdoctors have power, and Nshila has got it. I don't know how it came about – it's unusual in a woman – but it's there. More than that, since she came to this country she has made a study of witchcraft in England and grafted on a whole new skill set. You should hear her talking to that cat she calls Rasputin. It's a witch's familiar in the old tradition!

'Stop dreaming, Zach, and get on with your report. What was scam number three?'

'Pullinger got his hands on large quantities of older drugs, all made by reputable companies but now superseded in Europe and the USA. These were not harmful when properly used, but like many modern medicines there were conditions in which they were contra-indicated: there were words in the publicity that said something like "Not to be used by persons with a heart condition or any allergy". Pullinger substituted his own publicity. This made no reference to any side effects, listed more advantages, and suggested larger doses. Again, people died. The scam was eventually exposed. An experienced nurse in a Roman Catholic mission hospital found such drugs being pre-scribed inappropriately for a patient and made a powerful complaint. Pullinger managed to escape retribution by putting that particular company into liquidation.'

'Better, Zach. It's beginning to build up. Do you want a drink?'

Thankfully, I began to relax. I felt that the Witch Queen was beginning to ease up. Nshila turned to attract the barman and I reflected for a moment on how we had met. We had been doing an Open University MBA course and I was in a real panic about the final exams. My special skill is that I am an expert hacker: I was quite sure I could hack into the Open University computer in good time to study the exam paper and work up all the right answers. Now, this is the bit you really won't believe. They did not have any electronic version of the paper! How on earth can a reputable university be so antediluvian in its methods? Each professor wrote a question about three days before the exam, somebody put them together on an unlinked PC, and the paper was faxed to examination centres on the day of the exam!

It was terrible. I had done very little work, and it was my father who was paying for fees and subsistence – the lot. There would be the most awful consequences if I failed the exam and the news got back to him in Kano. Nshila was around when I was lamenting this, and a few days later she said: 'I might have a way to help you, Zach. Hacking isn't the only form of magic available'.

I have learnt that Nshila is dead crafty about her methods. She sees witchdoctoring as an uncertain science where the practitioner has limited control of the results. So she mixes it up with practical action. She does quite ordinary things side by side with the magical ones. With me to help, she used ordinary desk research and logic to check the incidence of questions in past papers. We found out who was setting the papers and what their interests were. We analysed what our lectures had covered and what projects we had been set. We made a short list of ten questions, reckoning that at least four would come up in one form or another and that four questions well answered would get a pass mark.

She then clammed up and said nothing for three days, before taking me at night to a disused cricket pavilion (pitch sold off to a developer). She had turned it into a temporary witchdoctor's domain and hung all the usual impedimenta on the walls (charms, bones and so on). One surprising feature was a plain white board of the type the OU has in its lecture rooms. The place was hot, and stank abominably. She dressed in her witchdoctor gear and did a Macbeth-type act with a cauldron. It was a fine mix of modern technology and ancient magic because the cauldron was heated from an LPG burner of the type you use for a barbecue. I have no idea what nasties were in the cauldron, but the smell was spicy and foul, and the surface of the liquid opaque and oily. I thought I saw some bones floating around in it, and an eye seemed to be watching me from the middle. It reflected things, although there was not much light in the place. Nshila made me smoke some sort of weed, smoked some herself, and commanded me to watch the cauldron while thinking hard about our lecturers. I don't remember too much after that, except that a lot of weird images flashed through my mind and Nshila moved round her cauldron stirring and muttering. I suspect she was in a trance.

We both lost consciousness, and must have been in that state for half an hour or so. When we recovered, Nshila immediately wrote seven questions on the white board. I wrote up two more. How did they come to me? Well, I realised that some symbols I had imagined in the liquid were actually the formula for discounted cash flow. I also remembered the face of one of our lecturers as it had been when she made a joke about statistics and sampling technique. I knew those subjects would come up.

So we had 19 questions. Eight of them came up in the exam. Six of those had come to us through the smoke of the cauldron and only two by logical research. I passed the exam with honours and my father gave me a Mercedes. I am scared of Nshila, but I am also very grateful. Nobody asked her to help me. It was unsolicited good will.

'Stop dreaming, Zach, and get on with your report.' I realised that the barman had placed our drinks in front of us and Nshila was getting impatient.

'Nshila, could we sit somewhere else for this next part? I've got a tape recording of Pullinger at work and we need some privacy.'

At a corner table, I explained that I had hacked into the systems of Pullmax Limited (his holding company) and investigated Pullinger's diary. It showed that he was due to meet a Mrs McAllister at Honeyridge Residential Home and there was a note in the diary 'approx. estate £2.5 million'. I had followed up the lead.

Con artists have been relieving old women of their savings for centuries, but he was bang up to date. The huge explosion of information we have suffered in recent times means that choosing is complicated and difficult. Years ago, as an old woman wanting your wealth to do some good after your death, you would have named a deserving local charity because you did not know much about any others. Today, your eyes and ears are assaulted by a great many charities competing for your money. They all present their cases aggressively, and you see television pictures of sickness and neglect and oppression and torture that they plan to alleviate. You are invited to make a donation by ringing a phone number immediately, and paying with a credit card. You are also made aware from other sources that much charitable giving gets diverted into the hands of crooked politicians and administrators.

Pullinger appeared to solve this problem through The Ethical Charities Evaluation Foundation, known as ECEF. Instead of worrying about how much to leave to Oxfam and how much to Save the Children and how much to

28

Amnesty International, the testator just left the entire sum to ECEF, trusting that delightful, considerate man Mr Pullinger to apportion it justly and effectively. It is true that he worked hard for his money. He spent a lot of time with each old lady and, while building up trust, gave sound advice about other aspects of their affairs. But the rewards he got from his investments were huge. One of the gems of his technique was to recognise the possibility of fraud and then impute it to other people. He would say:

'One way you can protect yourself is to insert a clause into your will that leaves the money to ECEF only if I am there to deal with it. You can say that if I die, or leave ECEF, then everything goes to just one charity, which you can choose now.'

In this way the old lady was putting her trust in that nice Mr Pullinger only, and avoiding all the sharks that lurked in the background.

I told Nshila that I had managed to get taken on as a handyman at the Honeyridge Residential Home and confirmed that Mrs Ethel McAllister was due to meet a visitor, Mr Pullinger, in Suite 3 of the visitors' wing at 2 p.m. on a certain day.

At that hour, in my role as handyman, I had grabbed some flowers from the pantry and marched boldly into Suite 3 to change the display. You can spin out an activity like this for as much as five minutes if you attempt an artistic job. That means, for instance, getting the new flowers nicely arranged and then deciding that some of them stand too high. Then you have to take the lot out and cut the bottom ends off the chosen ones with scissors. Then you re-arrange them all again. Then you spend time picking up the stems that you have discarded. I got a good look at Pullinger, but also, I am pleased to say, I heard a lot from Ethel McAllister. She was clearly not the sort of person who, when she had an audience, was going to stop singing her favourite song because some lowly servant was also in the room. The room itself was very ordinary. A typical place for occasional use, with tasteful but inexpensive decoration, a coffee table and four comfortable armchairs. The windows looked out onto the main driveway of the home.

I switched on the tape, and the classy, self-confident voice of Mrs McAllister came through. She had a distinct Scottish accent.

> I am a rich woman, Mr Pullinger. When I die there will be substantial sums left, I don't have any close relatives and some years ago I made up my mind that I would name some charities. Recently I have been disturbed by adverse reports on some of them. You know the sort of thing. A television channel sends an under-cover reporter to check out what is really going on, and then they make a programme that pillories the managers and trustees and employees and makes the whole thing look like a gigantic confidence trick. I heard a few days ago about a big-name charity that instructed staff to claim 'every penny goes to the right place' when the administrators knew quite well that this was not true.

As the words came from the tape, I remembered how Pullinger had nodded gravely to show his understanding.

> You are right that some charities have had adverse publicity recently, but only a minority, and we don't know for certain how serious it has been. Investigative reporters always have an agenda of their own and their findings are not totally reliable.

I could see Nshila listening carefully as she heard Pullinger speak for the first time. It was not at all the voice of a villain. It was a warm, deep voice, cultured and reassuring. He enunciated every word clearly, but was measured in his speech rather than slow. It was easy to listen to, easy to understand and carried no threat. Yet there was an undertone of power: a subtle suggestion that somebody so confident and knowledgeable ought not to be questioned too closely.

My memory flashed again. Mrs McAllister had seemed very determined to make her point, leaning forward and tapping Pullinger on the knee.

Perhaps. But some of the things that were said seem to have the ring of truth. It's said that some of them have got so big that their administrative expenses just grow and grow because the staff build themselves little empires exactly like industry and the civil service.

It can happen.

And then, some charities are better than others at getting the money to the right place and doing the right thing with it. I hear terrible stories about the money given for aid in Third World countries being passed to some government authority in the land concerned and disappearing into the pocket of a minister. I also hear of money being spent on advanced technology that will theoretically bring a benefit, but never does so because local people don't understand it and can't use it. You read about highly expensive equipment rusting to pieces.

The tape made a brief, loud screeching noise at that

point. I paused it to explain that I had moved a table without lifting it properly. Then Pullinger was heard again.

Mrs McAllister, I can't deny that such things happen. But a good proportion of the money does get through to those who need it, and is well used by them.

I paused the tape again. I told Nshila that Mrs McAllister had been very specific about her reasons for arranging the interview.

Mr Pullinger, I heard of your company when I was talking about the problem with some friends. It was said that you advised testators on the subject, and you responded to my enquiry. So far you have just defended the charities. Why is that?

Then Nshila interrupted and put her own finger on the pause button. She asked me, 'What was Pullinger like, physically?'

'Rather repulsive, I thought. He was in his early forties and had all the signs of a man who was good to look at when young and thinks it is still true. All over, he was that little bit too sleek and well-fed. The lines of his face were starting to blur, and a small roll of flesh showed over his collar, and his hair was a fashionable length but beginning to thin out. His hands were pudgy. His clothes were expensive and immaculate, but just a little too tight. I got the impression that he had told his tailor "You know my measurements. Just make one the same as last time".'

Nshila stared into the distance as if she was trying to picture Pullinger in her mind. Then she asked, 'Anything more?'

'You could smell him. The mixture was mostly cologne and after-shave with a hint of whisky and cigars. It was a smell of richness. It seemed to say "I couldn't possibly be after your money, could I? I am rich myself and don't need it." His speech was courteous, respectful and charming – but you would expect that since it was his chief weapon. I'll bet he was rather different when talking to his junior staff. I noticed that there was no hesitation in what he said and it seemed to be spontaneous. While he was speaking, it was actually true in his own mind. Such people can be in a different situation five minutes later, and conjure up a totally different image, and be just as convincing. But their belief lasts only as long as the conversation, and afterwards it's history. The contact goes away believing that a promise has been made while the words were only intended to convey sympathy and understanding.'

'Good enough, Zach. Start the tape again.'

We certainly do advise people, Mrs McAllister, but we don't see any of the charities as unworthy and we don't want to appear too critical of them. After all, it is a difficult thing to get right and mistakes are forgivable. But we do know them all very well and we have analysed their strengths and weaknesses. Testators often feel that if they can tell us in detail what causes they want to benefit, and in which countries, then our judgement about which charities to name is likely to be sound. It's true that in some cases we take charge of the money and pass it to the charities ourselves instead of just giving the testator our recommendations. It's not the best way from our point of view because it can expose us to critical comment. In fact, we actually charge a little bit more for that service than we do for advising only.

How does it work? I'm not in the position where a small extra charge is going to worry me.

Nshila stopped the tape. She said that Mrs McAllister seemed to view the extra charge in a positive light, perhaps taking it as evidence of Pullinger's credibility. Nshila also asked if I had still been in the room. I explained that I had left earlier, after hiding the recorder behind the flower vase. She pressed 'play' and heard Pullinger replying. He was now at his most confident.

The main feature is that you have to complete one of our questionnaires about the causes you want to assist, the places where you want your money to go, and any restrictions like maximum and minimum amounts.

I could do that easily.

There's a bit more. Believe it or not, we also ask you to write a small essay about what things you believe to be most important in life. It may seem an odd requirement, but sometimes when we have to choose between two equally worthy causes we like to ask 'What sort of person was the testator? How would she have judged?' We can't ask you the questions after you die, of course (*feeble laugh*), so we have to know something of your mind beforehand. Then you name ECEF in your will instead of the half-dozen other names you might put.

It strikes me as quite a convenient arrangement. You seem to be very careful about observing the testator's wishes.

There the tape ended. Nshila stood up, stretched, glanced round the room and sat down again. She thought for a minute, and asked, 'So she's still considering, is she? She has not yet signed anything?'

'Correct.'

'It adds up well enough, then, Zach. I shall know what to tell my client. You'll be sending me an invoice, I expect.'

I did not feel I needed to answer that one. But I had one thing more I believed I should tell her.

'Nshila, while I was working on this project I learnt that Pullinger is also an asset-stripper, using his holding company Pullmax Industries. He is one of those commercial criminals we studied in our MBA course. He does a great deal of harm that way. Do you want to hear about it?'

'Yes, I certainly do, but not now. Save it for another time. Go and buy us another drink.'

The serious part of our meeting was obviously over, and when I came back with a lager for me and a vodka for her, the climate was a social one.

I work for Nshila on a freelance basis. She became aware of my computer skills at the OU, and about a year after our graduation she started asking me to dig out information for her. That meant things that were personal and private, but dead easy for a skilled hacker to access. She paid well, and I found excitement in it. Then she started asking me for more general things, things that needed conventional research. I became skilled at that, too. I know how to locate sources and check their accuracy I am very useful to her. I don't ask any questions, but I can't help wondering about her projects. Is she some sort of high-class head-hunter who goes back to her client and says that a person is or is not right for the job? Is she carrying out research for a syndicate that specialises in blackmail, and pays huge sums for good-quality dirt? Is she checking out possible marriage partners for European royalty? I don't know. But in view of her special skills I wonder whether dark methods and dark ends are involved. I felt very uneasy when one of the people I researched for her met an unfortunate end a few months later. He attempted a simple repair to an electric toaster and was inexplicably electrocuted. Was she involved?

It's interesting that Nshila once told me I was into witchcraft just as much as she was. 'Look, Zach,' she said, 'whether you call it witchcraft or magic, it's only a matter of manipulating forces that you understand and other people don't. You can make pop-up messages appear on other people's computers, provided they are connected to the Internet. They have got no idea where the messages come from. To them, it's magic. To you it's computer science. Get it?'

I sometimes get to talk with Gillian Harker and Peter Grace, who work for her in The Rain Consultancy. That's a completely legitimate business that gives advice about the weather to people responsible for outdoor events. They work for her full-time and must know her reasonably well. But Gillian is totally absorbed in meteorology and notices nothing else. The only thing I got out of her is that she told one client to expect a bright sunny afternoon and Nshila over-ruled her, telling the client to expect a thunderstorm. Gillian could not understand why Nshila contradicted her – against all the available data – nor why there really was a thunderstorm. It never crossed Gillian's naïve mind that Nshila might have created the storm.

Peter Grace is a different matter, because he is country-bred, from one of the most traditional areas in England – Suffolk. He is fairly sure that Nshila uses some form of magic or witchcraft, but he likes Nshila and he likes his job, and country folk are reticent anyway.

I wonder whether I shall hear more of Pullinger.

Chapter Four

Love at the College

If I had stayed in the village and worked with old Kwaname would I have been his successor? I don't know. In one sense I later took on his role, but it was in an abnormal situation. Anyway, my time with him came to an end through one of those chance events that seem to have determined my life.

My eldest brother, Masuko, won the lottery. He was then in his last year at St Albans, which was the country's premier multi-racial boarding school.

The pupils were forbidden to play, of course, but the groundsman used to buy tickets on their behalf. Once Masuko had won, there was colossal pressure to let him keep the money. The headmaster, you see, was white. If he had stopped Masuko getting the money, Masuko being black and an academic star from a backward tribe, then the school and the headmaster would have been crucified. The final deal had three parts:

Masuko was to keep 70 per cent of the money.

20 per cent of the money was to be a gift from Masuko to the school.

10 per cent of the money was to buy full secondary education at the school for one of Masuko's relatives.

You have guessed it. After extended arguments, I was chosen. Masuko was vehement that his brothers lacked the brains to benefit from a European education – and neither of them much wanted it, anyway. Opposition to me was based on the appalling precedent of giving higher education to a woman. Things hung in the balance when I got my last gift from Kwaname. He let it be known that some nasty things would happen to the flocks and herds of anybody who deprived Nshila of this opportunity. Why did he do this? You would expect a witchdoctor to be ultra-traditionalist. I believe he was smart enough to know that the basis of all witchdoctoring – indeed all magic – is knowledge. He must have reasoned that if I returned to the craft, I would be a better practitioner with this huge new increment of knowledge. He might have been making what they call, at business school, an 'investment decision'. Thinking back, I believe that he was more worried than he ever showed about the invasion of European habits and was saying, in his own way, 'If you can't beat them, join them'.

I think kindly now of Kwaname, and see characteristics to admire. He did a necessary job and was a true professional. A tribe needs a witchdoctor. It needs somebody who is a store of knowledge, can communicate with the spirits, be a guardian of morality and can take unilateral action without endless formal meetings. In England, you still have a person called Archbishop of Canterbury, and one of his duties is to put the crown on the head of a new monarch – i.e. to legitimise the civil power. At times of crisis, such as a major disaster or a war, you set aside all the talk of being a 'post-Christian society' and rush to church to pray. Think of Kwaname in that light. He did his job well, and the outcome of his actions was almost always beneficial to the tribe. I think Kwaname got things right 80 per cent of the time. Such a person needs to be respected and feared, which demands savage behaviour from time to time. Being feared makes a person lonely, and I realised even when I was young that Kwaname was short of human contact. He was often angry, demanding, critical: seldom offering kind words. But his actions said something else. He never did anything cruel to me. He treated me as a thinking person – even when I was 9 years old. He gave me small gifts. He advised me, in a round-about way, how to behave myself in the harsh family environment. Perhaps the most important thing of all is that he never turned me away. If he was busy, he pointed to a corner of the hut and I waited till he was free. I felt that in some way he was pleased to see me and that my presence had value for him. He gave me an identity.

Anyway, you are now looking at 13-year-old Nshila, translated almost overnight from lying in a blanket on the floor of my mother's hut to the girls' dormitory of St Albans College. I have experienced many changes in my life, but that one remains the greatest.

The country had been independent for a few years. The government was black, except for a skilled Finance Minister and a tenacious Lord Chief Justice. Both had displayed political foresight by joining the majority party some years before independence. They were useful to the government in the sense that they exemplified the principle of equal opportunity and non-discrimination. They were token whites. That was pretty important because all other ministerial posts, and most significant public offices, were portioned out within the dominant tribe to the exclusion of all others.

St Albans had originally been a whites-only secondary school, imitating a middle-range English public school. I mean places like Malvern, Sedbergh and Blundells, whose alumni I meet regularly at parties and who Mike Fanshawe sees as marginally inferior because they didn't go to Eton. In my time, St Albans had been open to black people for about five years and to girls for three. All staff members were scrupulous in treating the blacks and the girls fairly, but their attempts often looked patronising. The white boys were mainly decent enough, once you had created an identity for yourself and earned a bit of respect. A minority were racist, fascist pigs without being aware of it. Those were capable of change. A few others were conscious RFPs and prepared to fight for their cause. There were 60 black boys who divided along tribal lines and devoted most of their energy to scoring off one another. There were 24 white girls and 15 black ones. Three of the white girls were rich and conceited and rude. The rest were friendly, especially my own best friend, Alison Packman. The 15 black girls were supportive of each other and stood aside from tribal conflicts.

Alison was tremendous. She was young enough – a few months older than me – to have no real colour prejudice. Everybody who has lived in a colonial environment knows that prejudice is not natural for children. At ages up to ten or eleven the children of the master race play happily with the children of the subject race and don't always reflect that relationship in their games. To Alison, I was like Eileen Mhonde, daughter of her mother's cook, for whom she had great love and respect. Alison actively enjoyed the opportunity to befriend me. She was also the daughter of the British Trade Commissioner, enjoying considerable status, and had an elder brother at the school to act as her protector or enforcer. The other side of the coin was Alison being dim. Not really backward, but slow to catch on to things and, left to herself, always in the lowest quarter of the class. The teachers had to tell Alison something at least three times before she grasped it. After I had settled down I was at or near the top of the class, and able to help her. Something I reflect upon with happiness is that Alison eventually scraped into quite a decent UK Polytechnic and can put BA after her name She would not have done it without me.

My first year at St Albans was occupied with adapting to the environment and the required behaviour, and with the content of the lessons. I did not think about witchcraft. But, looking back, I realise that my subconscious mind was already juggling with two different cultures. One of the books we read was Kipling's *Kim*, and I was impressed by the character's awareness of having 'separate sides to my head'. I noticed, especially, the European attitude to things supernatural. Though unaware of it, I was taking the first developmental steps towards the globally competent practitioner that I hope to become.

In my second year the two worlds began to clash. Abel Chiluba arrived as a new boy. When I saw the name on the list it meant nothing to me, but it turned out that he came from a neighbouring tribe and knew quite a lot about me. Apparently his tribe had suffered in past years from the witchcraft of Kwaname, and the tales included references to the witchdoctor's female helper. Me. So the whole school soon knew my past. You can imagine the excitement and controversy it caused. The white boys divided into the town-bred and those who came from remote areas. The former laughed at the whole concept. The latter had all heard stories about unexplained events attributed to witchcraft, and were inclined to treat it with respect. At least three had seen relatives sent home uncured from the mission hospital and restored to full health by the witchdoctor. The white girls showed the same division but were all to some degree frightened. The black boys were openly scornful but secretly scared. They did not believe that a woman could ever be a true witchdoctor, but the school culture lauded equality of the sexes as a moral good. Perhaps that meant that if, say, a career in medicine was open to women then a career as a witchdoctor was also.

What everybody agreed was that if witchcraft worked, it should be used for material benefit. And even if it did not work, nothing was lost by trying. The concept was also wildly exciting because witchcraft had to be secret. Requests began to dribble in.

'Nshila, that ugly cow Mrs Van Jaarsveld has a real down on me. Nothing I do is ever right. She finds fault with everything, however hard I try. But Meg Grant can get away with murder. Can you do anything?'

'Nshila, I'm off to the sports shop on the edge of town. Old Bangham is duty master. Can you fix it so he does not see me?'

'Nshila, I never looked at that chapter on Portuguese explorations. If Grimshaw asks me questions about it, I'm sunk. Can you make him ask other people?'

I tried. And soon I realised that common sense and intelligent action will get you a long way, without resorting to spells. For instance, you can stop a man looking elsewhere by making sure that he looks at you. If somebody is prejudiced against a pupil, just displace that prejudice by providing a new hate object.

I cast spells, too. After all, I had spent a long time with Kwaname. I had listened and watched and sometimes assisted, and I had some knowledge of the physical side. I knew what substances he mixed together and what movements he made, and what words he uttered. I could follow some of his procedures by rote, though I did not fully understand how it all worked. I did all right for an inexperienced young girl. I was aided, I can now see, by the fact that all my customers wanted to believe in the witchcraft element. They found it exciting.

How do you suppose my first big opportunity came? Love charms! It was a hot day and I was sitting with Alison in the shade behind the sports hut. A group of ten boys were at fielding practice about a hundred yards away. Alison left me to attend a tutorial and I was on my own. The scene comes back to me vividly. Close beside the sports hut was the heavy roller they used on the cricket pitch and two lizards were basking in the sun on the handle. Their colouring was so matched to the wood that one minute you could see them and the next you had lost their outline. At the foot of one wall of the hut was a hole. I could see the bottom of a cricket stump through it, and a flattened football and a shoe with a hole in the toe. I remember thinking that I must tell the staff that white ants were having a go at the hut. The sky was clear, birds were flying around and I could hear distant noises from the school buildings. It was a scene I have since admired often enough in England, when friends have taken me to their old school. The biggest difference, of course, was the grass I lay on. African grass is much coarser and thicker that the type you find in England.

The boys finished their practice. One of them hung back until the sightscreen shielded him from his friends. He came over to me: not running, but at a quick pace as if to lessen the chance of being seen. It alarmed me a bit. This was Patrick Quinn, a boy in the top form and a prefect. What did he want? Had one of my misdoings been uncovered? There was no chance he was interested in a junior black girl like me. Correct. He was not even sure of my name.

'Are you Nshila Ileloka?'

He made a few preliminary remarks about the school. Asked how I was getting on. Made a few comments about the teachers, and the food and so on. I wondered when he would get to the point. He talked about his home, and told a story about the gardener being cured of fits by a witchdoctor. Then he came out with it.

'Nshila, I've been told that you know a little about witchcraft yourself. Is that true?'

43

'When I was young I got quite friendly with our witch-doctor, but that's all in the past. I never give it a thought, here at St Albans.'

'But look, Nshila, can you sometimes make things happen?'

'Patrick, I really don't know. I have seen some strange things come to pass, and sometimes I felt I had caused them. But there were other reasons that might also have been the cause. I am pretty ignorant and the whole thing worries me.'

Patrick thought for a time. He asked me if I would keep a secret for him. Getting a qualified 'Yes' he crossed his personal Rubicon and blurted out:

'Can you make Mary Zonde love me?'

Once he had got the first words out, others followed rapidly. He thought she was absolutely terrific. He loved the way she did her hair. He admired her proud upright carriage. (Not hard to acquire if you carry water pots on your head long enough.) He had never seen legs like hers anywhere. She looked like a fashion model, even in our school uniform. It was classic adolescent male stuff. He could not stop thinking about her. He was losing sleep, and so on. Finally, he suggested paying for my help.

Wow! Your first paid job. Your first commercial success. Your first big sale. Your first client. Acceptance of your first article or painting. Can you remember it? I still remember that hot afternoon behind the sports shed when Patrick Quinn asked me to deliver Mary Zonde into his arms. But could I do it?

'Patrick, love potions don't have a big place in African witchcraft. In our society a man who wants a woman approaches her parents in the decent way and talks about bride-price and cattle. There's no need for magic!'

For a moment we were unable to hear each other. The groundsman had started cutting the field. His tractor and

44

gang mower roared past on the other side of the hut, and faded again.

'Really? I know a bit about witchcraft in Europe, and all the books say that love potions were a big part of it. In English Literature we have been doing *Tristram and Iseult*, where a love potion gets swallowed by the wrong man, and three lives are ruined because of it. Surely there are similar things that you people can do? And Mary is one of your people. She ought to be susceptible.'

That last comment raised another problem. All my experience had been within my own society. It was what the newspapers today call 'Black on Black violence'. Even if I prepared a love potion, would it work if one party was white? They have a sceptical attitude. Tell an African that a spell has been cast on him and the news will have a psychological effect. Tell a European and there might be none.

But the excitement was too much for me. Being asked for something by a male sixth-former – sharing a secret with him – really boosted my ego. I wasn't going to refuse. Perhaps I could make it work. At the worst, I could invent a dying grandmother, return home and get help from old Kwaname. But could I trust Patrick? Would he keep his mouth shut? Very doubtful, given the way boys boast to each other about their success with girls. How would the school react if the story got out? With horror. Could I deny it all? Yes. Would they believe me? No. Against that fear was the fact that I approved, strongly, of Patrick's choice. Mary Zonde was impressive. Almost a grown woman, she had curves in all the right places and a strong face with marvellous bone structure. She frequently smiled. She was intelligent and athletic. On the tennis court, she had a powerful forehand volley that left most opponents, including the boys, standing immobile.

People say I am 'good under pressure'. It's objective comment, and the number of times it has been said makes me feel they are right. But I don't feel confident, and I loathe those pressurised situations when I must make a rushed judgement. There was no way I could sort out the details, there and then behind the sports shed. How could I gain time?

'Patrick, when is your birthday? When is Mary's birthday?' He knew his, but not hers.

'I don't know if I can help you. I don't know if anyone can help you. But I do know that the first step would depend on your relative positions in the zodiac. All I can do right now is ask you to find out her birthday. And I warn you that the project may still be beyond me.'

'All right, Nshila, but if I get the date, will you promise to try?'

'Yes. I will promise that much.'

I realise now that by invoking astrology I was dragging in European concepts to supplement my own culture. I knew nothing about it at that time except that it was a white mystery and was connected with the stars. It has no place in African witchcraft, where the stars are the personifications of different spirits. The idea was good enough – just – to get me out of a hole.

I survived the encounter. Patrick might or might not come back with a date. If he did, I could still fabricate a story to kill the project. Maybe I had received a letter from a friend at Mapanda Academy (our bitter sporting opponents) telling me how a pupil had been expelled for practising witchcraft. It had scared me off, I would say. But it was also possible that I might have fixed on a workable plan.

Here's how I dealt with it. You may feel that my thinking as I report it was beyond the power of a teenage girl. Well, I am now using adult words to describe a child's thought processes. But I did truly think the thoughts. The problem had two sides – practical and political.

46

Practically, could I help Patrick? As regards pure witchcraft, I had never seen Kwaname make a love potion. I don't think he liked anybody enough to help them in that way. But I had seen him make plenty of substances that were supposed to cure aches and pains and sores and boils and keep ticks off dogs. Maybe I could use the same ingredients and mutter the same spells and add personal variations. It would be easy enough to get a scrap of Mary's clothing, strain some romantic potion through it, and tack loving words onto the spell.

But what about delivery? Spells of this sort – good or bad – with a physical element require that the patient eats or drinks them. In mediaeval European magic the boy obtains a love potion and somehow tricks the girl into using it. He lies to her, telling her that it is something especially tasty, or slips it into something that she is going to drink anyway. In *Snow White and the Seven Dwarfs* the wicked queen can prepare the poisoned apple but Snow White must bite it. How was Patrick going to manage this? He had little contact with Mary. He was admiring her from afar. I put that problem on the back burner.

I could provide some practical reinforcement by discovering what things Mary went for and letting Patrick know. I mean, if I knew that she loved boys with a crew cut and hated boys who told lewd jokes then it would be easy enough for Patrick to get the one and cease the other. It would also be possible to leak the fact that one of the prefects was quite wild about her. The excitement and uncertainty would put her in the right frame of mind. She would be expecting an approach. All in all, I felt I had a chance of success.

The political thing was much harder. Would it all come out? If it worked then surely it must do. The top form had twelve adolescent boys, and if Patrick got what he wanted then it was a certainty he would tell his mates. It is not the sort of thing a boy can keep to himself. The worst-case scenario was that, say, half-a-dozen boys would get paired up in this way. Some of them would have sex with their partners. Some of them would be caught by the teachers. One or two would be expelled. Whatever investigation the authorities carried out, somebody would open his mouth too wide and my name would come up. And the best excuse a boy/girl combination might offer would be 'Nshila bewitched us. We could not help it. We are blameless victims!'

Could I protect myself? If Patrick believed in witchcraft enough to ask me for a love potion then maybe he believed sufficiently to be scared of me. Could I threaten him with terrible consequences if he failed to keep quiet? I had learnt enough from Kwaname to have some skill at scaring people. But would it last? I did not believe that fear would be enough to stop Patrick boasting. And when he did, I would have to make the promised evils come about. I might be reduced to some dangerous action like poisoning the illegal alcoholic drink that the boys made underneath the stage in the assembly hall. No, the scare strategy was out.

I turned my mind towards blackmail. I needed to get something really nasty about Patrick and any successors that I could use against them. And then his words came back to me: 'I would make it worth your while, of course.' I had been certain he meant money. But was I right? Perhaps he meant some sort of reward in kind like fixing my inclusion in a team or club. Or did he mean protection from the persecution that goes on from time to time in all schools? Whatever he meant, the clear inference was that he was going to reward my services. If that were somehow recorded then I would have a weapon. And, since he was senior to me in age and the school hierarchy, I would also have the defence: 'He bullied me into it.'

I have told you before how one thought leads to another if you keep your mind open and active. Another of the texts they required us to read at St Albans was Marlowe's *Doctor Faustus*. In case you have never read it, the stupid fellow signs a contract with the devil, bartering away his soul in exchange for 24 years in which his every wish shall be granted. Why should I not have a contract? The idea of a contract with the forces of darkness would be hugely exciting to the boys. Not serious enough to make them run away, but serious enough to inspire a feeling of risk-taking, danger and bravery. Good enough! I would devise a contract, and make Patrick sign it with his blood!

Some might say that this was a gutless approach, but I still wanted to hedge my bets in a practical way. So when Patrick came back with Mary's birthday date, I pretended to make some obscure calculations – stealing out at night to the pitiful shelter where supporters were supposed to stand at Rugby matches – and decreed that the only time to brew and administer a really good potion was three weeks ahead. That allowed only two weeks before the end of term, and whatever the outcome I felt I could ride out two weeks of aggravation. I did make Patrick sign a contract. It was most impressive, written in blood, on parchment, with a quill pen and stating a fee of $60 US. A penalty of 'aches, pains and boils afflicting the private parts' was specified if due payment were not made. The document included some Latin phrases and used dollars as currency because our Shonina was hugely unstable.

My three weeks' grace was given over to research. Mary was not too difficult. She was two years senior to me: senior enough to have her own small cubicle to sleep in, out of reach of dormitory gossip. She was not in the same form as me. But we were both part of the drama group that was rehearsing a play for the end of term and that offered chat-opportunities in abundance. She was not particularly good at learning her lines, so I made myself useful by hearing her. I also presented myself as being quite obsessed with another of the senior boys. I picked an unimpressive one, which allowed Mary many chances to say why he might suit me but would never do for her. I got comments like:

'He never walks upright (first boy). I could not bear a man who slouched around with his nose to the ground.'

'If I was interested in him (second boy) I would insist on a decent haircut.'

'He's a wimp (third boy). Never stands up to anybody and accepts everything the teachers tell him.'

'He uses all those poncy lotions and smells like a chemist's shop (fourth boy).'

Two weeks into my research project I was convinced that Mary would respond best to an aggressive, masterful approach – sandbag the girl and drag her off to your cave – that sort of thing. But it would have to be done with confidence and panache.

The next step was the rumour-mill. Every school has one. I started one or two rumours that reflected rather well on Patrick and made the girls look on him as something of a hero. I attributed these to my departed elder brother, saying that he had been friends with Patrick's family and heard all about the incidents. This part of the strategy I had to share with Patrick, who might otherwise have denied the stories. He must have then realised that I was into 'assisted witchcraft' rather than the pure supernatural type, but that's the truth anyway. I am not sure 'pure' witchcraft exists.

I also mixed up the natural and the supernatural in what I told Patrick. I told him he had to act more aggressively in his ordinary life around the school. 'Be argumentative,' I said. 'Shout at people sometimes. Lose your temper once or twice. Have a row with one of the teachers.' I also told him to buy a razor and start shaving, even if he did not need to! With the instructions I gave him a few pills that were pretty certain to make him bad-tempered. I knew enough about chemistry to do that without casting any spells at all. Finally, I spent two hours just before and after midnight in that shed beside the playing field brewing up a potion and muttering spells. I did everything I could remember from my time with Kwaname and I squeezed the mixture through a handker-chief stolen from Mary's jacket. I crooned love songs over the mixture and spoke the names of Mary and Patrick several times. I poured the potion into an up-market, cut-glass phial that the Head Girl used for her perfume. The theft was never suspected.

The next day I met Patrick and put the potion in his hands.

'You must get Mary to drink this. All right?'

'No. Not all right. How on earth can I manage it? The girls and boys sit at separate tables for meals. You know that. And I don't have much contact with her at all. We're not in the same classes. What's to stop you from doing it yourself?'

I lost that argument, principally because he was right about my greater opportunity. But I got him to agree to an extra 15 dollars as 'risk money'. Next, I gave him his instruction for the big day. I told him that if he waited behind the big tree at the bend in the back drive half an hour after lunch, then my witchcraft would bring Mary walking past him, quite alone. The idiot asked what he was supposed to do! I told him to jump out, call her name and embrace her. Then the spirits would take over!

I quickly figured out a way to administer the love potion. Remember that St Albans was a boarding school. We had 'prep' late in the evening, and towards the end of it somebody was sent to the kitchen to collect what were called 'the rocks'. This meant a large jug of cocoa and a basket of buns, bread rolls and stale cake. We all had our own mugs. That evening I made sure I was in front of Mary in the queue and picked up her mug instead of mine. I had just tipped the potion into it, and filled it with cocoa, when she said, 'You idiot, Nshila, you've got my mug.' With a word of apology I handed over her mug and she drank the lot. Job done! You are going to wonder whether Mary noticed the different taste. No. The cocoa was always so foul that it smothered minor differences.

Next day I was due to meet Mary straight after lunch to hear her run through the big speech in Act Three. I asked if we could do it walking down the back drive because I wanted to see a bird that was nesting in the bushes beside the gate. Just before the Patrick Tree (that's how I think of it, now) I 'forgot' something and told Mary to walk on and I would catch her up. So there I was, about 25 yards away, hiding behind the tractor they used to pull the gang-mower and watching the outcome of my first piece of mixed-race witchcraft.

It worked! After two big scares! First off, Patrick failed to leap out as she walked past. But she had only gone ten yards when he finally woke up and shouted 'Mary' in a nervous, strangled voice. She stopped and turned round.

Patrick stood there like an idiot. His mouth moved but no words came out.

'Well, what do you want?' Mary sounded mad and intrigued at the same time.

'I love you!' He got it out at last and made a grab for her left arm, which was the nearest bit of her.

Mary hit him hard across the face with her right hand. Patrick drew back and they stood looking at each other, neither quite sure what to do.

'What was all that about, then?' Mary demanded.

'Mary, I'm sorry. I really am. I just want to walk with you and tell you things. I just didn't know how.'

'Sorry! You filthy reptile. So you should be! Are you out of your mind? I could get you expelled!'

'Don't! Please don't do that! I think you're terrific. I just want to be with you.'

'Liar. You want a lot more than that!'

Mary then behaved brilliantly. She was so cool and controlled, making a few comments about hot-headed idiots unable to control their hormones. Then she said. 'If what you want is to get friendly with me, you need a bit of education first.' She put both hands round his neck, pulled his head towards her and kissed him. It was not a polite friendly kiss. It was serious, sending him a message. I went back to the school building, wasted fifteen minutes, and returned. They were locked in each other's arms on the turf beside the tree. Not pleased to see me.

What made it work? Was it psychological, because I had put the right thoughts into the minds of adolescent people who think regularly about sex anyway? Was it chemical, because of some aphrodisiac ingredient in the potion Mary had swallowed? Was it genuine magic because of the spells I had muttered while making the potion?

So that's the story. I succeeded. They were together for the rest of the term. Then Patrick went off to university and Mary started the next year as undisputed queen of the sixth form. She worked hard, played hard, and enjoyed herself a lot – but never suspected my role in her first romantic encounter. Before he left, I gave Patrick an invoice and three weeks into the autumn term I received an envelope with the logo of Witwatersrand University on the back. I found nothing inside except six 10-dollar bills. He had paid the basic fee and ignored my 'risk money'. He still owes me!

At St Albans College, in the time after Patrick left, I kept well clear of practical witchcraft, and, perhaps because of my caution, got clean away with the episode. I told nobody about it at the time (though I did tell Alison Packman, many years later when we missed a connection at Peterborough railway station and sat drinking in the Great Eastern Hotel). Patrick was a risk, of course, but in the end his macho view of life made it impossible to admit that his suit had received outside assistance. He preferred to believe that Mary had surrendered to his irresistible male charm.

I worked hard during my next year because I had begun to dream of entry to a British university, preferably with some sort of grant. One of my subjects was biology, and through that study I picked up a mass of useful knowledge about poisons and antidotes and the many ways in which mammalian bodies can malfunction. I also made quite an effort during RE (St Albans' code for Religious Education). The teacher (Reverend Quick) was fairly broad-minded and devoted one term to what he called Comparative Religion. That was really useful, for it made me realise that human beings have an in-built need for some sort of supernatural belief. The need gives rise to all sorts of weird cults, and the major world religions only stand out because their myths have better literary expression.

And then, just before the end of my last-year-but-one, Kwaname died. My life changed again.

Chapter Five

Death in the Creek

At first nobody in the tribe was too upset. As he grew older, Kwaname had become difficult and demanding, and easily enraged. He seemed to do the tribe more harm than good. But three months after his death they needed him badly. There was an increase in cattle theft, attributed to a neighbouring tribe, and it seemed as if the thieves knew more about us than they should. For instance, cattle stolen from the herd of our chief would have had the whole tribe up in arms. So they disappeared instead from the small herds owned by low-status people: people who had difficulty winning support for punitive action. It got worse and worse.

I know something about what happened at the council of tribal elders, for Moses Maunga had to tell me why I was wanted. He came into it because he was a half-brother of Kwaname by his father's third wife and the nearest that Kwaname had to a friend. The council said to Moses, 'You are related to Kwaname. You must know something of his mysteries. Can you help?' I will paraphrase his answer:

'Yes. I can possibly help, but this is very dangerous work for somebody who is not an expert and I don't want to expose myself to stupid risks. You will remember that Nshila Ileloka spent four years with Kwaname and acquired some of his skill. I want her brought home to work for me. I will decide what must be done, and she will do it. If anything goes wrong, and the spirits demand some sacrifice, then it will be better to lose an unimportant woman than an experienced senior person such as I.'

Everybody knew that Moses was totally ignorant and that I was the person needed. But it was unthinkable that a woman should be considered responsible in such a matter, so Moses was appointed, as it were, Project Manager. Everybody knew that he would do no work and take all the credit if things went well. Everybody knew that I would do all the work, receive little credit if things went well, and possibly die if they went badly. I have seen things stitched up in an identical manner in sophisticated Western societies.

So I was back in my village. But now I was a bit more than a precocious child. I was attached to a respected member of society with a responsibility to carry out. When Moses told me the problem it was quite a shock. My first instinct was to follow any lead he could possibly give me and to accept a subordinate role. But as he talked, I came to realise that despite his authoritative manner he was completely ignorant and lost. He was looking to me, the schoolgirl, to provide answers and was finding it hard to get this message across without losing face. I might easily, then, have gone to pieces, Amazingly, I avoided doing so. From some external source there was a flash of inspiration telling me that there might be another option. I found the courage to ask, in a dignified way, for time to think about everything he had told me and make sure that I had understood it. He agreed.

Sitting quietly in the guest hut, I worked it all out in my mind. It came down to the fact that people were uncertain about how to treat me. They knew what I had been, but they did not know what I had become. This meant that to some extent I could invent my own personality. If I wanted to masquerade as a person of great spiritual power I might get away with it. I did not see myself as such a person, but the more I considered the matter the more I realised that I had a chance to become one. Here was a colossal development opportunity. Did I want the role? Well, it was a lot better than being a schoolgirl and could open further doors for me. Yes, I did want it.

My experience with Patrick was crucial, here. Without that memory I might never have seen the opportunity. A demand had taken me by surprise. I had felt fearful and inadequate. I had reflected, and taken the assignment, without at that moment knowing how I would cope. By imagination and hard work and determination I had succeeded. I could do it again. Those early-life events have convinced me that experience is the key to personal growth. Once you have done something the first time, even if you do it poorly, you have learnt what it is like. A similar task may appear difficult, but it is not completely unfamiliar: it has lost some of its fearfulness. Quite recently I watched a television programme called *You are what you eat*. It was about diet, and so on. I would say rather: 'You are what you have done.' Your experiences make you.

In my next talk with Moses we struck a deal. I would tackle the problem in my own way without interference or direction from him. On the other hand, I would tell him everything I was going to do well in advance so that he could explain to the tribe that I was following his orders. If we were successful, we would still maintain the fiction that he was the prime mover and thus enhance his status. This was good enough from my point of view, because a share of the glory would surely filter down to the operator.

At St Albans we had a lively theatrical society (I have told you a bit about that already) and I felt some drama was appropriate. I said that the first thing I must do was visit the hut under the baobab tree and commune with the spirit of Kwaname. I said I must do this alone and that nobody must come near the hut. I explained that this was a dangerous endeavour because I had no way of knowing how Kwaname would respond. He might choose to destroy me. (There's no harm in letting your client know what hardships you have endured on his behalf.) Alternatively, he might subject me to some form of test. Even if terrible screams were heard at night, nobody was to approach.

Where do ideas come from? We hear stories, and remember some parts and seemingly forget others. Then the missing bits resurface in some strange way and we think we are being original while in fact we are repeating what he have heard. The Witch of Endor, from the Christian Bible, must have been in the back of my mind, as I gave all these dramatic instructions. She was asked by King Saul to call up the prophet Samuel from the dead. What a wonderful image that is! The bottomless black pit opening up, and the witch staring into it, and something stirring in the depths, and getting bigger and bigger until it is obviously human, and then acquiring the features of an old, old man. Samuel! Not too pleased to be disturbed! Strangely, the Bible does not tell us if the witch was scared of Samuel. It tells us that she was frightened, rather, of Saul. Saul had given orders to root out all witches and soothsayers, and the witch feared that this was an entrapment operation. You read, today, about police working tricks like that, and then having the case thrown out in court because 'entrapment' is frowned on. Once again, there's nothing new in human behaviour!

I opened the door. It creaked – as it always had – and hot, heavy, spicy air wafted out. I went in and closed the door behind me.

You must have had the experience of revisiting a place well known in your childhood. It is romantic. Perhaps this is due to the place being familiar and strange at the same time. It looks the same, and yet it looks different because you have changed yourself. You are probably a good deal bigger, and the place seems to have shrunk by comparison. Certainly, your eyes are two feet or so higher up than when you saw it last, so you have a different perspective. If you used to look at the workbench at eye-level, you are now looking down on it. Part of you reverts to being the child, but part of you remains the adult. It is almost a schizophrenic experience. I remember Mike Fanshawe telling me about the top-floor rooms to which he was banished, as a boy, when the house was full of visitors. The bathroom had an old stand-alone bath with claw-hammer feet and there was just enough room for a small boy to hide between the back end of the bath and the wall. Mike revisited the place as an adult and was convinced that the bath had been moved. It was inconceivable to him that anybody, however small, could have squeezed in behind it!

Was there an atmosphere in the hut? Of course. A witchdoctor's hut will always have a powerful atmosphere, and a special one if it has been unused for some months. It was extremely hot. It was silent except for the buzzing of a few flies up near the roof. Sunlight fell through small holes in the walls and roof, throwing patches on the workbench. Everything was still, but I had an illusion that the place was changing and coming to life as my eyes adjusted gradually to the dim light. The bright patches became less dominant, and moment by moment other features took on an identifiable form. Sometimes, when I used to come before, he would be standing immobile at the far end of his bench, and I would be unable to see him because of the bright light I had come from. For a moment that image seemed to materialise before me. He wasn't there – but I could almost feel him. Stuck in a crack in the workbench I saw a cheap earring that I had lost years ago. I had been wearing it for a play at the primary school and the teacher had been mad with me for losing it.

What did I do first? I sat on the floor and cried. Why did I do that? He was a rather terrible old man, but he had given me something important. He had given me an identity. Because of his interest and protection I had graduated from being a nobody to being the witchdoctor's assistant: a person who might have something to offer. And now I was potentially an expert, and a tribal saviour. None of it would have happened without him. I am not ashamed of a few tears for Kwaname.

The memories came flooding back. I noticed a large collection of herbs and ointments, most of which I could identify and know their purpose. Masks hanging on the walls were familiar. There were the remains of a fire. Numerous small effigies lay discarded on the floor with nasty things sticking out of their ears and eyes and private parts. Some had been there since my childhood. Some had been made since that date. One really shocked me, because the huge hooked nose identified it beyond doubt as Morgan MacMillan, a British official who had made a great many enemies by cracking down on big-game poachers. I had read about his death a year before – trampled by an elephant. And here was his image, almost flattened – perhaps by the stone that Kwaname had sometimes used as a doorstop! That was a growing-up experience for me. Maybe other, non-spiritual actions had been taken against MacMillan but it was clear that Kwaname *had* made an image and *had* crushed it, and MacMillan *had* died in a similar way.

I also found a stock of paints that Kwaname had used on his own face and hands, and various pots of incense that would produce noxious spells when burnt, and the robes that Kwaname had worn.

I spent about an hour in complete silence, touching nothing. I did it to give Kwaname a chance to speak to me if he wanted to. Then I spoke to him myself, aloud. I heard no answer, but a sense of comfort and familiarity came over me. I burnt a substance that I knew would produce a lot of smoke and a foul smell, and rise through the hole in the roof to be seen outside. The people had to know that something was happening! As I did that I reverted to schoolgirl mode and had a fit of giggling. I remembered the Reverend Quick telling us how the smoke from the Vatican chimney declared the election of a new Pope. This time the village was going to know they had a new witchdoctor, but the principle was much the same – drama to underline the importance of an event. I giggled again at the thought of an infallible Nshila Ileloka!

I spent two full days and nights in the hut, eating nothing. My most significant activity was turning over all the bits and pieces I could find in the hut, recalling what Kwaname had done with them. I made a real effort to think myself into the role. Sometimes I did more than think. I made up some potions, because I found that the physical action stimulated my memory: when I asked myself theoretically 'what comes next?' I received no answer, but when the mixture was smoking in a pot, my hands somehow knew the answer of their own accord. It was an eerie experience, as if Kwaname had put his hands over mine to guide them. I muttered some incantations. I slept at times, and twice went into a trance state after using the right drugs.

For the benefit of the villagers, I provided coloured smoke through the roof from time to time, and made loud noises. I screamed, and shouted phrases in Latin. (Did I tell you we did some Latin at St Albans?) I chanted the rhyme from our Latin primer about prepositions that begins *Ante, Apud, Ad, Adversus, Circum, Circa, Citra, Cis.* I thought the villagers might take this as spirit language.

I have said that Kwaname did not speak to me, but that's not absolutely true. There was a moment when I distinctly heard three words. I had remembered that he used to keep certain charms of great power in an old biscuit tin that he buried below the mud floor, stamping down the earth to hide the location. He had often allowed me to see the tin, but never the burial spot. Believing, now, that I would need all the help I could get, I found a sharp, strong stake and began to probe for the tin. My arms froze. I could hold the stake, but I was physically unable to press on it. And I heard the three words – 'Not yet, Nshila.' It shook me. And then I relaxed. He knew that I did not need these charms for the present. He also knew that I might need them later.

A feeling of lassitude and boredom eventually overtook me. Fortunately I had brought some light reading with me. Witchdoctors don't often read frivolous romances from Mills and Boon. This was an exception to the rule.

I had already grasped the fact that image is all-important. That lesson has entered into my soul, and that's why I am, today, extremely careful about the impression I create. When the time was near for my reappearance I worked really hard at it. I used the materials Kwaname had bequeathed to me and the make-up from my handbag. (At St Albans girls in the fifth and sixth forms were allowed to have handbags, but they were a standard issue, which enraged us all. Every girl made an effort to personalise her handbag in some fashionable manner.) I also practised my slow, dignified walk, studying myself in the mirror – that same mirror which Kwaname had been looking into the day I collapsed on the floor. I used the eye-liner to make myself look older and shaved my hair at the back to create a striking and unusual feature. I walked up and down in front of the mirror and tried various postures that I had seen Kwaname adopt.

When I went back to the village I held myself rigidly upright and behaved with great dignity. I acted as if I was only partially in their world. I copied one of Kwaname's gestures, that people knew well. They noticed, and picked up the right message. It was really hard keeping that up all the time. But the Nshila previously known to the villagers was wildly different from the metamorphosed creature that now walked among them.

How did I start my assignment? By maximising my knowledge. Would-be taxi drivers in London are tested about their knowledge of the place before they are licensed. They call the learning process 'doing the knowledge'. I did not know it then, but in fact I spent three days 'doing the knowledge'. I listened and asked questions, and thought through the meaning. In particular, I listened to the children. They see an awful lot and talk to each other about it, and talk to adults if they feel comfortable. They often don't understand the meaning of what they have seen and just provide you with a procession of iconic images. But you can tease a great deal of knowledge from it.

I did something, quite naturally and spontaneously, for which I learnt a sophisticated name later on at the OU Business School They dealt there with some techniques of problem solving and one of them – from an American guru whose name I have forgotten – made a big thing about asking the question 'What has changed?' The idea is that if something is happening now that did not happen before, then it is probably linked to some other change that you may be able to identify. I asked myself what had changed in the village. One thing seemed to be our relationship with the neighbouring tribe. Their people knew about us, and we knew about them, in a way that had not been the case before. How might this have happened? What contact had there been? I discovered that a girl from our tribe had married away. It happens from time to time. Nobody is very keen on it, but there is no formal prohibition and if the bride price is right the thing goes ahead. Nadenda had left us six months ago and the cattle-thieving had entered its sophisticated phase – targeting the low-status owners – about six weeks later.

We had no proof, of course. Did I know anything else? Who had she married? What sort of person was he? The answers I got revealed that Moyo Kayesha was an ambitious fellow seeking to gain status in his tribe and one day usurp the chieftainship. Owning more cattle would improve his perceived importance. It would also replace the cattle he had handed over as the bride-price for Nadenda and even, later, allow him to marry a second wife.

A stumbling block remained. Would he risk being discovered? It might well mean war between his tribe and ours, which the elders of his tribe were currently opposed to. Peaceful co-existence was the policy. But then I learnt of Eli Sikara. He was a half-brother of Kayesha, recently returned from a job in the towns and holding a high opinion of himself. He, like Kayesha, wanted status, but felt it might best be pursued through his half-brother. It sounded good to me. Kayesha gets information from his new wife and uses it to direct the thieving of his half-brother Eli. If it goes well they both prosper. If Eli is found out, Kayesha throws him to the lions. A good strategy!

So I sat and waited, asked questions, listened to the answers, and looked wise. Three more days passed without my learning anything that suggested a better solution, and a few things happened to support my provisional one. Time to act.

I disappeared into Kwaname's hut and set about making an image. Nobody knew very much about what Eli looked like so I could not do what Kwaname had done with Morgan MacMillan. My answer was to make the image much larger than usual and write his name on the back. 'There,' I thought, 'whatever spirit handles these assignments should be in no doubt about who to go for.' I filled a large bowl with mud, and dunked the image in it seven times, finally leaving it face down in the liquid. During the process I repeated various rituals that I had heard Kwaname use. I did not remember exactly what they were all for, so I left out those that I knew to be inappropriate – like the pregnancy one – but included most of the others on the belt-and-braces principle.

The job only took me three hours, and I thought the villagers might be unimpressed by something that was so easily done. (No merit is gained by doing things quickly in an African village.) So I spent another three hours merely sitting in the hut. I read one of the set books for the school examinations. I thought about my witchcraft strategy. I burnt some incense to provide smoke and smells that the villagers would notice. Finally I had the brilliant thought of playing my tape-recorder loudly. One of my tapes was dirge music from a state funeral in the Congo. It was terrible – really dreary and ghastly and extremely badly played. I felt it would give the villagers something novel to talk about, and perhaps advance my status.

That's the magic part of it done. I went back to the village and allowed word to get round that the spell had been cast and the victim marked down. I had no means of telling Sikara directly, but these things get around fast. I also assured people that the cattle thefts were going to stop, and it was now quite safe to use grazing areas that they had temporarily abandoned. I mentioned one area where, so the spirits had told me, the grazing was especially good.

65

The Patrick affair had started me on a path rather different from the traditional witchdoctor. I had never perceived the unseen powers as totally reliable, and my first attempts to assist them by physical action of my own had worked well. I planned to use that strategy again. It seems, looking back, that this has become my normal modus operandi or MO as the police in England call it. (In the spy stories they would call it my 'handwriting'.) For three nights I left the village at sunset and walked to Kwaname's hut to commune with the spirits. Around midnight I dressed in his dirtiest animal-skin robe and made the two-mile journey to the grazing area about which I had told the tribe. I went bare-footed for silence, but carried the high-heeled shoes – four inches – that the girls used for dances at St Albans. The grazing area is easy of access on our side, but an enemy approaching it would have to walk down a steep path towards a stagnant creek and then walk for 50 yards beside the creek to the nearest crossing point. For two nights I hid in the bush getting very cold and miserable because nothing at all happened. I could sometimes see the movement of our cattle, and I could hear our herd boys calling, but that was all. I was really worried. Perhaps Sikara, hearing that he had become a target, was too frightened to try again!

People in northern Europe may scoff at the idea of anybody being cold at night in Africa. It's supposed to be burning hot, surely? Not so. Because heat is pretty normal, my people feel the cold much more than Europeans do and are miserable in temperatures that would be called warm in, say, Aberdeen. And at times we do even get frost. I have never seen this myself, but people in the village had said that Europeans in our country put the legs of tables in tin cans of water to stop white ants eating the wood. They say that on very cold days in the middle of our winter very thin films of ice form on those cans.

So we must get zero temperatures at times. Anyway, I was cold those two nights.

The third night I was rewarded. I heard him coming about two hours after midnight. He passed me, and went on down the path towards the creek. I put on my heels and stood to my full height. With my arms above my head, wearing Kwaname's witchdoctor outfit (the smell of it was almost lethal on its own) and screaming spells at the top of my voice I tottered after him. It worked. He looked back, gave the most awful yell and shot down the rest of the slope, losing his footing early on and plunging into the viscous mud of the creek. In broad daylight I would have cut a ridiculous figure. But on that night, moonless but starlit, the effect was everything I could have hoped for.

Now I have to tell you about one of the great unknowns. I had been psyching myself up to deal with him terminally if he looked like getting out of the creek. I had told myself that I would hold him under with a branch of a tree, or crack his skull with a boulder. My weaker self had been saying, 'Nshila. This is your Rubicon. If you kill this man by your own physical act then you are indisputably a murderer. Don't do it.' My stronger self had replied, 'The world will be a better place without him. When the time comes, Nshila, just close your mind and do it. You don't want to be an indecisive fool like Hamlet, do you, forever finding excuses not to act? Do it! Do it! Do it!'

Can you remember how your subconscious mind prepares you to succeed or fail? If you really don't want to do something then it causes you to forget some necessary item, and when the time comes to act you can't. If the bit of you that wants to do the business is stronger than the other part, then you have all the gear to hand. You tell yourself 'I am not committed. I can hold back if the spirits tell me to', but psychologically you have made the

67

decision. In my hand I had a large stone with a sharp edge.

I did not have to use it. He splashed into the green, muddy gunge of the creek and lay still. Maybe he had died of fright on the way down. Maybe he had struck his head on a boulder when he fell and was unconscious. Maybe the spirits had decided to intervene on their own account. Whatever the reason, he stayed immobile – face-down – for the half-hour that I watched. I walked slowly back to the hut, fell on the floor and slept.

At noon next day the village sent a small boy – shaking with fear – to knock at the door and see if I was alive. I went back to the village with him and said nothing to anybody – rendered dumb, I hoped they would think, by the magnitude of the task. The talk that I heard reflected news from the herd boys about spirit activity beyond the creek that they were too scared to investigate. Two young men eventually undertook the duty, and reported a body found beside the creek, partly eaten by jackals. Surely the remains of the cattle-thief, struck down in his wickedness by Nshila. Big celebrations, and Moses boasting about his management of the campaign.

Attitudes towards me were ambivalent. Everybody knew that I had done the real work, but I had created an uncomfortable social situation. There was no way a woman could be accorded the respect appropriate to my skills and value, but it was equally impossible to deny them. Nobody knew quite how to treat me. I went back to school quickly. I made academic work my top priority for the rest of my time and got a scholarship to the London School of Economics.

And I still don't know what would have happened if Eli Sikara had struggled to his feet. Would I have crushed his skull with the stone? I think the answer is 'Yes'. I think I would have felt so committed to the task that going ahead was less awful than turning away. But I don't know for certain, and never shall.

In the minds of the villagers, of course, there was no doubt at all. I had brought about the death of Eli Sikara. In my own mind there was doubt about the method. I had invoked spiritual forces, but for all the proof available they might have been quite ineffective. If that were true, I could absolve myself of murder by witchcraft. Physically, I had engineered the circumstances in which death was likely but had not struck a fatal blow. If you had asked me at that point in my life what my 'occupation' was (like they ask on the passport application) I would have said 'Student and unofficial, unqualified witchdoctor'. The word 'assassin' had not crossed my mind. I had been involved in only two deaths. In the case of Samuel Shonga I had obeyed Kwaname without full understanding. In the case of Eli Sikara I had taken justifiable action to protect the interests of my tribe. I was a goodie. I was on the side of the angels.

Chapter Six

Economics and Witchcraft

I spoke about the traumatic exchange of village life for schoolgirl life at St Albans. I think I said it was the biggest change I ever encountered. Maybe, but arrival at Heathrow at 5.30 a.m. on a cold, wet October morning comes a close second! A few hours after leaving your sunny homeland you are plunged into a murky environment where millions of people are swarming around you and life runs three times faster than you ever imagined possible. It took me the whole of the first day to find our embassy, make contact with the Student Liaison Officer and trek out to the remote lodgings that he had booked for me. I twice took the wrong tube train.

All the first winter I felt cold and miserable and poor. I had a grant from my government, but the exchange rate of our currency got worse every month. My tuition was paid for by my scholarship, and Masuko, now well-established in the school at Margate, gave me some money left over from his lottery win, but I was still poor. I hated walking around in clothes bought from Oxfam. The place was also dirty. In Africa the sun turns a lot of natural rubbish to dust, and the wind blows it away. They are nature's scouring agents. What happens when there is no sun at all and everything is packaged in plastic and the rubbish collectors are on strike? It's revolting. Yet they call this civilisation.

Because of the awful climate, I spent a lot of time in the college buildings or in a library. In that respect, England was great. I read a great deal and got right on top of the academic work. I had been frightened beforehand, thinking that England, the great colonial power, must be full of terribly clever people and that I would be ignorant by comparison. It was different. I learnt that the English people I met in Africa had been the more educated sort and had given me a misleading impression. England has its full share of less able people and the public education system is nothing to boast of. I was well able to keep up with the students of my year.

At times I was reluctant to leave the warmth of LSE and endure the misery of the Northern Line out to Golders Green. I found I could postpone it with coffee and a rock bun in the small refreshment area of the library: eating and drinking very slowly I could kill ten minutes there. Once, when most of the tables were occupied, a young man I had often seen in the library asked, 'Do you mind if I sit here?' and plonked himself down on the scratched, paint-peeling, wobbly plastic chair. We got talking. Naturally we started on the harmless stuff like, 'What are you reading?' and 'Where do you come from?'

I never saw him again and I'm not even sure of his name. I think it may have been Peter Widgeon. But he represents another turning point in my life because he jumped on the fact that I came from darkest Africa. He had been sorting out the books belonging to his recently dead father and been held up for twelve uninterrupted hours by *King Solomon's Mines*.

'What a book!' he exclaimed. 'Straight old-fashioned adventure from the days when the world still had unexplored places. Full of larger-than-life characters. You've got the grizzled old hunter, Quartermain, and the naval officer on half pay with an eye for the girls, and a centuries-old corpse in a cave on a hill-top. It's terrific.'

I liked his enthusiasm. I asked, 'Which of the characters did you like most?'

'The witch-woman Gagool. She's old beyond belief and looks like a bag of bones but she has her army of trained assistants who help her smell out her enemies. And at the peak of the smelling-out ceremony she does the raving, devil-inspired dancing as well as anybody.'

'She sounds ghastly.'

'Yes. But what a character! She never gives up. Even when the goodies have nailed the tribal chief, her protégé, and entered the cave to collect the treasure she is trying to trap them there and leave them to a horrible death. You really ought to read the book.'

I took his advice.

'It's written by a European,' I thought to myself, 'and he is obviously fascinated by African witchcraft. Do Europeans have none of their own?'

Clearly they did. I was well on top of my academic work and was soon deep into the study of witchcraft in Europe. It was great. Three subjects really grabbed me: shape-shifting, transformation and foreknowledge. Shape-shifting means that the witch can change her physical appearance and work unrecognised. So if a man and his wife are having a terrible row, the witch may see and hear it all while sitting under the table in the form of a mouse. No reliable evidence exists to prove that anybody worked this trick. How could there be? It is all rationalisation sparked by the fact that a person has unexplainable knowledge. But if the shape-shifting possibility is discounted then the unexplainable must still be explained. Could it be that the witch has just made deductions about what is likely to have happened, based on deep understanding of the people and careful observation of their behaviour?

73

I mean, if you visit a house just after the husband and wife have had a major row, you can often see signs of it. I am not talking of broken china smashed against the wall, but observable constraint in their behaviour. I told myself, 'You can do that, Nshila.'

Shape-shifting also covers dressing up. The words are often connected with children's parties, but that is what witchdoctors do for certain rituals. It is also what witches did in Europe. If you assume the appearance of some animal – like a leopard – by wrapping the skin of one around you and letting the skull hang down over your face, then superstitious people will believe that you are endowed with the qualities of a leopard, and are in sympathy with other leopards, and able to command them. You have been endowed with their power and capability. Is this shape-shifting? In one sense it is. You have changed shape in the perception of others.

Transformation means that one actually becomes the creature instead of merely acting the part. It is a wildly exciting idea and features in numerous witchcraft stories where the witch or wizard mumbles a spell and immediately becomes a peacock or a toad or a woodpecker or whatever. Possibilities are endless, because the capabilities of living creatures are so varied. I laughed at some of the images conjured up. What happens, for instance, when one protagonist in a duel has become an octopus and the other an albatross? Some very elaborate games are available in the shops today which exploit the idea of transformation. But outside the make-believe world of games, it's a non-starter. Yet I have to tell you that it is something I have never experimented with, just in case there should be unexpected power there. Suppose I changed myself into a lion or a grouse or an elephant and could not manage to change back? I don't fancy being shot by some gung-ho American on his tailor-made safari, or blasted out of

74

the sky on 12 August. For if you become the creature and assume its characteristics then presumably you lose all the qualities that you possess and it does not. If the lion you have become can't do much witchcraft-wise, then you can't either. And what about physical health? I was in agony last week in the dentist's chair and he comforted me with the assurance that the crowned tooth would last a lifetime. Lions have no dentists. If their teeth wear out they can't kill any longer, and have perpetual pain in their jaws. No thanks!

The big things, of course, are the werewolf and vampire legends. They are so old and so widespread that one has to assume some grain of truth buried within them. Mike Fanshawe was shocked that I had never read *Dracula*. We were doing a weekend at that palace his people have in the country and he searched out a copy from the family library. I read it all in six hours curled up in a huge leather armchair. Afterwards I could talk of nothing else.

'Give over, Nshila. Stop talking about it. We're off to a dinner party in ninety minutes. I don't want you sinking your fangs into your neighbour's neck.'

Foreknowledge is called by other names as well, such as second sight or prophetic vision. Some instances are easily explained away. Take the story from the Bible – the 22nd chapter of the First Book of Kings. There you find the King of Israel, Ahab, asking his prophets 'Shall I go up to Ramoth-Gilead to battle?' The whole lot of them say, 'Go. You will win!' That's just saying what the boss wants to hear. There's no foreknowledge in it. But Ahab is a bit suspicious and calls for 'A prophet of the Lord'. Along comes Micah, who says, 'Go into battle and you will get chopped.' Was that foreknowledge, or was it the judgement of a well-informed man based on sound military intelligence?

Other cases are a bit harder to explain. I remember

Kwaname describing something when he was in a trance state. 'I see him ... He counts ... He searches ... One is missing ... He is walking now beside the flood ... The cow is mired ... He grasps it ... He pulls ... He struggles ... It is free...' I knew from earlier words that he was talking about Enoch Bengono who is always careless about grazing his cattle too near the river. But I also knew that Enoch was at that very moment fast asleep beside his hut. Kwaname could not possibly be seeing what was happening now But a few weeks later something similar did happen. There was more rain than usual and Enoch very nearly lost a cow that way.

Was it all a con-trick? Did Kwaname just know that the nature of Enoch Bengono and the weather at that time of year made this sort of scenario likely? Did he sometimes fabricate instances of foresight to advertise his skills? It is not too difficult if you select carefully and choose vague words. For instance, don't be too specific and don't include too much detail. Make sure that what you say can be interpreted in more than one way. If you already have some sort of reputation, people will do your work for you. Someone will say, 'That's exactly what was foretold!' Others will go along with it. Nobody will be quick to pick holes in the vision if everybody is scared of the visionary.

Observation is vitally important. Remember how much Sherlock Holmes was supposed to be able to deduce. 'Well,' he says in the story, 'I know nothing about you apart from the obvious facts that you are, etc. etc.' Observation enables one to maximise available information and separate the probable from that which is only possible. Atmosphere is another key factor. Words spoken in a dark, smoky tent, or in a seance or by a palmist, an oracle, or a person expert in interpreting the tarot cards, are invested with a dramatic quality and the mind of the listener is more likely to perceive a link with things that happen subsequently.

Is hypnosis witchcraft? Is witchcraft a form of hypnosis? We have abundant evidence that in some circumstances one person can so influence another that the latter will follow a course of action prescribed by the former without knowing why. I can't answer. My studies have not been slanted that way. But I do know that I have consciously used dramatic effects to make a person sensitive to certain phenomena. And by doing so I have made him less sensitive to other phenomena. That is to say, I have made it more likely that when he has to make a choice he will choose according to my will.

I ought to have mentioned broomsticks. I really love the concept of a black-gowned witch with her pointed hat flying around like a microlite enthusiast. It could be done easily today, but I don't believe the stories. I think they are another rationalisation. 'How can she know these things? She must have seen or heard them. How did she get there? She must have flown. How does she fly? You know that old broomstick that is always outside her door? She flies on that!'

Flight is terrific. I wish I had been alive to help Elmer, the eleventh-century monk at Malmesbury Abbey whose Abbot gave him a small budget for flight trials. He made some wings and launched himself from the highest tower available. He managed half a mile of flight and survived with nothing worse than broken legs. It's true!

I have said little about spells, though the making and injuring of images is a powerful example and I have covered that well. My problem is that a 'pure' spell is only the utterance of words, an incantation, without additional elements. Suppose I cast a spell upon you, using words only, that causes you to find a poisonous mushroom in the field and eat it. That would be a pure spell. Alternatively, I might cast a spell upon you that caused you to eat the poisonous mushrooms that I had swapped for the harmless ones in your supermarket trolley. That would be an 'assisted' spell and the magic would lie in the fact that you were unsuspicious, and ate them, and that I had chosen poisonous mushrooms correctly. How much is magic and how much is logic? Think again of the wicked queen in *Snow White*. She prepared a poisoned apple and delivered it. She went in disguise to the home of the seven dwarves and persuaded Snow White to eat it. No magic so far. But how about the result? The poison in the apple caused Snow White to fall into a trance that could only be broken by the kiss of a prince. That is big magic.

Chapter Seven

Going Professional

I got through my first year with excellent marks and a big increase in my knowledge about the supernatural. The second year was not much different except that I linked up with three other girls to rent a flat. It was a lot better than lodgings because we were free to do what we liked when we liked. But it had a downside, too. The building contained six flats and we were afflicted by other people's radios and televisions, not to mention the worn-out plumbing and decrepit heating system. We had the usual quarrels about who was responsible for buying what, and when, and in what quantity, and who should pay for the electricity this month. The worst thing was the high rent.

Then came the adventure of Frikkie Verloppen. The rumour-mill caused Walter Vokes, a man I had never met, to seek my help. He had contracted to rid the world of a person called Frikkie Verloppen, and was finding the assignment tough. Could I help him?

I think Walter lacked the qualities needed to be a good assassin. He had completed some minor assignments in a small West African republic and thought too highly of himself. He had now taken on the job of killing two white South African police officers. They were known for their brutality and at least six people had died in custody at

79

their hands. Walter had tracked them north into a lawless neighbouring state when they went on an illegal hunting expedition. Walter managed to kill one of them. They had been crossing a river in a canoe and Walter had shot one of them from a concealed position on the bank. The survivor had paddled fast enough to reach cover before Walter could aim accurately again. Ozzie Van Vuren was the dead man. Frikkie Verloppen survived.

Frikkie decided to spend the rest of his leave in England. He thought that a crowded island like this would make things difficult for an assassin. Walter had never been to England, and soon regretted his hasty decision to follow Frikkie.

He was out of his depth. Amongst his old university friends from Witwatersrand University was Patrick Quinn – Patrick of the love potion story. Patrick told Walter about my identity as a witchdoctor and Walter had enquiries made in my tribal area. Well, you know how past exploits get exaggerated! Walter became convinced that I was a powerful operator with at least three deaths to my credit and that I could more or less make the moon stand still. So Walter hung around LSE drinking in the local pubs long enough to identify me. He struck up an acquaintance-ship on the basis of places in Africa we both knew, and in due time brought the subject round to witchdoctors and witchcraft

'Nshila, I have African friends who tell me you killed a tribal enemy. I find that very interesting.' That was Walter's way of sounding out my status and attitude and hinting that he was in the business, too. The con-versation went round in circles, neither of us wanting to reveal more than we must do in order to force the next move from the other. At the start, of course, I had no idea what was in his mind. By the end I had gathered that:

- He was an assassin, albeit a beginner with only one substantial hit to his credit.
- He had accepted a contract to kill two people and had missed out on one of them.
- The surviving target was in England.
- Walter felt inadequate to operate effectively in England.
- The fee for the total job was considerable, and Walter could afford to pay me a lot of money.

I got hold of these basic facts and went home to West Kensington with my head in a whirl. Luckily the other girls were all out and the electricity bill had been paid. The lights worked, which meant the cooker would work too. I turned on the gas fire, threw Jenny's underwear off our only good chair and sat down with a very large vodka.

My first thought was, 'This contract and that sort of money are going to put me in a different league. Fame beckons.'

My second thought took a different direction; 'I have never attempted this sort of thing before. Can I do it? Am I good enough? What will happen to me – in this country – if anything goes wrong?'

You know the saying about people getting cold feet? At that point I thought it might be more than a proverb because mine really were getting cold. Well, that happens, doesn't it, when the gas runs out? I found a few pound coins in the jam jar that Isabel calls her strategic reserve and shoved them into the meter. Warm again.

'Look, Nshila, this is an opportunity. Grab it. Make a start and you will grow into the job.' The risk-taker inside my skull was getting vocal. 'You were just as much in doubt before the love potion business and before the cattle thief affair. But you succeeded. You owe it to yourself.

81

You owe it to Kwaname. And how will you feel in a week's time if you run away from this one?'

The next day I did a deal with Walter. I would carry out a feasibility study, for a substantial fee, to be paid in advance and not refundable.

I have not presented myself as somebody interested primarily in financial gain. Nor am I. (I have even done some *pro bono* work, removing a blackmailer to oblige the Women's Institute.) But remember that at the time I describe I had been two years in England, leading the life of a penniless student. I had begun to have aspirations. In fact, I don't believe it's possible to live in London, and encounter all those rich yuppies, without feeling that some of the wealth should be coming your way. I very much wanted to get a place of my own to live in, and I had been seduced by the comparative freedom that one gets from owning a car. I know that London traffic is appalling, and you can't park anywhere without major expense, and that you often get there quicker by bus or tube, and that every car owner is contributing to atmospheric pollution and endangering the planet. But if you own a car you don't have to fit in with schedules made by other people and you can choose, or change your destination. You can also shout and scream your frustration, which most people refrain from in public transport. So the money looked good to me.

The downside was that I would be arranging a death for money: something I had never done before. I would have become a professional assassin. Could I live with that? Well, this was just one assignment and I did not have to do it again. If I was quite certain that the world would be a better place without Frikkie, then I could do the job and afterwards take up some harmless occupation like pig farming, and put it all behind me. Anyway, I was only agreeing to a feasibility study, and the first part of that was establishing his rating as a target. I could still say that he did not deserve death and I wasn't going to do it.

I made a lot of enquiries through friends, and by letter, and by trawling South African newspapers and by e-mail. The replies left me in no doubt at all. Frikkie Verloppen and the late Ozzie Van Vuren were extremely bad people.

So I banked the money and got some more details from Walter. He gave me the date when Frikkie Verloppen had entered England and the place of entry – Heathrow. He had a photograph, too, that showed Frikkie receiving a merit award from the Commissioner of Police. He gave me details of Frikkie's appearance, height, weight, habits and interests. But he no longer knew Frikkie's whereabouts.

Finding one person amongst the 60 million or so in these islands is hard, but not quite impossible. For a start, a visitor like Frikkie has to give an address on the immigration form. The form gets filed somewhere and the data may or may not be entered to some database. A determined hacker may be able to raid that database. Of course, the data may not have been entered, or it may be false, or the address may be correct but the person never went there. But you have to try. I spent £3,000 in that direction and got nothing useful.

Where in these islands might he be? Theoretically, he could be visiting an aged great aunt in Stornoway. But was it likely? He was not really coming to England so much as escaping from South Africa. If he wanted to get lost in a crowd then he was probably in London. Would he have the patience to maintain a low profile for a long period? I thought that was unlikely. Surely he would do something to indulge his special interests. Were there any clues in that? Yes. Frikkie was a policeman, and they are notorious for sticking together. He would feel safe with them. Frikkie was almost certain to have contacts among British policemen and would try to meet them. Unfortunately, my contacts in the police were junior officers and unable to see the engagement diaries of likely senior men. But if Frikkie met anybody, then he and his contacts would certainly adjourn to one of the waterholes where policemen are known to drink. So another strategy would be to brief an enquiry agency and have watchers screening the pubs around Scotland Yard. A fact that gave this strategy a slight plus rating was the ease of recognising Frikkie if one should see him. He was over six feet tall, heavily built, and a piece of his right ear was missing.

I also looked at the other enthusiasm. South Africa had a rugby team touring the British Isles, and their first match was against England at Twickenham in two weeks' time. The Springbok team included two men with long records of foul play, and these were balanced by two similar Englishmen. The match was expected to be close, exciting and violent. Frikkie was certain to be there. I needed watchers scattered through the crowd.

This looked a dangerous strategy. I would need a minimum of twelve operatives, and if Frikkie was eventually assassinated in a way that got big headlines then there would be twelve people who might see his picture in the press and say 'I was paid to finger this man!' Someone would open his mouth.

There are some safeguards available if you take this approach. First off, choose the agencies with care, favouring those that will accept a commission through an intermediary or by post or telephone. Avoid any that make a serious attempt to assess your standing and responsibility. If you have to appear in person, use an alias. Stipulate that extra copies of the photograph are not to be made, and all those you provide, returned. Remember also that fingering the subject and killing him are separate activities. If it should ever be proved that you spent money finding somebody, and the somebody later died, the two events would still have to be connected.

My spending on private eyes was less than I expected because of a brave (and lucky) initiative of my own. I went into the main reception area of Scotland Yard and enquired at the desk for an imaginary officer who had, I said, given a very interesting talk at LSE. While the lady at the desk was establishing that they had no officer of that name I studied the staff notice board. One of the larger notices advertised a block booking for the South African match and asked for the names of officers who wanted to go, with the names of any guests. Three quarters of the way down the list was Inspector Hawkes plus F. Verloppen (Guest). I now knew where Frikkie would be on that Saturday, down to the block number and a range of row numbers. I only needed two operatives to identify Frikkie and follow him back to wherever he was staying.

But why did Frikkie want to go to Twickenham with British policemen who would be cheering for the wrong side? If he spent all his time urging his champions to inflict illegal injuries on the Brits, would he not earn some himself? I did not need to answer the question, of course, because the thing was clearly going to happen. But I did speculate. I concluded that the things they shared – a profession and a love of the game – would prove more important than national loyalty. Perhaps having an enemy amongst them might add a dimension to the beer-driven arguments afterwards.

Anyway, it all worked. By 11.30 p.m. on the evening after the match I knew that Frikkie was staying at a mid-range hotel in South Kensington. I enlisted a friend who was heavily into rugby and engineered a meeting in the bar of that hotel. I took the precaution of being lightly disguised. When Frikkie and my friend were deep into past matches and their third pints, I picked Frikkie's key out of his pocket and was shortly in his room. The next day I called on Walter for his help.

'I need some of his hair and some clippings from his fingernails or toenails. It will be far easier for a man to get them than a woman.'

'But not easy enough! All right, I can find out where he gets his hair cut and watch it fall to the floor and pick up some pieces when I sit in the chair as the next customer. But nail parings are a lot harder. How do I know when he cuts his nails, or where?'

'Look, Walter, you just figure out some way to get them, or you can forget the whole project. There's no witchdoctor in the world who is going to cast an effective spell without physical parts of the target person to work on. I'll give you one idea. A man like Frikkie won't last long in London without sex – probably with prostitutes. Find where he goes and bribe a girl to get you samples. They'll find it quite easy. "Oh! Frikkie! You're scratching me with those filthy long talons of yours. Let me cut them!" In my village Kwaname used devious tricks like that.'

I did not tell Walter what I had found in Frikkie's room and how I intended to operate the practical, non-witchcraft part of the assignment. The principal thing I found was a diary, showing that Frikkie intended to go to Cardiff two weeks later to watch the Springboks play Wales, and that he had a date with an official at South Africa House on the Monday after it. I also checked out his luggage, which consisted of one suitcase, one battered holdall, and a fairly new briefcase of a common make. It was the kind that has combination locks for the two latches. It was open, and on the lid inside was a typed note of the combination numbers. This discovery made me fairly sure I would kill him with an anti-personnel device.

My twin-track strategy involved burning his hair and nail clippings in a suitably impressive ceremony and killing him through a bomb in his briefcase as he walked down Trafalgar Square to South Africa House. The first part I knew I could complete with panache. The second involved detailed planning. As at first envisaged, it called for me to travel to Cardiff and back on the same train as Frikkie and switch his briefcase for the one containing explosive and detonator and radio receiver. I then had to get him crossing Trafalgar Square on foot on Monday morning when there were not too many people about so that I could kill him without collateral deaths.

How did I start? I waited impatiently, until Walter produced the goods. I did not ask him how he had done it, though I congratulated him, since five days is excellent time for that sort of task. I pressed him hard to check the reliability. Was there any possibility of a mistake? Could the samples have come from any other person? Was he trying to deceive me by offering parings from his own toenails? I could not be sure just how much Walter believed in the witchcraft element and I had to be pretty tough. 'Look, Walter, these physical tokens are the critical link between the fate I am going to unleash and the person who is going to get hit. If these are bits of your toenails and I work the magic right, then whatever was planned for Frikkie Verloppen will come straight at you.' I embroidered the facts a little bit to throw a real scare into him and he swore that the bits and pieces truly came from Frikkie.

What sort of workshop could I create for myself? The hut under the baobab tree was hundreds of miles away and I was a student, sharing digs with three other girls. The etiquette is that you can ask the others to keep clear for a short time if you have an assignation with a man. You can't ask it for anything else. You can't say 'Please will you keep clear of the flat between 9 p.m. and midnight on Friday the thirteenth because I want to cast death-dealing spells against my latest target.'

87

The unromantic solution was the old boiler room in the basement of LSE. It is called 'old' because they now have an up-to-date plant in another place that heats most of the school, and does it very well. The old boiler room is kept in use because it heats a limited area in the oldest part of the building which is remote from the site of the new plant. Like much old technology, this boiler is simple and unsophisticated and not computer-controlled and therefore never breaks down. People seldom visit it. I hung a few black curtains, brought in a brazier to burn the herbs, hung various charms and masks around the walls, scattered old bones on the floor and sprinkled blood around. Don't ask me how much of all this was necessary. I don't know. Remember my mixed cultural heritage. The educated side of my head says that since none of it has any effect at all then it does not matter what I have remembered or forgotten from my time with Kwaname. The tribal side of my head says that Kwaname got results, and I should try very hard to do the things that he did, in the manner in which he did them, and in the environment in which he did them. So I have to work in somewhere dark and hot, and it has to smell pretty awful, and I have to have all the impedimenta that I can remember and obtain. I reflect with gratitude on the impulse that caused me, when I first came to England, to bring some of my witchdoctoring gear with me. I certainly have one skull and one hank of hair that came from the hut under the baobab tree. They look incongruous beside the distilling flask that I stole from the school science lab when I visited my brother in Margate. Anyway, after all the right preliminaries, I mixed a paste containing the hair and the nail parings and spread it thickly on an enlarged copy of Frikkie's photograph. I poured acid on the photograph, murmured the words of death, and watched the paper disintegrate.

I did all this before taking any action on my 'physical' plan for his destruction. Why? Would it not have been better to get everything on the physical side set up first, and then cast the spell at the last moment to make sure the plan worked? Once again, I have to tell you that there are a lot of things we don't know. We don't know by what method witchcraft operates or what rules cover its timing. Perhaps it does not operate directly upon the target, but upon the circumstances surrounding the target, placing him in a certain position at a certain time and giving the hit a better chance of success. Perhaps the spirits operate psychologically upon you yourself, the witchdoctor, leading you to do things that are conducive to success. When you hear about the adventures I had when setting up the physical side, you will see that disaster might have struck at several points. It never did. Maybe it was because I had already cast the spells.

Getting the briefcase was not too hard. I had contacts who could take an identical item and fit a thin slab of plastic explosive into the base, taking up so little room that in normal circumstances nothing would be suspected. The detonator and radio receiver would go into the handle. But would Frikkie take his briefcase with him when going to a rugby match? It would not be natural. I prepared a thick document apparently coming from the South African Embassy and marked URGENT in red lettering. I caused it to be delivered by messenger to Frikkie's hotel shortly before he would be leaving for Paddington. I waited across the road to see him leave, having two return tickets (first and second class) already in my handbag. I got it right. He obviously decided to read this important document on the train, and he left the hotel with his briefcase in his hand.

He travelled second class which suited me well because the coaches are fuller and people are not surprised to find others seated close to them. I managed to get a seat that placed us back-to-back, so that we did not see each other but it was natural for our two briefcases to be side by side on the rack overhead. All I needed was for him to make a journey to the buffet car or the toilet. I did not really expect either move before we passed Reading, nor was I surprised when Swindon went by without him stirring. By Bristol Parkway I was getting edgy and by Newport panic was coming on. I risked a look round the seat and was disgusted to see that he was asleep. What was Plan B? I would just have to waste a day in Cardiff and camp at the station during the late afternoon so that I could catch the same train as Frikkie back to London.

Then I saw a silver lining to the cloud. Perhaps security at the gates of the rugby ground would search his briefcase. After all, it was a strange thing to carry with you on such an occasion. If that happened, it was far better that the staff should search his own briefcase rather than the modified one that I had failed to exchange. I took some comfort from that thought, and spent a peaceful day in the public library reading up on witchcraft in Wales. It contained some good stuff, especially in connection with hallucinatory drugs, and the plants from which they come. But it gave too much space to Druids, who seem to have been a fine mixture of con-artists and savage murderers.

I walked back to the railway station in the late afternoon. I picked a vantage point at the top of the stairs that lead up to the London platform and waited.

That's when the mistake of the day became apparent. My shoes. Image being important to me, I like to make the most of my height and I had chosen fashionable shoes with a decent heel. After all, I had thought, most of the time would be spent sitting on a train. The library had not been a problem because I had kicked them off. Now, standing on a wet railway station, my feet were in trouble.

The pointed shape was giving my toes hell, and my ankles wanted to die. I could feel the cracks in the paving stones through the thin, damp soles.

Two trains had gone and I was getting seriously worried when a battered and unstable Frikkie climbed the steps. I assumed that he had shouted too loudly for South Africa when close to aggressive Welshmen. But he was here, and he still had the briefcase. The train arrived, and once again I was able to sit back-to-back with him and remain unseen. Would I be any luckier this time? All the beer he had drunk would surely send him to the toilet at some stage, but would he sleep it off first? Before Newport he bought coffee from the refreshment trolley. As we emerged from the Severn tunnel, I looked round the seat and saw him asleep. Just after Swindon I heard him snoring. I tried to formulate Plan C and got nowhere.

I need not have worried. We were passing through Didcot when Frikkie grunted, woke up, left his seat and walked down the carriage. I acted the moment he had passed from view, achieving the whole thing quickly and neatly without a fumble. There was a good three minutes to spare before he came back and sat down. All his papers were in my briefcase: my briefcase was in the place where he had put his. His briefcase was behind my seat. The deed was done. I relaxed and closed my eyes.

Was that the end of the day's excitement? No. Would you believe it, at Paddington Frikkie got up and walked down the carriage leaving his briefcase on the rack. The stupid oaf had forgotten it! I grabbed both briefcases and hurried after him. On the platform, then, at Paddington, I actually confronted the target face-to-face and said, 'Excuse me, sir, did you leave this on the rack beside mine?' It was a terrible risk, because he might have remembered me from the brief earlier meeting.

He was obviously pretty tired and hung-over and took

a moment to register what I had said. He also showed some resentment at being addressed. Could that have been because I was black? He stared at me for a moment, and I saw something in his eyes. In books they tell you that some character perceived qualities in the depths of another person's eyes. I never believed it. An eye is an eye is an eye, it seemed to me. But looking at Frikkie changed my mind. I thought I saw greed and cruelty and viciousness in those eyes. Perhaps I was conditioned by my knowledge that prisoners had died in his custody. I don't know. Anyway, he recovered in a moment and spoke the appropriate words of thanks. Then he asked. 'Which one?'

What a fix! There I stood with an identical briefcase in each hand and for the life of me I could not remember which was which! I was, and looked, confused. Luckily his need to be macho and decisive caused him to act. He picked the one in my left hand, opened it, saw all his own papers and said. 'This is mine. Thank you.' Just think what might have happened if he had picked up the other! He would have opened it with his own combination and found nothing in it. He would have smelled trickery immediately. In my relief I was unable to resist a final comment. 'That's OK. Have a good weekend!' I avoided saying 'It's your last!'

When he got back to the hotel, he found a message from a secretary at South Africa House asking him to alter the time of his appointment on Monday to 8.15 a.m. The message said that his contact apologised for the inconvenient time, but had been detailed for an out-of-town meeting later in the morning. Who arranged the message? I did. It removed one remaining danger relating to collateral damage that would be caused if I exploded his briefcase when other people were too close to him. I needed about ten yards space around him. My plan envisaged Frikkie walking down the east side of Trafalgar

Square, and at 8.00 a.m. I expected a much better chance of his being alone. Maybe you also want to know why I planned on that location at all. Well, I had discovered by now that Frikkie was a tube man rather than a bus man. It was logical that he would take the Piccadilly Line to Leicester Square and walk down St Martin's Lane till it meets the east side of Trafalgar Square just above St Martin-in-the-Fields. But perhaps he would walk the whole way? Well, I would be waiting outside his hotel and would know how he travelled. If by some chance he did walk, then things were better than ever for me because he would cross the whole width of Trafalgar Square and give me more opportunity.

I was there on schedule. He walked to Knightsbridge tube station and rode to Leicester Square. I followed him discreetly when he left the tube station and then overtook him to reach a position on the west side of the square with a good field of view and well within the range of my transmitter. It was a clear fresh morning and I remember feeling excited and invigorated.

There were more people around than I expected because an early service was just starting at St Martin's. But I could see that when he was about ten yards south of the entrance there would be a clear gap. My finger was on the button when disaster struck. Disaster in the form of an extremely large shaggy dog that found Frikkie a novel and exciting acquaintance. He must have had a special smell about him. No way was I going to kill a beautiful creature like that. I cursed under my breath as Frikkie and the dog neared South Africa House. (In my mind I had somehow named the dog – Fumph, I called him – I don't know why.) I was resigning myself to the aggravation of a postponement. Suddenly, Fumph deserted Frikkie and disappeared down the entrance to the tube station. Frikkie was alone! I pressed the button as he took the first of the steps up to the building. Excellent! No danger to the reinforced windows. No doorman outside at that hour to impress the natives. No person close enough to Frikkie to suffer more than a mild shock wave. Farewell, Frikkie!

Now let's get back to the witchcraft bit of it. I can think of three things that might have gone wrong. I might have left the train at Paddington before Frikkie did, and never have known that he had left his briefcase on the train. I might have given him the wrong briefcase when I accosted him. Fumph might have stayed with Frikkie right up to the doors. I think Fumph's behaviour is the most remarkable thing of all. Unaccompanied dogs don't normally disappear down the steps of tube stations. Have you ever seen it happen? I have never seen it before, and never seen it since. So three turning points all fell in my favour. Was that because of my spell-casting?

The aftermath was interesting. A question of jurisdiction had to be sorted out, because an embassy is legally part of the country it represents and the Metropolitan Police had long arguments with South Africa House about the exact point at which Frikkie had died. South Africa House won, but soon realised that the need to be assertive had blinded them to their limited investigative capability. It took a week for their Head of Security to admit this fact and agree to a joint investigation. His great-grandfather's farm had been burnt down by the British in the Boer War and his grandmother interned. He did not like the British.

The investigation started with the obvious questions. How was it done? Why was it done? Nobody was in doubt that Frikkie had been killed by a radio-detonated bomb, but these days such a thing can be produced in a bathroom by anybody who has access to the Internet.

The bomb had been placed in his clothing or briefcase without his knowing. So his habits were reviewed and his

94

hotel room searched. The police officers who had been to the rugby match with him were able to suggest what sort of person he was, where he was likely to go, and who he was likely to meet. But no suspicious contacts could be identified. The staff at the hotel reported that Frikkie had often been in the bar. He had made conversation with other customers and on two occasions people had come to meet him there, apparently by appointment. The staff were able to give descriptions of these people, including 'a smart black woman who looked like an up-market hairdresser', but they could remember no names, and no diary was found in Frikkie's room. That line of enquiry also faded out. Enquiries were made from the police in Cardiff, but no leads were found.

Who might want Frikkie dead? They had an excess of suspects. A great many detainees, guilty and innocent, had suffered from his attentions as a policeman. But a trawl through police records in Pretoria found only twelve people who had been arrested by Frikkie, had left the country legally, and were still absent. Seven of those were in the USA and were eliminated. Two were in Russia and could not be found. Two were in England. They were now themselves police inspectors and were on a course at the Bramshill Police Staff College. They had been attending a lecture on 'Limitations of DNA Testing' at the moment of the murder. The last person was Elimelech Olonga. His treatment in prison had left him with head injuries and personality disorders. He looked a likely suspect until it was found that his relatives had placed him at a renowned British hospital and that he was playing football with other inmates at the time of the death.

The authorities soon realised that the investigation stood little chance of success and was costing a lot of money. They began to look for alternative solutions. They reflected that Frikkie was not the sort of policeman really required in the new South Africa and that they were better off without him. It was known that, in talks with his contemporaries, he had expressed extreme dislike of the post-apartheid regime and said that he was only hanging on to get his full pension. Finally, the authorities came up with a truly bizarre solution.

Frikkie had been a suicide bomber, the cover-up said, who saw no future for himself in the new South Africa and wanted to strike a blow against the regime. Why, then, the media asked, had he detonated his bomb outside the building and not waited till he was at least at the reception desk? Well, answered the authorities, he may have stumbled on a loose stone or been stung by a wasp and pressed the detonator by accident! Perhaps the bomb was actually on a timer and Frikkie had regrets at the last minute and delayed his entry to save lives! Where had he got the materials for his bomb? If this question was pursued, the answer might blow a hole in the fabricated story. So the South African authorities suggested that Frikkie had brought them into the country himself.

Nobody believed any of this, but 24 hours later there was a freak rainstorm in Wales and the media rushed off to report on a drowned village. Frikkie was forgotten.

How am I able to give you all this detail? Naturally, I took great interest in all the reports. I had never before killed somebody in England using, so far as they would believe, purely physical means. Killers make mistakes, and the British police get things right in the end more often than not. I was afraid. Later on I got a good deal of information from my friend at Scotland Yard and from Mike Fanshawe, who had handled transactions for three different clients in South Africa House. The thing was a top subject at parties for at least six weeks, Mike heard a lot about it, and I got most of it repeated to me. I even met one of Mike's clients at a party and brought the

96

subject up. He found the final solution most amusing because, he said, 'I have a strong sense of the ridiculous. The idea of an oaf like Frikkie having the skill to make a bomb is about as daft as you can get. If a man like Frikkie loses a finger in an accident then he's no longer able to count beyond nine.' He was also of the opinion that whoever got rid of Frikkie ought to come to the embassy and get a medal. I liked the man.

Chapter Eight

A Very Good Cover

I failed to make the Verloppen case a one-off event, after which I would put all clandestine affairs behind me. Success went to my head, or maybe my pocket. I still had a year to go at LSE, and in that time I had two other approaches. I accepted both, and in both I had a good result. So by the time I walked up to the Vice-Chancellor to receive my First Class Degree I had become a professional assassin. There you are. I have admitted it. Is the label really so awful? Later on I will argue a good case for the social usefulness of my profession, but right now I must make clear that I am the most selective assassin of all time. Only the most deserving people get hit. You can tell that from the exhaustive enquiries that I caused Zach Kawaro to make about Pullinger. Believe me, I have rejected more assignments than I have accepted. Of course, I never set out to be an assassin. When people asked me 'What are you going to be when you leave school/university?' I never gave that answer. I became one by accident, by acquiring a certain mix of skills and knowledge, and by my inability to refuse a challenge.

Towards the end of my time at LSE, I came to see that I needed a genuine business to act as my cover, and that it had to be legal and successful. I enrolled at the Open University for an MBA degree, intending to equip myself as a businesswoman. As I got towards the end of that course I scoured the trade papers for a suitable purchase.

How did I end up as owner of The Rain Consultancy, which deals in meteorology? The search was difficult, because there had to be an overlap between activities I was engaged in legally and my work as a witchdoctor and/or assassin. I mean, if my legal work was running a shoe shop and I was discovered mixing poisonous herbs in my kitchen I could not very well pass it off as a business-related activity, could I? But if I was a chemist then maybe I could create doubt in people's minds. There had to be the possibility of confusion between my roles. So running a petrol station was out, as were many lines of business in which the practical and the pragmatic dominated. I toyed for a while with a betting agency, which has plenty of unknowns and plenty of dark corners, but I discarded it as too complicated and risky. Then a day came when the column included a 'For Sale' advertisement for a weather prediction business. It proved to be run by a dedicated 85-year-old meteorologist. He was beginning to make mistakes in interpreting data, and felt that he could no longer give his customers a fair deal. Rain-making! What an opening! My mind flew back to the hut under the baobab tree and I could almost hear Kwaname speaking to me. Translated, he was saying 'Go for it, girl.'

I went to see the owner. He was a wonderful old fellow. He was sharp and precise most of the time, but twice during our meeting he lost his way completely and sat motionless in a trance. He was up-to-date in knowledge of modern techniques but distrusted their reliability and did not apply them. Another factor must have been the cost of modern equipment. I told him, 'It's amazing that you have remained in business so long.'

'I enjoy the work, Ms Ileloka, but the driving force is escape from my sister-in-law. My wife died five years ago and her sister decided I must be taken in and cared for.'

'Was that so awful? At eighty, weren't you grateful for a secure home?'

'A different home, maybe! Margaret, my wife, was an understanding, laid-back personality who believed that following your star was far more important than what the neighbours thought. Like me, she was eccentric. She was the world's top expert on the historic development of tapestry. Her elder sister, Vera, is the archetype of prison wardress. A week after Margaret died, Vera marched into the house and said, 'You can't live in this tip any more. You are coming home with me.' Her own husband was twenty years dead and she was desperate for somebody to boss around.'

'Why didn't you refuse? Age does not stop you living alone if you can still cope.'

'You haven't met Vera.'

'So this business is your refuge?'

'Yes. And I am lucky to have it. There were two large sheds in the garden, and by knocking them together and giving them an inner shell I managed to get enough space for a laboratory. Vera never comes in here. If I turn up for meals when the bell rings, I can survive. But what it will be like when I have sold the business, I don't know. Perhaps I will grow silkworms, like my grandfather did when he was old.'

I would have liked to tell him I was an assassin and could eliminate Vera for quite a modest sum – paid by instalments, if he liked, with 'Nought per cent finance' as they say in the car advertisements. But Vera's crimes were not vile enough. Also, I had a mental flashback to village society where a man who kills another in a fight is compelled to take responsibility for the dead man's wife and children. The idea of permanently caring for Keith

101

Manning – that was his name – was unwelcome. Our negotiations went smoothly, and I ended up paying not much less than he was hoping for and very much less than my maximum budget. What did I get for it?

I got a huge quantity of recorded weather data, that took Gillian ages to integrate later with a purchased database. I got maps and charts and drawing instruments that were still serviceable but were, as a method, made redundant years ago by computer programs. I got a lot of small-time customers who were active but not creating much revenue. I got about 25 serious customers whose business yielded a good profit. I acquired an existing business with all the right registrations and documents, which saved me a lot of time and effort. Finally, I had a network of observers all round the country who received a tiny payment for reporting any significant local weather phenomenon. Some of these had not reported for a year or more. I asked about this.

'Look, Nshila, many of these are men and women of my own generation. You get some natural wastage. Jim McTavish on Skye, went for a walk on the mountain in a blizzard and was never seen again. Wilfred Manfold in Aberystwyth went mad. His last three reports all referred to a monster in Cardigan Bay which was spewing pebbles out of its mouth to spoil the sandy beaches. Helen Nutley in Scarborough was forbidden to help any longer by her daughter. I got a very rude message saying the old woman was endangering her life by taking observations from the top of the hill in bad weather. But some of them are still very helpful.' (That proved to be true.)

Last of all, I got a fir cone.

'When I was a boy in Devon, my grandfather told me that these were the best ever prediction tools. "It opens out," he told me, "when fine weather is coming and closes up before wet weather". All my life I have kept one handy.'

102

'Does it work, Keith?'

'I'd love to say "Yes", but the truth is that it reacts to change rather than predicts it. But I'm always happier about a prediction when my cone agrees with it. This one here is Cone Number 259 in the series started in boyhood. Would you like to take it?'

I, too, am fond of the old ways. 'Look, Keith. I'll give you another fifty pounds for it, and I will keep up the tradition.' I did so. I am now on Cone Number 272.

An extra satisfaction in this deal was that I love water. Meteorology is mainly about water – or its absence. Things like temperature and winds and sandstorms are part of it, of course, but an awful lot is about water: whether there will be rain or not, and how hard and for how long. That is especially true in England because it happens all the year round with no 'dry season' like in my country. Water is great. Quite apart from being essential to life, it is beautiful, providing dew on the grass and sparkling leaves on the trees, and streams and waterfalls and rivers and the sea. It cleans things. It twinkles in the gutters and disappears mysteriously down drains. It even comes up drains at times: after a heavy storm you can find drainage points in the street performing as if they were springs. It is powerful, producing waves and floods and landslides. It is great to drink – a better friend in need than the concoctions man makes with it. It fills water barrels beside country cottages, and the over-flow runs twinkling down the path. It makes streams that you crossed in one stride into challenges that can barely be jumped. It makes motoring an adventure. I was travelling once in the Fen country, after heavy rain, and the road disappeared underwater beside a measuring post that showed the 'maximum depth of water ahead' as 4ft! I barely got through. Water creates tiny prisms everywhere, splitting the light into different colours. Go out on a bright autumn morning while dew is still on the grass: you can pick any dewdrop and walk around it till you get blue and yellow and green and bright red flashing at you. Magic!

That's rain in England. In Africa it is different but just as exciting. Colossal storms shot through with lightning: dumping water so fast and heavily that you can hardly see ten yards through it. There is not too much noise inside a thatched hut, but I have been in the houses that the Europeans built, which always had a corrugated-iron roof. The noise in a storm was so deafening that people gave up trying to talk. I get a faint echo of that sound when an English thunderstorm breaks over London and the rain falls on the skylight in my bathroom. The Europeans built an administrative centre not far from my village: it had the shape of a hollow square with a ridged roof to each of the four sides. That meant that there was a gully at each corner. In a storm, the water shot down those in four streams and met in the centre of the square to form a lake. The noise was terrific. You get erosion, obviously, during a storm: deep grooves open up in dirt roads, large enough to bring you off your bicycle. The same can happen when you ride into a heap of sticks and stones and earth that has built up when the water carried it against a blockage. Most dramatic of all are the flash floods that can happen when there is a heavy storm over a dry riverbed or gully. A huge volume of water collects in that riverbed and rushes downhill. You can be standing downstream in a place that is quite dry – no sign of rain at all – and suddenly you hear a strange rumbling and a wall of water comes charging down at you. People have been drowned that way.

Most marvellous of all is the smell of the earth when the first rain falls after the dry season.

Not far behind is the day-by-day excitement as the river rises over the flood plain when the rainy season gets under way. You walk a path on foot one day, and two weeks later you are following the same track in a canoe. Months later, the water recedes and forgotten landmarks emerge. You wake up one morning, for instance, and say, 'I can see the old mooring post where we spotted a crocodile last year.'

Back to Keith Manning. I was also keen to buy from him because rain-making was one of the first activities into which Kwaname initiated me. It fascinates me because, like other forms of magic, it is imprecise and unprovable. I know all the right spells, but sometimes I can make rain and sometimes I can't. Looking back, I ask myself whether Kwaname really did make rain or whether he simply knew that it was coming and cashed in on the fact. He was an intelligent, observant old man and he knew the seasons of the year. Perhaps he had a stock of small signs that built up in his mind to a near-certainty of coming rain. And he was the one who responded to any request from the villagers. If he knew no rain was coming, then he just said 'No' and they thought he had used his influence to deny their request, when in fact he had done nothing at all.

If rain-making is a con trick, and it is really only rain prediction, then it's logical that there should be a local element in it. In Europe one hears the expression 'Old Wives Tales', and at times these refer to perceived links between local signs and coming rain. The old wives have lived in the same place for many years and they know these signs. If an old wife were taken, say, from Cornwall to Cromarty, would she be as accurate? I doubt it. My own ability to make rain is increased if I am in a familiar place.

But if magic is unreliable, scientific methods are also limited. The meteorologists have the most marvellous data-collection and data-analysis methods. They have computer

105

programs that will predict the movement of blocks of air, and the conditions that will affect them. But they can't say: 'There will be a cloudburst over Mugglesham-in-the-Moor at 3.30 p.m. tomorrow'. To do that, they would need the exact conditions pertaining over Mugglesham immediately before the specified time. It would hardly be a forecast. By that time the black clouds would have sent all the Muggleshamites running for cover.

So my deal with Keith Manning went through. I changed the name and have ever since been Managing Director of The Rain Consultancy. We have the top floor of a small office block in Eastcheap. I found it through another of those knowledgeable, well-connected people in Mike Fanshawe's circle. I think his name was Rupert – or it may have been Percy or Archie – they are all so alike.

'Nshila, Mike tells me that you are looking for office space, and being asked astronomic rental figures. Is that true?'

'Yes. I think the problem is the amount of space. I don't need very much and all the property owners want to deal in large areas. The less you need, the higher the rate per square foot.'

'Well, for many tenants the place I am thinking of has disadvantages. But they might not be serious in your case. I think Mike told me that you were not worried about street frontage or modern architecture or high-speed lifts and so on.'

'No. My business is specialised and discreet. But I don't want anything seedy.'

Then the conversation was interrupted. We were sitting in a wine bar in Fenchurch Street where I was due to meet Mike and two of his friends. Mike and one other had been held back by some sort of crisis. The third person had been sent ahead to keep me happy. The others now arrived and the usual greetings had to be exchanged.

It was ten minutes before we got back to my need for discreet but non-seedy business premises.

'I understand. I am talking about a small building in Eastcheap. It is a lovely old place that escaped re-development ten years ago. Either side of it, several buildings were demolished to make way for large office blocks, but the ownership of this one was in dispute and the developers could never get title to it.'

'I don't want a whole building – even a small one.'

'Let me finish. Like many office buildings it used to have a resident caretaker who had a flat on the top floor. Those days are long gone and the owners want to convert it for renting out. The money they want is modest by present standards.'

'Why? What are those disadvantages you talked about?'

'The lift does not go all the way up to the flat. You have to climb a spiral staircase. There is a water tank and an air-conditioning plant on the roof: both are noisy and you have to allow technicians access to them from time to time. And ninety years ago the man who was then caretaker was poisoned by his wife.'

I took the place. The geographical situation is perfect, giving me a respectable address but a low public profile. Anybody looking for me will find the discreet brass plate in the foyer that says 'Rain Consultancy – 4th Floor and Stairs'. Nobody is likely to find me by chance. The water tank and air-conditioning plant are indeed an annoyance, but you get used to them in time. I have office space and living space. It is gloriously peaceful on a Sunday. My office block will eventually disappear and become part of some mile-high development with a striking, fashionable award-winning shape – a pineapple, maybe, to match that remarkable thing called The Gherkin that they erected in the early 2000s. But it won't happen yet.

The Rain Consultancy is a Limited Company and files

all the proper returns at Companies House. You can go there and read our accounts. It provides me with a wholly legitimate persona. I have a National Insurance number, and all the usual credit cards in the name of N. Ileloka, Company Director. If I ever need to go on the dole and claim state benefits, I shall have no trouble at all. However, I have the documents for two additional identities hidden in a small wall safe under the rear end of the bath.

We provide detailed advice about the probability of rain. We gather information from everywhere in the world and we are right just as often as anybody else. Why do people consult us when such information is freely available from respectable government bureaux? I can give several reasons. The first is that clients often have large sums of money depending on a 'Go' or 'Don't Go' decision and our fees (time-related) are small in comparison. Another reason is that a huge number of people favour a belt-and-braces approach. They like to get two opinions, and if the two opinions coincide then they feel more secure. It works in our favour, because in most cases we will agree with official opinion: we are using the same raw data and analysing it in the same way. A third reason is that we make a positive prediction. Every government department in the world will hedge its statements with warnings and conditions and the Meteorological Office favours phrases like 'Sunny, with significant intervals of rain'. We say GO or DON'T GO. People like that. They feel that somebody else is taking the risks with them. They feel they are getting something for their money. Psychologically, there is also the fact that people don't like admitting they have paid out money unwisely. It is much more common to argue that they paid out for the very best advice (meaning the most expensive) and that if even the best advice is wrong, what more can one do?

We are also popular because we talk to people. What's

so strange about that? Well, technology is now so cheap and the cost of employing people so huge that more and more firms are using menu systems to determine what sort of information a caller wants and then directing the caller to a suitable recorded response. It allegedly saves money for the firm, but it is intensely annoying. The customer rings up, expecting to get a human being on the line, and hears instead a long list of possible reasons for the call, and instructions about which button on the phone to press for each reason. The recording starts too soon for the customer to find pen and paper, and goes too fast to write it all down. If and when the right button is identified and pressed, there will sometimes be a human being on the line, and sometimes only another recording. The killer punch is often: 'Thank you for calling the XYZ Company. Your call is valuable to us. All our customer liaison staff are occupied at the moment. Please wait!'

The Rain Consultancy is old-fashioned in that respect. If you ring our number you may well get an engaged signal. In that case it has cost you nothing and you try again later. If you get an answer you will have reached Gillian Harker or Peter Grace or me. We will listen to your request, ask suitable questions, and give you our best advice. We will give you our time and attention. Being friendly pays off. Here's an example. Mum rings up for a prediction about the weather for her daughter's wedding in Herringbone-under-Edgecliffe. She certainly wants to know about the weather, but she is also desperate to off-load her latest worries about some bad habits she perceives in her future son-in-law and which she can't moan about in her family. Assume that she gets Gillian Harker (Peter and I are not quite in her league at this sort of thing, though we do have other specialities). She will get the facts about the weather plus sympathetic attention to her other worries. She will feel an awful lot better, and she will be well-disposed towards The Rain Consultancy. She will never notice that the advice cost her four times as much as if she had given the bare details and listened to our prediction.

Yet another bonus is that we have gathered, and can pass on, a stock of helpful advice. You would be amazed how often people go into an event hoping for the right outcome but taking no precautions for the alternative. Customers are frequently grateful for the most basic tips like: 'Have a stock of cheap umbrellas behind the door with amusing messages on them' or 'Get a box of cheap wooden clogs so that ladies can take off their designer shoes if it gets muddy'. I once overheard Gillian talking to a customer about that idea:

'Mrs Angard, here's something really novel you can do with clogs. Paint pairs of matching words on them like "Bacon" and "Eggs" and "Sunshine" and "Shadow" and "Snow" and "Ice". Then a woman with one word on her clogs goes round looking for a woman with the corresponding word. It's a great way to get people mixing.'

Silence, while Gillian listens.

'It does happen sometimes, Mrs Angard, but they can't very well express their dislike of each other in public, can they? And when you made up your guest list you would not have included too many people that hated each other, would you?'

More listening. I was listening, too, and my imagination created a vision of Mrs Angard. A worried, mousy woman, my imagination said. Somebody who expected things to go wrong but would never take drastic action to prevent them. Pretty, my imagination told me, in a rather faded way. Correctly dressed, but always having some small thing out of order and thus suggesting incompleteness. What was her objection to our idea? How would Gillian cope?

'Well, yes. You have to plan it a bit, Mrs Angard. You

don't want to put names like Adolf Hitler and Eva Braun on the clogs. But I think you'll find it a real success. It does wonders for the ego of a girl who buys her shoes at Marks & Spencers that she can face up to somebody who buys from Gucci!'

Here's a bit of advice we offer about marquees. People think that all you need do to shelter from the rain is get under the canvas. They don't realise that heavy rain on dry ground runs under the sides and creates big muddy patches. So dig a small trench just inside the walls. The moat will fill with water and the rest of the floor will be dry.

Gillian Harker, a meteorologist, and Peter Grace are my only employees. Gillian is God's gift to a semi-legal operator like me. She is a dedicated professional, utterly absorbed in meteorology, and utterly naïve about everything else except badminton. Badminton means that she is athletic beyond belief and has incredibly swift reactions. She works all our electronic equipment so swiftly that I can barely see her hands move. That is useful, for our technical area is stuffed with sophisticated appliances and we have comprehensive databases about every aspect of the weather. We are forever interrogating them. I could never do without Gillian. It never worries me that Gillian is a rather serious girl with a limited sense of humour. Jokes sometimes have to be explained to her. What does worry me is that she suffers badly from cave-man syndrome, and the latest example is Alfred. Alfred is mountainous and strong and sweaty and poorly-shaven and dumb as an ox. Gillian loves him, and he does exactly as she tells him all the time. I am terrified that she will marry him.

I tell myself that Gillian knows nothing about the illegal side of my life. But maybe she knows more than I think, and prefers to shut her eyes to it. She knows that I sometimes use the equipment to pursue special interests

111

of my own and she knows that for every megabyte of data we hold about the weather, there is another megabyte about my 'special interest'. She accepts that from time to time I have consultations related to that interest, and she acts out the receptionist/secretary role for me. If any of her friends ask her about the consultancy she portrays me as a woman who received a substantial legacy and runs the business as a hobby. She tells people that the job suits her, that she is well paid and that she has the very best equipment to work with. What more could she want?

Well, professional integrity, I suppose. There have been a few occasions when my work as an assassin required me to interfere with what was expected. I needed it to rain or not rain at a particular time and place and I wanted to send a prediction that was in line with my intentions. I remember two cases in particular. In the first, my target was staying in a small country town and there were two events scheduled for the local festival. One was an outdoor pageant and the other was an art exhibition. The hit was planned for the art exhibition and I could not take the risk that the target might prefer the pageant. The organisers of the pageant were paying us for a prediction and all the signs were good. Gillian would normally have sent a GO. I over-ruled Gillian, sent a NO GO, and worked hard to make it rain. I succeeded, and the plan worked. Gillian was furious.

'That was wrong, Nshila. You should never have overruled me. Our reputation – mine as much as yours – depends on honest use of the data. I'm not putting up with that sort of thing!'

'But it did rain, Gillian. I was right, and the client will only think how good we are.'

'That's beside the point, Nshila. You may have had an accurate hunch, or have developed second sight or something, but all the scientific data said there was no rain about and we should send a GO. We're supposed to be scientists, not on-course bookmakers.'

I eventually pacified Gillian, saying that I sometimes got these extraordinary flashes of insight and felt compelled to act on them. It did not happen often, did it?

Gillian had to agree. 'Not often. But when they happen are they always right?'

'Seldom. I lost a lot of money once on a horse called Tangled Knight which was supposed to win a big race at Doncaster.'

'Serves you right!'

The other confrontation arose when I had a hit planned for a fete in the precincts of Snodholme Cathedral and the Bishop rang Gillian to ask for a GO or NO GO. Gillian was convinced we should send a NO GO and I over-ruled her. 'Unprofessional' was, in that case, the most polite word she used to me. I had to do a lot of apologising and smoothing-over. But the target got caught in the machinery of a fairground ride and died to the sound of 'Rule Britannia'.

But Gillian does look at me strangely from time to time and suspects me of being what the Scots call 'fey'. She has sometimes seen me when I have been working in disguise and failed to remove all the traces. I make obscure remarks, sometimes, about my background and the strange events I witnessed in the dark continent. I think she makes excuses for her credulity on the grounds of my origin: and perhaps she does it quite deliberately to avoid any obligation to probe deeper. Twice she has been openly suspicious about visitors I have received. Gillian believes too much of what appears in the media and is inclined to think that Arab equals terrorist. If she opens the door to a properly dressed Arab she gets visibly disturbed.

You might ask why Gillian does not work for the

Meteorological Office itself. She did. But most of them have to do a stint presenting the weather forecast on television and she got an awful lot of comment about her personal appearance and dress sense and the shape of her legs. Most of it was complimentary, but she did not like it. Finally she experienced or imagined a degree of sexual harassment. Gillian left. But having left, she never took them to a tribunal or sued them. That tells you that she is a lovely girl, or hopelessly naïve, or out of touch with the modern world. Take your pick.

She finds working for me very enjoyable and I value her highly. But I don't care for Alfred.

Peter Grace was the son of a farmer in East Anglia and helped on the farm from an early age. By the time he was 16 he was stuffed full of country lore and expert in weather prediction, much of which knowledge he got from his grandmother. He did well at school and was accepted by The University of Essex. Then a financial crisis occurred in the family. His uncle died, and was found to have been heavily in debt. Immediately the farm was short of money and without one of the men who had worked the land. Peter had to endure a year of hard work and poverty. That was when he started his career as a thief. It began in a small way, stealing motor car parts from the stockholders and selling them by mail order. Peter was pleased by his success and found the risks exciting. He went on to bigger and better thefts, gave up the idea of university and reduced the financial crisis on the farm to manageable levels. After six years he was amongst the top industrial thieves. The peak of his career was reached when the police visited a manufacturer of propeller shafts.

'Have you lost three cases of prop shafts for the Maxwell Cicada?'

'What on earth are you talking about? You can't lose huge items like that. We have certainly not lost them.'

114

'Well, will you make a quick check, please?'

'All right... Now here's our computer print-out of warehouse stocks. All the figures match.'

'We do have a good reason for asking. Will you please go to the warehouse and make sure those crates are physically present?'

And when they went to the warehouse, they found the crates missing.

'How did you know?'

'They have just turned up in Tel Aviv.'

That was not the transaction that let Peter down. It was, rather, a mundane one involving lorry batteries from a small factory in Sussex. Peter was fond of saying, 'I should never have bothered with a piddling outfit like that. The firm was small enough for the left hand to have some vague idea what the right hand was doing. I ought to have gone for a government department. The MOD for example.'

Peter had an easy time in prison because he was seen as 'clean' and clever and rather enterprising by the other inmates. Smart theft from large organisations was in their view a commendable life-style. However, he did not think the odds were in his favour should he continue with that career and he decided to give honesty a go. He could not revert to farming because, while he was inside, his father had sold out. He came to my notice when I made a prediction about the weather for a fun fair and took the unusual step of attending myself. He was there, helping a friend who owned a steam traction engine. I love those things – the noise and the massive flywheel, and the smoke from that huge funnel, and the bright paint and the brass trimmings, and the image of ponderous power. We got talking. My prediction (Go Ahead) looked unhappy at midday, when heavy clouds began to build in the east.

'Not so good,' said Peter, looking at the sky. 'I think

115

the expert they consulted about the weather is going to have egg on his face.'

'Her face. It was my company they asked.'

'Well, well. You're in that sort of business, are you? I must say I would have agreed with you. None of the signs I use suggested bad weather for today. Will they ask for their money back?'

'Not at all. Everybody knows it's an imprecise science. But if anybody asks them for an opinion about my company they will be bound to say I failed. It happens at times. I don't like it but every business has risks.'

While we talked the wind changed direction and those heavy clouds moved off southwards. They had a big storm five miles away, but we had unbroken sunshine. I was relieved.

The happy feeling made me more talkative than usual, and when Peter said he would love to know more about my operation, I invited him to come and visit. Things developed from there. He spent two days with us, and got on well with Gillian. On the second day Gillian was busy on the phone and I was downstairs having a moan at the doorman. The second line rang, and Peter answered. He started off by getting the details with a view to saying, 'I will get Ms Ileloka to call you back.' However, we have a big board along one wall on which we plot the most significant recent data. Now, when I say 'white board' I don't mean a piece of white plastic. I mean the things they introduced in schools in the early 2000s that are linked to a computer and can produce the most sophisticated displays at the touch of a few keys. Peter had been playing with this, and as he talked he realised that he could manage quite a good answer to the questions himself. He did so. I returned in time to overhear most of the conversation and I was really impressed by his manner: direct and helpful and friendly, and obviously listening carefully to the caller.

Just why I offered him a part-time job that day is still beyond me. Business was good enough to justify some extra help, but I did none of the things one ought to do when considering an applicant. Maybe somebody bewitched me! But I did it, and he came, and it worked well. Eighteen months later he works full-time and I am very pleased to have him. I suffered a major shock when his probation officer turned up one day and I learnt that I was employing an ex-convict. I might have sacked him, but the probation officer was such a poisonous interfering, humourless character that I would have done anything to spite him. Peter's reaction was an attempt to re-assure me.

'Look, Nshila. I went down for stealing major items of equipment: things like engines for motor cars, and trailers, and street lamp standards, and garden machinery. What have you got here that I am likely to steal? And I succeeded because most of my thefts were unnoticed for days or weeks. How soon are you going to miss anything I nick from here? About two hours, maximum.'

So Peter is still with us. He does not have the meteorological knowledge that Gillian has, but he learns very quickly. He understands the meaning of her forecasts, though not the details of how she made them. He is extremely good at putting them into layman's language and making callers feel that he is on their wavelength. In that respect he is better than Gillian, who sometimes blinds people with science. Together, the three of us make an excellent team.

I sometimes think that Peter can make a good guess at my other activities. He says nothing at all, but being a countryman he regards unseen powers as quite credible. He is a long way from scoffing at them and told me once that he had a 'wise woman' in his ancestry.

Peter and Gillian have become good friends, but when you see them together the contrast is startling. Gillian is

117

pretty much an English rose; slender in build, with long, fair hair and a creamy complexion. She blushes furiously when she is upset. Peter looks like a minor villain, which he was, of course. His face is swarthy and he has one short-sighted eye, which protrudes slightly and gives him an unbalanced appearance. He has the thickest, blackest eyebrows imaginable and is, like Esau in the Bible, 'a hairy man'. The backs of his hands are well-covered, and if any buttons on his shirt are undone you feel you are talking to a gorilla.

Chapter Nine

The Buyer of Death

That brings my story up to the start of the Pullinger affair. I had been established in Eastcheap for a few years and thought of myself as a Londoner. Frikkie Verloppen was history, as were three or four very nasty – and otherwise untouchable – evildoers.

Assignments come to me through selected intermediaries who screen the clients and give me time for research: research of the type Zach Kawero did on Pullinger. It helps me to decide whether the target does or does not deserve to be hit. When I have satisfied myself that elimination is deserved, and can be satisfactorily accomplished, I have a single face-to-face meeting with the client. When I say 'face-to-face' I am twisting the phrase, because I always use a disguise and the client is promised a meeting with 'an associate' rather than the assassin in person. My reason for such a meeting is twofold. Firstly, I like to know the motivation: assassination is expensive, and the client must have some overpowering reason for wanting the death. Do I find the reason credible? Secondly, I won't work for people I actively dislike. So the meeting confirms or reverses my decision to take the job. It may also reveal facts about the target that were not picked up in my research.

The Pullinger assignment came to me through Julian

Jessop. He is one of the two people at the top of what I call my 'Supply Chain'. He and Dick Scarman are the only ones I ever speak to personally.

The meeting was scheduled, after the usual safeguards, for the Embankment Gardens. The client was coming into London by train. He would arrive at Charing Cross and would have to walk down Villiers Street. I planned to watch the steps that lead down from the concourse into that street. I might, armed with his description, be able to identify him and check that he was not being followed.

I chose clothes that were respectable but drab and bulky. I put some grey into my hair, selected a pair of steel-rimmed spectacles, padded my cheeks and gave my face a few lines. On my way to the bus stop I diverted to one of the charity shops that have sprung up everywhere, even in the City of London. They equipped me at rock-bottom price with an overcoat. When I emerged, I was one of those cheerful, slightly fat, middle-aged black women that you see singing lustily in church choirs.

I left the bus in Trafalgar Square and waited a few yards down Villiers Street, but that part of my plan failed. I picked the wrong man, and he turned right at the bottom of Villiers Street instead of left. Never mind. You can't win them all.

If you do turn left into the Embankment Gardens and walk a hundred yards eastwards along the path, you will leave an outsize image of Robert Burns on the left, and come to my favourite statue on the right. London is littered with statues and memorials: most of them feature boring old men whose memory has faded and whose images evoke nothing at all. This memorial is different. The plinth is only six feet high and the figure standing on it is a camel, with a soldier perched on top. He has his rifle across his knees and is staring into the distance. It is very lifelike. These are the words on the side:

120

To the glorious and immortal memory of the Officers, NCOs and Men of the Imperial Camel Corps. British, Australian, New Zealand, Indian, who fell in action or died of wounds or disease in Egypt, Sinai and Palestine 1916, 1917, 1918.

On plaques around the plinth are the names of all the dead from this campaign of the First World War. The whole lot, I mean, not the officers only. Naick Muzaffer Khan is there in equal honour with Major F.C. Gregory, MC. It creates an image. An army of mixed races and origins struggling through a hostile environment with traditional transport and eyes skinned for sight of the enemy. An army unified by adverse conditions so that death from disease was not less to be honoured than death from an enemy bullet. An army that wanted none of its members to be forgotten.

A bench stands opposite my favourite statue and at 4.35 p.m. I found it occupied by one smelly hobo in disgusting clothes (Jessop) and a yuppie-type in a smart business suit sitting as far away as possible. All that was according to plan. 'Go to the bench by the statue at 4.35 p.m.,' the client had been told. 'If there is a frightful, dirty hobo sitting at one end, that's the signal to confirm the meeting. Wait till there is nobody on the bench except the hobo. Sit down yourself, immediately. The hobo will soon get up and go. The next person to sit down – whatever they look like – is the contact.'

The yuppie left. A middle-aged man in black trousers and an anorak sat down. The hobo left. I sat down. Passwords were exchanged and we were in business. 'Tell me the story, Mr Crooksley. Full research has been done on Pullinger, but your personal views will give us something extra.'

'I am doing this because he killed my wife.'

121

'That's a good enough reason for wanting somebody dead, but more detail would be helpful. How? And when? And did he kill her by his own hand? Things like that.'

'I am a Chartered Accountant and an amateur archaeologist. Because of my hobby I was very pleased when my firm offered me a tour of duty with our office in North Africa. There are some interesting digs going on there, and volunteers are welcome. I was able to take part quite frequently, at weekends and public holidays. I enjoyed it a lot. My wife came with me. She also enjoyed it because she is interested in the full range of Mediterranean and Arab cultures. She was a wealthy woman, and travelled all round the historic cities of North Africa and the North West Sahara. A year into our tour of duty my wife fell sick and the firm booked her into a private hospital, for which we happened to be the auditors. It was thought to be an efficient and well-run place. About two weeks after admission my wife died suddenly and unexpectedly. The doctors came up with one or two possible reasons, but admitted that none of them were very convincing. They were puzzled.

'Naturally, I was very upset at the time and in no state to demand any extraordinary investigation. My wife had died, and even if some mistake had been made, nothing was going to bring her back.'

I could see that he was distressed: re-living the time was hard for him, and his voice quavered. We sat in silence for a moment and watched two teenage girls who were chattering away on a seat outside the café. Truants from school, I supposed. Then the client resumed.

'Six months later I was auditing the accounts of the hospital and noticed that certain drugs, one of which had been used to treat my wife, had not always been bought from the same supplier. One of these unusual purchases had been made shortly before my wife fell ill. My first enquiries were casual, subconsciously assuming that I would find a good explanation. It turned out differently.

'This is what I eventually discovered, with the help of a newspaper reporter and a private detective. The drug supplier normally used by the hospital had at one time been unable to supply certain items, due to production problems experienced by the manufacturer. In the emergency the hospital had turned to an alternative supplier who had stocks available. The particular drug used to treat my wife (and this was officially confirmed by later investigation) was an out-dated formula which had been re-packaged by the supplier and sold as if it was the latest type.

'The older version was normally effective. It was not a bad drug at all. But it had some nasty side effects, and for patients with certain medical conditions or allergies it was seriously dangerous. As marketed by reputable companies in Europe, these contra-indications were clearly stated in the descriptive literature and would have been observed by any hospital. In the translated literature provided by the rogue firm they never appeared at all, and the recommended doses had been increased.

'The latest formulation of the drug did not have these side effects, and my wife could have been safely treated despite the fact that she suffered severely from one of the allergies. The hospital, believing they were using the latest formulation, treated her with the old one. She died.

'The drug supplier had been buying up stock of the discontinued formula at a give-away price, re-packaging it as if it was the latest type, selling it under a misleading label, getting rich, and putting the lives of patients at risk.'

Mr Crooksley said it all in a cold monotone. He had established control of his emotions. I put some questions to him.

'Mr Crooksley, you have obviously made a connection between this drug scam and the man Pullinger. Tell me about it.'

'Well, my own enquiries led me to the drug supplier and revealed the name of the owner. It turned out to be a false name. But when the hospital became aware what had happened they put the matter in the hands of the police and there was an official investigation. It found that Pullinger was the true owner, and responsible for the fraud. When the police got too close, Pullinger simply closed the operation down and left the country.'

'It seems strange that the scam resulted in only one death – that of your wife.'

'Hers might not have been the only one. There may have been others for which some alternative explanation was accepted. And remember that the danger only arose in cases where a patient had a particular medical condition. Of the patients treated with the obsolete drug, she might have been the only one affected. Patients without any of the conditions would have responded to treatment in the normal way.'

A man and a boy passed in front of our bench – the man talking loudly: 'Hurt? Of course it will. But not half as much as my dentist hurt me when I was your age.' The boy's response was inaudible, but I remember thinking that he was lucky to have a dentist to hurt him: our village never had one. I probed my client's story a little.

'Surely one can argue that Pullinger is no murderer. Can't you see him as an ordinary criminal keen to make a fast buck? I mean, buying up old stock and selling it at twice the original price is not a new scam. If I was Pullinger, I would say that I never intended any personal injury, and that the drug had been used for years in Europe, and any alteration in the literature was an unfortunate error in translation.'

'No. No. No. Pullinger is an educated man who must have known what he was doing. Just getting hold of the drugs cheaply would have been illegal. He probably did not intend to cause death, but he knew it might happen and he dismissed it as less important than getting rich. I want him dead.'

'Killing him won't return your wife to you, and it's an expensive job.'

'I know it. But I want his life ended before he does more evil. Put him underground, and you will save an awful lot of future victims from misery or illness or death. Leopards don't change their spots. As to the money, I told you that my wife was a wealthy woman. She had a very big holding in World Oil Inc., and the shares have been rising sharply. They are all in my name now. I can pay the fee and still live comfortably. Few of Pullinger's victims are in a position where they can act against him. With the help of your principal, I am. I have a duty to all the others.'

'All right. I will recommend the assignment to the principal. Unless you hear from us to the contrary, you can assume your contract has been accepted.'

He visibly relaxed. Somebody was at last going to help him. Then he spoke again.

'There's one thing more. If it can possibly be managed, I want a shameful form of death. I don't want him dying like a hero in an attempt to rescue a dog from a mine shaft, or even passing away peacefully in his sleep. Ideally, I would like him to die by rat poison and have the obituary say that he got what he deserved.'

I was shocked. Professional assassins try to keep personal feelings out of it and operate clinically. What a depth of hatred to find in such an ordinary-looking person! But I felt sympathetic, too. It must be terrible to lose your wife as a by-product of a cheap commercial scam.

'Mr Crooksley, we can't guarantee that sort of thing. This is not like adding an extra blob of paint to a picture or writing an extra paragraph to a book. All I can promise is that we'll keep it in mind and go for a shameful death if possible. If we succeed we shall certainly expect a bonus.'

I left the Embankment Gardens at the eastern end. In doing so I passed the statute erected to commemorate Mr Raikes, who invented Sunday School. What strange phases English culture has been through!

Chapter Ten

Reconnaissance Begun

How does one decide time and place for the deed? Some-times it needs the most detailed planning, and sometimes it is dictated by fortuitous events. One of the latter cases, I remember, involved a yellow plastic duck. I had, as part of the research activity, stayed in the same hotel as the target. There was a duck in each bathroom with a charming note from the hotel saying: 'This duck is provided so that stressed-out businessmen can relax in the bath.' When he was paying the bill, I heard the target tell the receptionist, 'I just loved the plastic duck. I always play with bath toys whenever I find them.' I knew he was a fitness freak and I knew he went to a certain leisure centre. So I bought a duck and left it in the shower cubicle of the men's changing room. My duck was quite small, about three inches from bill to tail, coloured a few shades darker than lemon. It looked like a satisfied, well-fed duck. The bill was large, and wide open, and bright blue. It also had dark glasses. These were so large that they concealed the eyes, and much of the forehead. It was a self-important duck, fashionable and pleased with itself, and having a lot to say. It was a Yuppie among ducks. It had character. It was eminently playable-with. It was also filled with plastic explosive and had a voice-activated trigger tuned to the target's voice-print. He spoke to it and the duck responded!

The Pullinger assignment demanded more planning and more decision-making. I had three addresses where he might be resident long enough for me to set up a hit. One was in Albany Road, Blackheath. Another was at Corner Wood Hall near Pluckley, in Kent. The third was Garden Lodge, Greymoat Hall, Billericay, Essex. I set aside a day to check out all three. It promised to be a tiring day because I would need three different appearances. I decided to be a student at Blackheath, and something more like myself at Pluckley. Then I would stop at the Bluewater centre on my way back from Kent and get a suitable new outfit to cross into Essex. That way, I would only have to carry one spare set of clothing.

Why the student persona for Blackheath? I wanted something that would arouse minimal interest at 7.00 a.m., for that was the likely time of my arrival. Too early for meter-readers. Too early for delivery vans. Too early for Jehovah's Witnesses. But it is common for penniless students to be tipped off a jumbo jet at 5.00 a.m. and be struggling round London two hours afterwards looking for their lodgings. So I started out in a dirty, creased raincoat, a beret, trainers, and thick glasses. I would probably be remembered, but there would be no connection with the smart elegant figure that is the real Nshila. Under my raincoat was the business suit I needed for Pluckley and in the car were my black court shoes.

An early start – about 6.15 a.m. – and over Tower Bridge onto the South Bank. I love the river, and I love the bridges over it. I love the Albert Bridge, illuminated at night. I love the graceful modern, slithery appearance of Waterloo Bridge when the tide is high. It reminds me of that French phrase 'Ventre-a-terre'. I love Westminster Bridge because of Wordsworth and his sonnet. I love Tower Bridge. I am amused by the crass over-statement the Victorians were given to: Tower Bridge is a fine example.

Now for the Old Kent Road. I have friends (including Mike Fanshawe) who are dedicated Monopoly players and treat the OKR as if it was something romantic. The reality is different. A long succession of cheap shops boarded-up to await redevelopment and cheap shops struggling to survive until their turn comes. Mixed up with them, some sixties-style developments and the odd drive-in fast food outlet. The traffic, which used to be horrendous, is now relieved by state-of-the-art road layout. You can still see a few historic public houses, but are they all open? I like the Dun Cow. I like the Lord Nelson. I like the evocative sound of the Kentish Drovers. I get a real kick from the Thomas à Becket. It reminds me of the dramatic happenings when King Henry II asked, 'Who will rid me of this turbulent priest?' Four knights decided they would do the job right now and earn some brownie points with the king.

They were assassins, like me, but what a mess they made of it. All four of them took a swipe at Becket: they needed five strokes in all to do the business, and even allowed themselves to be seen. Henry would have done better to employ a single professional, and keep his mouth tight shut about the whole project. Beckett had confined himself to his cathedral because he thought he was safe inside and at risk outside, so an assassin would have had no difficulty in finding him. And what a location for a surprise hit and a discreet exit! Have you ever been in Canterbury Cathedral? It is a maze of passages, corners, staircases and split-levels. A skilled assassin would be spoilt for choice about where and when to do it. He or she would also have been swifter and less messy and would have escaped unseen. Those thugs were grossly un-professional.

Blackheath at 7.00 a.m. was clean and fresh. I am always surprised by the short distance between the drab area down below and the openness of the heath with its solid Regency buildings. At that time of day I parked easily, realising then that I had made a mistake. My personal appearance did not match my transport. I left the scarlet BMW in the meanest street I could find and made sure I was unobserved walking away. Close by was a corner shop which turned out, amazingly, to be run by an Englishman.

This true-Brit shopkeeper was immensely helpful. I asked directions for Albany Road and got precise instructions. I also got a comment: 'If you want that Pullinger fellow – that industrial mega-thief – then he'll be out jogging. There's a host of keep-fit types that grind all round the heath and even down to Greenwich. None of them will be back for thirty minutes yet. Best watch for the dog.'

'He has a dog?'

'He's got a smelly little Jack Russell that he sends here for his newspaper every morning.'

I could have followed the directions and walked to the address, but if Pullinger was out jogging I would end up loitering and looking conspicuous. Another option was to scour the nearby streets in the hope of meeting him. There might be something in his appearance or his route, or any companions he had which would give me ideas. Or possibly I might meet him passing a roadwork site where they were digging right down to the sewers. A quick push would see my mission completed.

But unpremeditated, instant action is dangerous. Just pushing him down a hole would be unlikely to cause death. The event might be seen. Worst of all, I knew Pullinger only from Zach's description. Would I recognise him? Would I attack some local worthy by mistake? Not a good idea.

Waiting for the dog seemed best. I could then follow

it back to the Pullinger home and be close by when he opened the door. I might get a good look at him, and even speak for a few moments by accosting him to ask directions. I had half an hour to fill in. How do you do that early in the morning without looking conspicuous? If I mingled with people at a bus stop they might talk to me, and remember me. I walked purposefully in one direction for half a mile, knocked at the door of a seemingly empty house, waited a while, made gestures of annoyance and walked purposefully back again. Then I sat on a bench, read a paper, and looked at my watch at intervals to give the impression of waiting for a lift.

I was getting seriously bored when I saw a small brown and white dog trot into the corner shop and emerge minutes later with a tabloid paper in its mouth. I am not doggy enough to tell a Jack Russell from other small, short-haired breeds, but there can't be too many such trained newshounds in one small area. Nor could I be sure it was the *Sun*. But I felt confident.

Then came something I had not foreseen. The directions to Albany Road had been clear enough in terms of first left, second right, and so on, but I had never asked the distance involved. What is the best way to follow a newspaper-carrying dog unobtrusively? Small dogs can move fast when they want to, but this one was stuck with a responsible job and was doing no more than trot. If he was going any distance then I was going to attract attention. Would I be tagged as a suspected dog-napper? Are Jack Russells a valued species? Is there a market for them? And suppose the dog did not like black immigrants. Suppose it attacked me?

You have to make decisions, don't you? I waited on the bench till the dog was nearly out of sight and then walked after it at a normal pace. I had the advantage of knowing its route, unless it took some canine short cut through a private garden. Thankfully, it stuck to the roads. It led me dutifully to the door of a house in Albany Road, where it sat on the step, scratched and barked. The door opened and I had a sight of Pullinger. This was not the suave, slightly overblown version that had, according to Zach, done business at Honeyridge. Not impressive. He had a pasty complexion (perhaps he had been wearing make-up the other day) and without exquisite tailoring his weight and paunch were obvious. He was dressed in the bottom half of a track suit and a dirty vest. A bald patch was visible as he bent down to take the paper from the dog's mouth. Still, I must give him credit for the jogging habit, and most men do that straight after getting up. They don't tart themselves up till they get back.

What progress had I made? I had seen Pullinger. I knew he had a dog. I knew he jogged. I knew that he sometimes stayed overnight in the Blackheath house. Sherlock Holmes considered it a capital mistake to 'theorise without data'. But once you have got even a small amount there is no harm in speculating. In my MBA course I picked up the idea of brainstorming. You are supposed to spend time writing down every possible solution to your problem, having no regard to reality, and listing every idea, however ridiculous. Nobody is allowed to comment: the ideas all get written up on the board. Later on, the group reviews every idea in a disciplined manner, and something that seemed at first sight to be totally stupid may trigger a complementary idea in a different member. You then get contributions like, 'That idea looks stupid as it stands, but if we also did *this* then it might be more credible.' So here are some zany ideas that came to me in Blackheath. (This is from memory. I put the original list on my laptop when I stopped at a layby on the A2. It has long been erased.)

132

- Attach explosive to the dog's collar and detonate it by radio as Pullinger bends down to take the paper from its mouth.
- Intercept Pullinger during his run and offer him a drinking bottle, the way you see supporters doing for marathon runners. (Poison, of course.)
- Sell him a poisoned hair-restorer that has to be taken orally to affect his hormone balance.
- Go jogging myself. Stick a syringe into his rump as I overtake him.
- Booby-trap the front door of his house while he is out jogging.
- Shoot him with a tranquillising dart and hope he falls under a bus.

It is not entirely a joke. You have to make a start on a project even though you can't see many steps ahead and may be wasting time and effort. The process forces your mind into action. Years ago, at school, I sometimes found myself trying to answer an exam question, and formulating an idea, and then writing down some words. As soon as I saw the words on paper I knew they were wrong. The moment that knowledge arrived, I also knew how to make them right. It seems to be a law, for me: I have to get the wrong answer first and only then can I get the right one.

I felt I had learnt all that was possible in Blackheath and got out my map to check my next move. The A2 was about to become the M2 and I could get off at Junction 3 to drive a few miles south and hit the M20 as it loops north of Maidstone. Then the M20 passed quite close to Pluckley. However, I saw no exit at that point and I rejected going on to Ashford and turning back. I hate backward moves. I would leave the M20 at Junction 8, take the A20 to Charing, and then turn southwest for the last few miles.

It worked out well, with the bonus of a marvellous view as I came down Blue Bell Hill towards Maidstone. On the A20 I saw from the signs that I was within a mile of Leeds Castle. I made a detour to look at it. There was a time when they used pictures of Leeds Castle to advertise something or other. I've forgotten what the product was, but the pictures were outstanding. Was the reality anything like as good? Yes. I looked it over and marked it high. When you look at things like that you have to agree that European civilisation is impressive. It took them a century or two to finish such structures but that is a testimony in itself because of the continuing motivation. There are comparable things in Eastern cultures, but Africa has little to match it. Great Zimbabwe is fantastic but it's only one item. Europe is littered with these things.

I almost missed the turn-off at Charing, but spotted the sign just in time and wiggled around past an apparently deserted railway station and off into open country. After a main road, those tiny lanes make you feel you have been driving for ever, but just as I was starting to worry I found a large notice saying Pluckley. I went over the brow of a hill and suddenly I saw buildings on my right, then more on my left, and I shot down a steep, narrow hill with old-world houses both sides. When it levelled off I was in open country again. I had done Pluckley! The whole of it? Maybe not. I turned around and went slowly up the hill looking for a turning to the left that I had glimpsed briefly. Yes! Church and pub a little way down that turning. What was it called? A real old-fashioned English name. The Plantagenet Arms. The inn sign was terrific. So many of these signs are standard efforts now, and you see the same White Lion or Coach and Horses outside different pubs. It's almost as if there was one firm doing all the signs, and the brewers phoned in asking for a 'Black Bull' and the firm offered three stock designs.

This one was unique, and must have cost the earth. It showed a fearsome hunchback figure with a crown and a dagger, stuffing the body of another into a huge vat of wine. It had to be Richard III (final year special subject at St Albans) getting rid of the Duke of Clarence. The wine was shown spilling over the top of the barrel – as it would if you stuffed a body inside – and Richard's feet were obviously getting wet. One of Clarence's shoes was about to fall off. The butt of wine was clearly labelled 'Malmsey' and the colours were clean and vibrant. I love Richard. He really wanted that crown and took positive action to get it. Nothing indecisive about him at all. And the imagination and opportunism! He saw his chance and took it. I wish I had an incident like that on my CV. The sight really lifted me. There might as well have been a notice 'Assassins welcome'. I pulled into the car park and stopped. I was outside a traditional English pub, which is usually a great place to gather local information. Above the door were the names of the licence-holders. I wondered whether Mick and Jessica Grant, and their customers, would reveal all the facts needed about Pullinger and Corner Wood Hall.

Reflecting on Richard III from a professional angle, I realised that getting away with the Clarence murder was not much of a worry for him. Once you are king, as he soon made himself, retribution is unlikely because those seeking it run a big risk of being chopped themselves. The message gets across – 'mess with this fellow and it might be the last thing you do'. So the more people who knew that Richard had drowned Clarence, the better it was for Richard. That was the exact opposite of my case, since I needed to conceal any connection with Pullinger's death. Richard was more nearly in the position of old Kwaname, who used public knowledge of what he had done to reinforce his power.

Chapter Eleven

The Plantagenet Arms

Mick Grant was arranging bottles on the shelf behind the bar when he heard Jessica fold her newspaper and push back her chair. A moment later she came through from the kitchen and stood beside him.

'It's a great day for you, Mick.'

'Why do you say so?'

'I have done the accounts: the Plantagenet Arms has made its first monthly profit. And your horoscope mentions a fascinating black stranger.'

Mick Grant had been made redundant at 45. After long discussion, he and his wife Jessica had decided to try their luck as inn-keepers. They had applied to a large local brewery, quickly learning that prospective tenants were carefully screened because of the colossal failure rate in the early years. That was the time, the brewers said, when people discovered how hard the work was and how much the reality differed from the romantic image. Mick and Jessica had worked hard and waited a long time for a suitable tenancy. Finally, the brewery rang them with good news.

'The enquiry has ruled against the landfill refuse site at Pluckley. It is the end of a planning battle and means a new life for The Plantagenet Arms. We shall start immediately on major refurbishment and the place is yours if you want it. Better still, the decision releases an adjacent parcel of land for sale. We might be able to extend.'

Mick and Jessica were soon working on the structure and furnishings and layout of the pub in cooperation with the consultant hired by the brewery. Jessica wanted the place to be attractive to present-day pub users, and was critical of old traditions. There were times when she spoke forcefully.

'Most men can't escape from the spit-and-sawdust image of a pub where they got drunk when they were young and lied to each other about their success with women.'

'That's not fair. I have not been in a place like that for thirty years.'

'All right, I'm exaggerating. But these days a large minority of pub visits are made by husband and wife, or boy and girlfriend or even women on their own. And most pubs are still lacking in the amenities and ambience that women want.'

'Well, I agree that things are moving in that direction. Maybe there are things I would never think of that are essential from your point of view. I am willing to listen.'

Jessica was still in an aggressive mood. 'You are going to do more than listen. There will be times when I make the decision and you put up with it. I want the Plantagenet Arms to be the sort of place where a smart woman can come in on her own and feel entirely comfortable. I don't want the slightest hint, by way of slower service, for instance, that women are not every bit as important to us as men. But let's cross those bridges later. What sort of place do we go for? Do we aim for a five-star rating?'

'It's one possible option. These days a business has to have a clear identity – something that distinguishes it from others and makes it a place people will drive a long way to visit. Suppose I consider the female viewpoint. You like to dress up for the evening and you are never much impressed by the scruffy men you find around you. What about a "Men wear ties" restaurant? That would be distinctive enough.'

'We can't go quite that far. There will still be local people who want to walk around the corner from their houses, sit in a cosy atmosphere, and drink beer from pint mugs. We have to work out a compromise.'

It took Mick and Jessica about six weeks to agree their strategy. Those six weeks were full of anecdotes about what they had liked or disliked in the past, and conjecture about what customers wanted today rather than yesterday. They never actually came to blows, but they certainly shouted at each other. In the end they were both happy with the solution. The Plantagenet Arms would put quality first, even if it meant higher than average prices. The ambience would be upmarket, well-designed in the first place and carefully, conscientiously maintained. It would be spacious, clean, and free from the smell of yesterday's cooking. The furniture would be solid. The food would be excellent but not extravagant. The beers, wines and spirits would be carefully selected, and kept under the best conditions. The service would always be efficient and friendly, but not servile. Ideally, no customer would have cause for complaint, but if it did happen then the failure would be rectified immediately without any attempt at justification or excuse.

Mick and Jessica lived through the first two years and put up with all the hardships and setbacks. The promotional strategy was slow to pay off. Suppliers let them down. There were faults in the building work. The refrigeration plant failed. Two highly-paid chefs left them because they found Pluckley too remote. One was so ambitious that the same dish differed dramatically from one night to the next. But they survived.

One of the good things that came along was Jemima.

She was a Danish student who had set out in her gap year to travel the Celtic fringe before studying archaeology at university. Her planned itinerary had been Scotland, Ireland and Wales, returning through Southeast England to Harwich. She was on the way home when somebody mentioned The Garden of England. She asked where it was and was told 'Kent'.

'How do I get there?'

Jemima was told to turn off the M25 at Junction 3, go down the M20 for 25 miles and then turn right. 'If you reach Folkestone you have gone too far.'

Jemima arrived outside The Plantagenet Arms at 11.30 on a spring morning. 'Am I in the Garden of England?'

'Yes. Pretty much in the middle of it.'

'I like it. Can you give me a job?'

It was a most unusual interview, but Mick found Jemima a great asset. Her outward appearance was the classic dumb blonde – tall and slender, with shoulder-length hair. Somewhere in her 18 years she had learnt that dumb blondes could raise a laugh. She cultivated the image. Temporary employment as barmaid and waitress soon became permanent. Male customers liked her for obvious reasons: women liked her because she was efficient and polite.

Jemima was also good with the occasional staff. She changed their attitude to work. Starting out, they were sometimes inclined to think that serving other people was a demeaning role to be performed in a grudging, surly manner. Jemima convinced them that helping people enjoy themselves could be a pleasure. Her enthusiasm and friendliness infected them. The Plantagenet got known as a friendly place to go. Life was promising when Mick looked out of his office window at 11.15 a.m. to see a scarlet BMW drive into the car park. No door opened for a few minutes, but he saw a flash of light from

140

the vanity mirror. Then the driver got out and stood looking at the view. Mick saw a tall slender black girl dressed in a black suit, finishing just below the knee: no hat: smart but sensible shoes with a medium heel. When she turned to walk towards the doorway he saw a gold necklace and earrings, but otherwise the image was black all over.

What was her errand? Mick knew how deceptive appearances are, but the first thought in his mind was Public Relations. Somebody scouting for a location to entertain backers or buyers for an expensive lunch or dinner. Should he go to meet her? Negative. No point in paying unasked attention. Maybe she had arranged to meet an elderly aunt and had picked Pluckley as a convenient spot. Another thought: Jemima was on duty in the bar and it would be amusing to watch the interaction between two such contrasting women. Negative again. Good publicans are not voyeurs. Not that the girl would lack for people staring at her. Horace Ashbee was in the bar along with Nick Horam from Spiders Cottage. Both were recently retired: one a salesman of agricultural machinery and one a builder. They were unlikely to ignore such a visitor. Mick shook his head and went back to the products and prices offered by wine merchants. How far should he go in favouring the New World and Antipodean wines? The Australians and Californians were among the best, but a number of customers still wanted vintage wines from France. And how about the really expensive ones? It looked good on the wine list to have a few priced at £100 or more, but things would be pretty dire if somebody actually ordered one and he did not have it.

Ten minutes later, his curiosity about the visitor overcame him. He went into the bar and stood beside Jemima. As expected, he found Nick Horam and Horace Ashbee sitting with the visitor and attempting polite small talk. It was

141

easy for the host to introduce himself and ask, 'What brings you here?'

A business card was offered. 'This tells all, Mr Grant. I like your pub, by the way.'

Mick held the card at arm's length. 'No good: the print's too small.' He took his glasses from his breast pocket and tried again. 'At least I know how to address you now, Ms Melville. But I never heard of this outfit JUNGLE REFUGE. What is it?'

'Well done. That's what you're supposed to ask. It's a charity. We are concerned with the environment in its broadest sense, and particularly with the world's few remaining jungles and the creatures that live in them.'

'Then why not feature some special animal?' Horace joined the discussion. 'Why not elephants or tigers or giant gorillas or anacondas? I could get excited by the idea of an endangered hippopotamus, but the jungle in general seems rather vague.'

'We think that field is over-crowded. We want to be different. Also, the ecology of a jungle depends on plenty of creatures that are rather nasty to human eyes: it's not all overgrown pussy-cats and apes with near-human faces. There are snakes and poisonous spiders and creepy-crawlies too. They all make a contribution and we worry about the whole lot of them, so we take the environment in our title, not just one resident. Our advertising presents the jungle as a mysterious and exciting place: both fascinating and frightening.'

'I can buy that. You need product differentiation these days. It's like the fancy names for the beers and lagers I have to keep in stock. Are you here on business, Ms Melville, or recreation?'

She smiled at Mick. 'The "A" on the card is for Amanda, Mr Grant, and if it's your name that I read over the door then you're Mick. Nice to meet you, Mick. About your

142

question: it's business, but the type of business that gives me a fun day out and lets me meet nice people. I'm on reconnaissance. Several others like me are out, too. Our board have developed a strategy of going for the big bucks and we're supposed to search out promising areas. We aim to find and identify rich people who, if they give at all, will give large sums. You could say that it's foot-in-the-door salesmanship taken to the top of the market. That's why my ears flapped when these gentlemen were talking about your clientele, and mentioned some heavy spenders.'

Horace picked up the large glass bottle on the counter with the BARNARDO'S label and shook it to hear the five-pence pieces jingle. 'We certainly have some of those, but for others the charitable giving is at this level. But what do you really mean by big bucks? What will you get from any responsive target?'

'Put it this way. If anybody gives us less than five hundred pounds, we won't be back to try again. We have worked out that the full cost of putting the right representative on the right doorstep at the right time is £410.55, so anything less and we have lost out. Plenty of the calls we make are fruitless, so one is hoping for a thousand or more from the others. Of course, people don't always give at once. The cautious ones always call HQ to check our identities.'

Nick Horam looked out of the window. 'Here are some more of our regulars arriving. But not the big-bucks men, yet. That tired old Landrover is Frank Halliday from Cork Tree Farm and the big Volvo is Joan Gresham and her half-brother Vince. This pub really has three types of customer. There are locals, like Horace and myself: people who live in or near the village. Then there are various incomers, and people from farther off. They have a slightly different lifestyle. They eat out a lot (often here), drink

143

wine more than beer, and travel all over the county for entertainment. Some of them are heavily into horses. They get on well with us locals but there are no deep friendships. Then there is the smart crowd.' Nick faltered and stopped.

'What about them? I want to know!'

Nick's answer was still hesitant. 'Well, I never know quite how to describe them. You can't point to any one thing that unites them, except money, yet some of the other groups are not badly off. And even some of us locals have got a bit stashed away. What distinguishes our smart set is that they are careless spenders.'

'Go on.'

'You get the feeling that long-term misfortune is beyond their understanding. They seem to think that because they have never experienced hard times, then hard times must be an old wives' story. They buy things on an impulse, and run up huge debts, and never consider that they might one day run out of credit. If it ever did happen, they seem to think, they would just go out and get rich all over again! They have an astonishing self-confidence, yet they don't seem particularly intelligent or knowledge-able.'

The visitor was interested in Nick's general comments about wealth. 'You may think it strange, but I could tell the area had promise before I reached your village. I saw horses. They are one of our indicators. Horses cost the earth to look after. If you drive through an area and see horses everywhere, you can be sure there is money, too! In the half hour before I got here I was stuck behind a horsebox three times. I thought it was a good sign.'

'Got you,' Nick responded. 'Horses, we have in plenty. Now your visit makes sense. If you make us a target area, what happens next? I want to know so that I can put my savings safely under the mattress.'

Greatly daring, Horace put his hand on Amanda

Melville's arm. 'Don't look now, but one of our big spenders is just getting out of that Porsche in the car park. It's Donald Crosier. He's a well-known art critic. And the other car driving in is Janet Hare. She's in your sort of business but right at the other end. She collects for the Cottage Hospital.'

A group of six people was soon together round the corner of the bar. Amanda Melville, Nick Horam, Horace Ashbee, Frank Halliday, Janet Hare and Donald Crosier. Mick Grant and Jemima were still behind it. Amanda was clearly the focal person in the group, but somehow everybody seemed to be included. Frank Halliday told Donald briefly who Amanda was and what she did. Donald followed up on the introduction.

'I don't think I'm quite in your target league, Ms Melville, but the environment is certainly one of my priorities and you can phone me sometime, if you like.'

'Thank you. I will.'

Frank Halliday spoke again, 'Are you going to be in this area frequently, Amanda?'

'I'll be somewhere near for about three days a week for the next three weeks. This afternoon I have to go over the river to keep an appointment in Billericay.'

'Billericay? I have a call to make there some time soon.' This was Donald Crosier. 'I've heard of an artist there, said to have some very provocative work on her easel. The name's Groveman, I think. Searching out new talent is a major part of my work.'

Nick Horam reverted to the theme of potential rich donors. 'I suspect that this new man Pullinger is one of the wealthiest around. He paid the full asking price for Corner Wood Hall. It's in a terrible state and needs huge sums to put it into repair.'

For a time the conversation centred on Corner Wood Hall. Everybody offered brief comments.

'Is the place really that bad? It looks good enough from the outside.'

'It's different within. The floors of the top rooms are rotted and there are places you could fall right through. Some of the window frames are so far gone that they would fall out if a person leant against them, and take the person with them. There are treads missing from some of the stairs, and the cellar is an absolute death trap.'

'Yes, I've heard that. I've also heard that the sewage tank is leaking into the Bait Brook. A few months ago Mrs Jansen fell off the footbridge and spent two weeks in hospital.'

Frank Halliday gave the talk a new direction. 'Pullinger may be rich, but I have met him once, and I did not like him at all. My daughter Susan pointed him out to me because she had seen him at Corner Wood Hall through her field glasses.'

'That's a strange way to get to know somebody.'

'Well, Susan has a bird-watching project in the sixth form and she spends hours upstairs observing them. From our attic room you can see Corner Wood Hall quite clearly and everything that goes on there. She noticed how seldom he was at home. Something like one weekend in three is his attendance record so far. An absentee owner, I reckon, and they don't contribute much to the community.'

'Is your Susan going to be a "twitcher", or whatever they call them, then?'

'I think they prefer the title "birders" these days. But, yes. She is getting quite interested in it. I am trying to persuade her join the local society.'

Nick Horam was more interested in Pullinger than the doings of Frank's daughter. 'But, about Pullinger, is he any worse than the last owner? There is a story here, Amanda, because the property includes the ruin of a small castle. It is usually called The Keep. It was one of those things built in the wrong place at the wrong time by the wrong man, and it never amounted to much in terms of warfare. But the last owner had grand ideas about making it a tourist attraction. He generated a story about it – mostly fiction – and created special lighting effects and had a tea-room at the gate and advertised it as "Living History".'

Mick Grant had said little in the past few minutes. 'I'm hoping that Pullinger won't have much use for The Keep. Some of the stones used in the building would be just perfect for a storage shed I am planning. I aim to make him an offer.'

Janet Hare had a different view about the previous use of The Keep. 'I thought the "Living History" effort was quite imaginative. Most people emphasise warfare when they tart up old castles, but he worked on other things as well. He got amateur actors in and portrayed scenes from the social life of past times. There were off-duty guards drinking outside the buttery, and ladies on horseback setting off for a visit and men-at-arms training in the field. On an upper floor there is a wide ledge with a carved stone beside it. He had a woman sitting there, with a knight kneeling at her feet, proposing marriage. He called it "The Proposal Chair". It was amusing.'

'Getting back to Pullinger,' said the persistent Nick Horam. 'I was over at Gloria Sandmart's stables the other day and Pullinger was there, negotiating the hire of a hunter. I could tell Gloria did not want his business, but he was very insistent. I heard her state a price, and I know she uses price as a weapon to put people off without actually refusing. She asked twice the amount she asks me for my occasional day out, and he agreed straight away. I asked her later what she had against him. She said she disliked his manner, but, more importantly, he did not appear a very competent or considerate rider. She saw him as the sort of person who wants to be seen in the field for status reasons and social reasons.'

'You can see that in the way he drives a car. Fierce and noisy. Always revving the engine, always in the wrong gear, always slowing or stopping in a scream of brakes and a smell of burnt rubber. He's got no feel for machinery.'

'The man is a classic evil squire type.' This from Fred Basing, who had entered the bar in time to hear the last exchanges. Fred was a tall man, distinguished by very white skin and black hair that fell in a kiss-curl over his forehead. Admirers described him as 'Byronic', which pleased him greatly. 'He has started proceedings to evict Helen Snow from that cottage beside Hanger Wood. She has been there since her husband died and old Sir Glynn promised she should keep it as long as she wanted with rent rises linked to inflation. Pullinger reckons he's not bound by that promise.'

'I believe that's true, Fred,' Janet Hare intervened. 'But you're against him anyway because he tried to make up to your wife in the Golden Goose over at Six Way Green. You had to take a telephone call out in your car because of all the noise. Remember? Polly had to fend him off for ten minutes and chewed pieces out of you for not being there!'

Donald Crosier remembered the event also. 'You can't blame him for trying. Your Polly is a highly attractive woman, and knows it. She just can't bring herself to hand out a harsh put-down.'

'That's all true, but I disliked Pullinger before that.'

Vince Gresham spoke up from the far end of the bar. 'I know him a little from business. He thinks he's God's gift to women generally, but he falls heavily for a certain type, and your Polly belongs to it. He has a big weakness, there. I've heard that the only people who have beaten him in business deals have been women.'

148

The numbers in the Plantagenet Arms increased as time moved towards 1.00 o'clock. Stools around the bar filled up and several of the tables were taken. Jemima was joined by Mary Fetcham. There was always a group of three or four people around the visitor. Always men. Her combination of youth, smartness, skin colour and social skill made for a honey-pot effect. As Mick went about his business he heard odd pieces of the conversation, which were frequently about local people. Not surprising, I suppose, Mick thought, in view of what she claims to be.

The visitor ate a prawn sandwich, then cheese and biscuits. She stayed two hours in all and said a formal farewell to Mick before going. 'My assignment demands more visits like this before I can report back, but my first feelings are favourable.' She asked directions, and asked also, 'Will that take me past Corner Wood Hall?' She seemed pleased to learn that it would be obvious, on the right-hand side after about three miles.

As they were clearing up after the lunch time trade Mick asked Jemima, 'What did you think of our surprise visitor – the elegant Ms Melville?'

'I was scared of her. She is a very clever, dangerous woman. But you daft men can't spot it. Did you notice how little she drank? Two glasses of white wine. She was manipulating the conversation all the time.'

Horace Ashbee objected. 'She made the day for most of us. If a woman like that wants to manipulate me, I'm going to sit back and enjoy it. And what about you, Jemima? We all pour money into Mick's pocket just to sit and chat with you. Isn't that manipulation?'

It was the art critic who had the last word. 'I think her charity must pay its staff well. Did you recognise that perfume? I did. The present rate is about £200 for 15 millilitres.'

That was hard work. I really loved the pub, but digging for information is a slow old business. Men are a good source when you get them going (whoever tagged women as gossips?) but they constantly stray from the subject. Several of that lot were well over forty but their hormones were talking more than their brains.

But I did learn more about Pullinger. He was a recent incomer, and had created a poor impression. He wanted to look good, and intended to hunt, even if it cost him a lot of money and risked injury. He was capable of evicting old ladies from their homes. Late in the conversation I also learnt that he was a bit short-sighted and had poor dress sense. I had also seen Corner Wood Hall, and the grounds in which it stands, and the Bait Brook (a foul-looking stretch of slime), and the vicious bend in the road where the back drive from the Hall comes out. Better still, I had seen The Keep. It was larger than I had expected from the deprecating way they spoke of it. I had to find a way to see more of it. Perhaps I could get invited to that house that overlooks it. What was the girl's name? Yes. Susan Halliday. That option, of course, would need a change of appearance and personality.

I also got way-out ideas about methods of execution, which I recorded on my lap-top for brain-storming later:

- An accident in one of the insecure, dangerous parts of Corner Wood Hall.
- Thrown from his horse while out hunting.
- A fall into the poisonous waters of the Bait Brook.
- Trips over a stone and falls into the sewage tank.
- Interference with his car, so that his furious driving proves fatal.

150

- A bullet fired from the attic of Susan Halliday's home.
- Seduced to his death by a woman.

Then it was north over the Thames to find Garden Lodge.

Chapter Twelve

The Artist and the Barn

'Loyalty card, miss? Anything from our shop?' The girl in the service station was young and keen: perhaps in her first job, or a student earning tuition fees.

'No thank you. Just the nineteen-fifty over there on Number Five.'

After signing, the driver asked, 'Do you know a place round here called Garden Lodge? Can you tell me how to get there?'

'I've heard of it. I think it's part of the old Graymoat Hall estate, but that's so huge you could lose an army in it. I don't live here, you see, just come over on my bike from Hobsfall to do my shift and bike back again after. Sorry. But ask at the store in the village. There's a post office inside. They'll know.'

The village was a minor miracle – space to park the car right in front of the store (Cunninghams Convenience Corner Store) and another miracle inside – two post office clerks and no customers waiting. Between them, they knew the answer.

'Garden Lodge, Maggie? Surely that's the fancy new name for the old potting shed down the east drive of Graymoat?'

'That's right, Emily. It happened during your maternity leave. A little money spent on turning the place into some sort of residence. Tarted up and given a fancy name and let out to get some extra income. They need it badly enough, poor sods.'

'Well, we know where it is, Miss. Go out on the Duegeld Road, take the second right and look for two oak trees on a right-hand bend. Just after them there's a dirt track going off to the left.'

'Wait, Emily. Look, Miss, when Emily talks about a dirt track, you might get the wrong idea. Is that your car outside? Yes? Well, it's a foul, muddy track with deep ruts and you might have trouble getting in and out in a private car.'

'Garden Lodge, is it, Emily?' A new customer arrived at the counter and dumped a large parcel. 'Getting there won't be your only problem, Miss. You can bang on the doors and shout and scream and blow your horn for hours and she won't take any notice. Artist, she is. Lives alone with her son. Shuts herself up in her attic, or in that smelly old barn, gets absorbed in her work and ignores the whole world.'

Another voice joined in: 'That's what she wants us to think. My bet, she owes money to half the world and won't answer the door in case they have a court order on all her goods. That place is a perfect hideaway. She's probably one of those people we hear of on the telly who have twenty credit cards and run up fifty thousand in debts and then feel cheated when they're asked for money.'

'Don't be too harsh, Mrs Gates. None of us really know her. We're guessing. She's our local mystery, Miss, and we like making up stories about her. We are not even sure of her name. Sometimes it seems to be Groveman and sometimes it's Pullinger.'

A third customer arrived, but nobody seemed in a hurry to transact Post Office business. 'What day of the week is it? Thursday? Then you don't need to rush off to

Garden Lodge at all. Thursday afternoon she takes an art class at the primary school and most often she stops in at my Lavender Team Room afterwards. Go over there in a few minutes and take a break. You'll know her if she shows up. Looks like an artist ought to. I can't take you myself because I am going in to Billericay. My daughter is in charge. Try my lemon cake. And you'll hear most of the local gossip for a bonus.'

I found a corner table. I ordered the lemon cake as recommended, and a large rich concoction with cream on top. Also Earl Grey tea. I deserved a treat after the fast drive from Kent. Quite soon, two women entered the Lavender Tea Room and sat down. One of them seemed to have 'artist' written all over her. They dumped coats and bags and gloves and were soon deep in conversation.

'Thanks very much for the lift, Millie. I did not fancy the walk back to breakdown point, and teatime is a bonus, too.'

'It suits me. Peter met me at the school gate and asked if he could go off with Jim and his mum, and play computer games. I have three hours to myself. Peter will enjoy it, and Jim's mum will run him home. Afternoon tea in this place is always pleasant. What about that wreck of yours? Where is breakdown point this time?'

'Half a mile this side of the place where the mud track hits the main road.'

'What's wrong with it? Do you know?'

'No. And I don't want to know. I just wish it was something that could be cured by a smart kick to the back wheel and a string of curses. But it's not. I tried both.'

'Come on, Priscilla. You have to know something. What were the symptoms? Did it go "bang" and give off smoke and flame? Were there grinding noises? Did the steering fail? Is it just out of petrol?'

'Nothing dramatic like that. More like T.S. Eliot: 'not with a bang but with a whimper'. The thing stuttered and died. I did some quick sums and worked out that if I started straight away I could walk to school in time for the lesson. If I wasted time on that tin can, I would be late. No contest!'

There was a break in the conversation while their order arrived. They were splashing out on the cream cakes and the waitress had difficulty fitting it all onto their table.

'Priscilla, I'm going into my Good Samaritan act.'

'Have you got oil and wine ready?'

'No. What I mean is Good Samaritan by proxy. George is at home today and he is magic with motors. I will ring him on my mobile – if it's still got power – and get him to drive over and fix it. Then he can come in here and report.'

'How is he going to like that? Won't he tell you to get lost! Drop whatever he's doing and rush out to mend a motor belonging to a friend of his wife? Never!'

'Liking is nothing to do with it. At work George is terribly important – or so he tells me. Captain of a thousand or ten thousand or whatever. When it's just the two of us alone he does pretty much what I tell him.'

'Wow! Your experience of marriage is different from mine.'

'Marriage is a lottery and it's daft to praise yourself for a good result or blame yourself for a bad one. I made a lucky choice – so far.'

The mobile obliged. The conversation – as heard in the tea room in Millie's distinct tones – was a mixture of denials and encouragement. 'No, I don't know... It just sort of died ... of course there was petrol in it, Priscilla's not a moron... Well, take your tool box ... of

156

course you can... Remember how you fixed that broken sprocket or whatever outside Exeter... Just get on with it, this is a distressed damsel we are talking about... Mount your white charger and ride to the rescue ... all right, the Landrover... Bye!'

'Now we just wait, Priscilla. Let's have some fresh tea and perhaps some of those weight-enhancing chocolate biscuits. George will take about an hour.'

'I still find it pretty amazing.'

'You fall into behaviour patterns that suit you. George is very aggressive at work and when he's home he wants to be conflict-free. I am quite strong-minded so he finds that being obedient is more relaxing.'

'I don't think Brad and I ever had a clear behaviour pattern. If I had been more street-wise I would have got a better maintenance settlement – or maybe still have a working marriage and black figures on the bank statement.'

'Priscilla, why is the maintenance payment not larger? I often read the business pages, and sometimes the name Brad Pullinger comes up. He is obviously a serious player, and none of those are poor! He ought to be paying you many thousands.'

'What ought to happen and what does happen are wildly different. Do you know how these things work, Millie?'

'Not really. But common sense would say that if he has money to spare and you are on the bread line then the payment should be enough to make you and Angus comfortable. I've been your friend long enough to know that you struggle at times.'

'It's not a secret, is it? Anybody calling at Garden Lodge is going to make some deductions. Not to mention anybody seeing my car.'

'True enough, but at least we don't live in a snobby area. There are enough residents nearby who have had financial misfortune of one type or another. People don't despise you just because your life is a bit rough.'

'Yes. I know that and I am grateful that I don't live in an area like Crankstow. That really is snobby. Did you ever see the vehicles driving into Painters School to pick up children at the end of the day? I went there once because they thought they might need an extra art teacher. Range Rovers, Jaguars, People-Carriers, Off-Road vehicles, BMWs even a Ferrari. If I mixed with that set I would have gone from a friend to an *untermensch* in five minutes when my lifestyle changed.'

'What's an *untermensch*?'

'I think – I'm not sure – that it's a German word for a sub-human species. I can't guarantee the spelling. But I like the word. German has some very descriptive words.'

'I'll believe you – until the mobile library comes around and I can look it up. But let's get back to the maintenance. I saw a picture of your ex and some cronies on a boat, and the caption said that it was his motor-cruiser. You don't operate a thing like that unless you are loaded with money.'

'Millie, it was partly my bad luck, and partly the way the system works, and partly his falsehoods and the crazy, credit-dominated way people manage their affairs today. You see, at the time I did have a reasonable job and I did have some assets – or so the court thought. The job was overtaken by technology and I got very little redundancy money because I had not been in it long. The principal asset – as the court saw it – was a commission for a portrait. I was daft enough to dress smartly for the hearing and they tagged me as a successful professional woman who was not seriously in need. The redundancy was still in the future, and nobody was interested in how many other commissions I had (none) or whether I would be paid for the current one. They never knew that the client

158

was an African tribal chief and that the government of his country was going to introduce exchange control two weeks later. It did not help that I had been on regional television the week before, billed as a rising star in the art world. I am nothing of the kind, of course, more of a struggling amateur in a garret, but you know how the media tart it all up.'

'And you never got the money from the chief?'

'Not a penny. I don't have the portrait, either. It's sitting in a crate in a warehouse at Freetown. The shipping company owns the warehouse and they won't release it to the chief until he presents the bill of lading. The bank won't give him the bill of lading until he gives them the agreed price in sterling. He can't get the sterling. Impasse.'

'But he owes you the money, surely?'

'Oh, yes! Nobody disputes that. If my executors were working out my estate they would count it as a debt due to me and add on the full figure. But debts are not cash.'

'And I suppose your ex did the other thing, did he? Played down his wealth?'

'Of course. But in one sense he did not really need to because he takes good care not to own things personally. Everything officially belongs to one or other of his business enterprises and are lent to him, or leased to him. That boat, for instance: whatever the paper said, you can be sure that it was owned by some limited company, or hired by them. He talks to everybody about "a day out on my cruiser", or whatever, and everybody assumes that he owns the thing. Not true.'

'What did the court end up believing about him, then?'

'They tagged him for a middle-management executive on a salary of 40,000 a year with assets of another £20,000 and not much else.'

Neither woman spoke for a moment. The window was blocked by a large delivery lorry and the tea room was

159

almost blacked out. The noise of the engine was very loud. It moved away, and the conversation resumed.

'Priscilla, there's something I don't understand, here. If he owns those companies, and they can afford to own things like motor cruisers and pay out huge sums for entertainment, then they must be quite successful. Their shares must have a value, and large chunks of shares must be in his name.'

'True, but he is too cunning to leave loopholes. These are private limited companies, not Plc's and he makes sure that some of them lose huge amounts of money and appear worthless on paper. He has a few cronies who operate the swindle with him, and they swap shares depending on how they want to present themselves.'

'How does that work?'

'Well, let's give them names. There's my ex, Brad, and there's Eric Holtman, who is his closest crony. Say Brad wants to look rich. He swaps his apparently worthless shares in Braderic Frozen Foods for Eric's shares in the profitable Braderic Computers. That assumes, of course, that Eric does not mind looking poor for a time. When their needs are reversed, they swap back. Simple.'

'If somebody examines the records, surely it looks suspicious?'

'It does, but who can prove anything? Why do people buy and sell shares anyway? It's a personal choice. That's what Brad and Eric say, and who can prove it's a lie?'

'Do they trust one another?'

'So far, it has held up.'

'The ideal scenario, then, is that Brad dies when he is sitting in the rich chair and you make a claim on his estate.'

'That would be just great. But there are too many "ifs" for me to spend much time hoping for it. I don't know in what circumstances an ex-wife can ask for a re-assessment.'

'So what was the outcome? Oh! Sorry. I ought not to ask that.'

'It's all right. You are not a paid-up gossiper. I was deemed to be fully capable of supporting myself and I got what the court felt to be an adequate maintenance figure for Angus. I don't blame the court. On the evidence they made a defensible decision. I do blame Brad. He misled the court with no other motive than punishing me for the divorce. His ego demanded punishment for a woman who had the appalling cheek to find him wanting. He felt I had insulted him and shamed him in front of his mates.'

'You divorced him, then? Not mutual consent or the other way round?'

'Oh, yes. I was the one who called time. No way was I going to put up with that creature when his true persona came out. Things are tough right now, but even if you had told me exactly what they were going to be like, I would still have done it. I made the right decision, no question. Nobody's going to treat me like he did and get away with it! He makes things worse financially, of course, by regular failures to pay, and feeble excuses when he is chased. I can tell you one story. He was over in the USA at a time when the dollar was falling rapidly against sterling. He wrote a cheque in dollars that would have exchanged into £1,000 on the day it was due. He then delayed posting it for ten days so that I had to exchange it at a lower rate and only got £990. He did not save himself a penny, but he scored another nasty little point off me. That's what he's like.'

'What if he dies while the present state of affairs lasts?'

'Not much change. The settlement provides for continuing payment from his estate. But his will is just another expression of spite. With a great fanfare of trumpets it leaves me his entire 80 per cent shareholding in Braderic Domestic Ltd and appoints me as Managing Director. It's a company which used to make and sell tin openers. The big laugh is that it has a lousy product, has never made any money, and has an asset value approaching zero. That is Brad Pullinger's idea of a joke.'

'Won't it be worth anything at all? Surely an existing Limited Company must have some value?'

'Millie, Braderic Domestic can easily be worth zilch, or even less than zilch if Brad runs up debts in its name. Theoretically, he could do that, die, and leave me obligated to cover outstanding debts up to the nominal value of the shares I own.'

'Wow!'

'At times it is briefly rich because he acquires particular assets from companies he has bought and broken up. He then wants to assign those assets to companies he already owns and which might be able to make use of them. Once or twice he has found no better place to park those assets than Braderic Domestic. Seeing my present shareholding is 20 per cent, I once owned 20 per cent of a tin-mining concession in Peru, and once I had 20 per cent of a haulage firm on the Isle of Skye. Neither lasted long.'

'So Brad's meanness leaves you stuck in Garden Lodge? Is that right?'

'Partly, but there are a couple of other things. One is education. I want the best for Angus and I have worries about the lottery of state schooling. It would be great to think that I could afford a fee-paying school if I have to. So I try to put something aside.'

'I can understand that. We went private for a time. What's the second thing?'

'Art. In a word. And this is where you may think me an idiot. I am a reasonably competent traditional painter and in the years before my marriage I made an adequate

162

living from commissions. I did portraits, and houses and favourite pets and horses. The better-off clients paid quite well. It's not enough.'

'Do you mean the commissions fell off, or the money they could pay?'

'No. I don't want to paint like that. I don't want to spend my life as a fifth-grade hack artist. I have this stupid belief that I can somehow do better. Express something about the conflicts and triumphs and idiocies of our age.'

'Oh, no. Don't tell me you want to have a montage of dead parrots hung in Tate Modern, or something like that!'

'Not that bad. But abstract would certainly be true. It would be – no, it is – colours and shapes and suggestions and recognisable figures set in other-world contexts. Have you heard that I sometimes won't answer the door?'

'Yes. I've had several people tell me that.'

'It's true. I get completely absorbed in the work and block out everything else. Sometimes I hear the knocking and calling and horn-blowing and ignore it. Sometimes I don't even hear it.'

'I don't think I have ever experienced that degree of concentration.'

'It's born of frustration. Any job is easier if you have a clear vision of what you are trying to achieve. Sometimes I do and sometimes I don't. I don't know for sure what I want to say or how the expression would come out on canvas. There are partial visions in the corners of my brain. Sometimes they are internal, sometimes they are sparked by what I have painted. Always there is something marvellous waiting just out of sight. Stop working, and everything has gone. I sometimes think of trying the less harmful drugs, but so far I have held off.'

'Can you go on for ever like this?'

'Not for ever. I give maximum effort to whatever is the

163

imperative of the moment. Until the next disaster happens I can just keep myself and Angus warm and clothed and housed, so I put all the "mights and maybes" out of my mind and paint. In one sense this is a good time because painting is emotional and my emotions are all in top gear due to the slimeball Brad. If you looked at the pictures in the barn right now, you might just describe them as a visual representation of anger.'

'So Brad has helped you artistically has he, without knowing?'

'Well, there's a fire in my work that never existed when I was painting dogs and cats and horses. I suppose anger and hatred are some sort of spur.'

'Are you sure you want the financial situation changed, then? If he turned up with a bunch of roses and a cheque for £50,000 and a please-come-back-I-beg-you call, would that be good or bad?'

'Bad. It would confuse the whole issue. Right now he is an inspirational hate-object and I have creative moments when the canvas really begins to talk.'

'Can you concentrate hard enough to blot out the environment, too? I remember that barn as dirty and smelly and dangerous.'

'It still is. But I know my way around and I can stay out of harm's way. If I employed anybody then there would be massive safety issues. It's full of old agricultural equipment with rusty blades and sharp edges and spiked wheels. The loft has holes in the floor and the ladders seem to shed a rung whenever I climb one. There's an unfenced sewage pit just beyond the end wall. Its very foulness gives it character. With nobody but me there – and me the tenant – nobody bothers.'

'What about wild life? There used to be owls there, and surely there must be rats?'

'There are. The two biggest and oldest sit and watch

164

me painting. I call them Hansel and Gretel. They will qualify as art critics if they remember everything I have told them.

'They also know a good deal about Brad. But they might be a bit confused about his future because I switch from Plan A to Plan B and then to Plan C or D without rhyme or reason.'

'Oh! You make plots against him, do you?'

'More like visions. Some of them are set in his world and some in mine. I picture him falling overboard from his cruiser and getting shredded by the propeller. I see him tied to the spiked wheel of one of those agricultural machines in my barn. I see him hiding in the loft and falling through the floor when it gives way underneath him. I even see myself shooting him. Do you remember that wonderful Sherlock Holmes story when the villain gets murdered by a previous victim while Holmes and Watson watch from behind a curtain? The dialogue is something like "You will ruin no more lives like you have ruined mine! Take that ... and that ... and that" as she empties her revolver into him. I would love to end him like that.

'It would be even better if he was seduced towards his fate by a woman. There's a certain type of woman who fascinates him. He could easily be lured into a trap.'

'Heavens! You've got real violence bottled up inside you, Priscilla.'

'There's a bit of humour, too. In the vision where he falls through the floor, his jacket gets caught up on a nail and he hangs there with his feet two inches off the ground. My rats eat his feet.'

'You call that humour! But, seriously, he is never likely to turn up here, is he?'

'The odds are against it. But he might show up if my attempts to get a better deal from him ever showed any prospect of succeeding. He would enjoy trying to bully me into giving up. And if I was in trouble, he might well turn up to watch.'

'What sort of trouble?'

'Well, suppose I couldn't care for Angus properly. Suppose the school decided they could not afford a part-time art teacher any more. Suppose my rent went up. Suppose some nosy citizen told the social services that a child was living in squalor in a remote cottage with an unreliable single parent. Brad would happily come down here to separate me from Angus. He would not look after Angus himself, of course – simply allow him to be taken into care.'

'What about him and Angus? Do you have to let him see Angus, and does the boy get worried because he has no father?'

'I'm spared interference from him. That's one thing I have to be grateful for. Physically, Angus looks very much like me, and Brad's dislike has spilled over onto him. I think he has more or less written Angus off. As for Angus, I think it does worry him from time to time, but he's an extrovert child with plenty of friends and so far there has been no crisis. It's a help that broken marriages are so common today. Half his friends are missing one parent or the other and it's no big deal.'

'I don't think your money problems are going to get any worse. The school is obviously pleased to have you. Angus looks happy and healthy. He's not smartly dressed, but what do you expect in boys of that age? You look a bit weird at times, but everybody puts it down to the artistic temperament. At least your life is not dull, Priscilla. You enjoy painting, you feel you may be getting somewhere artistically, and you're not starving or cold and you have a cause to get enthusiastic about.'

The speaker hesitated before putting a question that

166

might not be welcome. 'I don't suppose your anger with Brad is just a defence? I mean, you're not secretly hoping for a reunion?'

'You have to be joking. I certainly found him attractive in the beginning. That huge scar across his forehead makes him look like a war hero. Another attraction to me, oddly, was the fact that he has large, powerful hands. They somehow projected an image of strength. It's all gone now. I know exactly what he's like underneath.'

'Sorry, one has to ask these things. Sometimes it's not as bad as one thinks.'

'That's all right. Millie, you're a great encouragement. I feel much better than when you picked me up at the school. Maybe tomorrow will see a massive change for the better. Maybe I'll be discovered by some famous art critic like Donald Crosier. Hey! There's my motor outside. Your call worked.'

Coats and handbags were gathered up and the bill paid. As she moved towards the door, Priscilla brushed past me and murmured an apology. I smiled an acknowledgement through my heavy spectacles.

A few hours later I was back in Eastcheap at the end of my data-gathering day. The immediate needs were to open a bottle of wine and ring the Indian take-away. Also to watch rugby on television. Not England, but Australia against South Africa in Perth. My sympathies were with South Africa and I watched all that male aggression with delight.

There are some disciplined people who make an immediate record of important events. They write it down first in chronological order and then re-organise it under headings that match their intentions. Do you remember them from school? Those are the people who listen to

167

what the teacher says about making a plan before they write an essay. It all comes out neatly and logically and some of them get to be teacher's pet. But there's no life to it – no heat – no zing – no fire!

I brood over a subject and let ideas mix around at random, fuelled by a spot of alcohol. After an hour or so they settle into a pattern and I start writing a summary. It starts out with just a few scribbles, but I get drawn into it, and by the time I am reaching for the black coffee there will be an outline plan.

What had my day's work told me? I deemed Blackheath unsatisfactory for hitting Pullinger. Too many people would be out and about, and the houses themselves were too difficult to get into: a front door onto the street and a back door into a garden that was overlooked by all the neighbours. Compared with that, Garden Lodge at Billericay would be easy to reach and leave unseen, and offered some beautiful opportunities. Sadly, Pullinger seldom went there. The best place, from what I then knew was The Keep at Corner Wood Hall. But what I then knew was not nearly enough.

Another consequence of my day was a massive liking for Priscilla Groveman/Pullinger. That really was a brave, feisty girl who deserved a lot better out of life. Listening to all that stuff about Pullinger shifting the assets of his companies around had given me the first sniff of an idea. By reading through my OU notes again about company law, I might be able to find a way of making Braderic Domestic asset-rich at the moment Pullinger died. That would be fun.

Was I getting too ambitious? If I counted up the things I would really like to achieve, it got rather frightening. I wanted to kill Pullinger. I would have liked his death to be ignominious. I would have liked him to die before Ethel McAllister died, so that her money was safe. I would have liked his death to benefit Priscilla. What were the priorities? Well, the only contract issue was Pullinger's death. I must stop the side issues interfering with it.

One immediate practical action needed was to brief my press cutting agency that I wanted every mention that came up about Ethel and Priscilla and Pullmax. That agency has always been extremely useful. They have an extensive list of subjects that interest me, and they don't miss much. I have told you before that information is the basis of successful witchcraft.

I also pondered the problem of viewing The Keep. Maybe, I thought, I could get friendly with Susan Halliday (the 'twitcher' or 'birder') and study the place from her window.

Chapter Thirteen

Susan's Story

I never expected that meeting to provide me with an interesting new friend. But it did. I had talked a lot about going, but as it came closer I felt nervous. The subject was great, but the people might be old, dreary and critical. I saw the notice again when I was in the White Lion for lunch with Mum and Dad. 'Go along, Susan,' said my mum, 'you really enjoyed that bird project you did, and these people are enthusiasts.'

'Mum, they'll all be your age and more. I'll look ridiculous and they'll treat me like I don't exist. The project was only school stuff. They'll laugh at me.'

Dad started in. 'Susan, if you're interested in something you have to make an effort. We're talking about the grass roots of a subject, here. There would never be high-powered experts doing wildlife programmes on television if they had not started at the bottom. Go there and find out. If you come out knowing half-a-dozen things about birds that you did not know before then you have spent your time well.'

'I know I might learn something, but if they are stuffy and unfriendly then I won't enjoy it. I'm better off walking in the woods with my bird book and field glasses.'

'Look, daughter, you sometimes have to put up with discomfort to get what you want. Think of it like wearing

171

some of those ghastly clothes that seem to be necessary to stay in with your friends. You can't tell me you enjoy freezing your kidneys because teenage fashion tells you there has to be three inches of bare skin between your top and your jeans. As regards their attitude, I can give you a few clues. Make a virtue of your ignorance and ask a few dumb questions that any of then can answer easily. People who know something just love showing off to those who don't know it. Stitch a smile on your face, listen politely, and you will find you have made a friend.'

'How's that?'

'The person who tells you all the things that she knows and you don't know will feel good about herself. And who made her feel that way? You did! So she likes you. Easy.'

'Dad, that's cynical and manipulative!'

'So what? It will get you the result! Anyway, what do you call it when you want your mother or me to buy something for you, and you wheedle and whine and purr and persuade till we give in. Isn't that manipulation?'

My mum was less aggressive, but mostly she supported Dad. I was almost an adult, she said, and I must learn to deal with adults. Why not get some experience? She reminded me how often she had dumped on me with her frustration about the Women's Institute, which she chaired. 'But mostly they do what I want, don't they? Why do you think that is? It's because I work much the same way your father does. I listen to people. I let them sound off. I agree with what they say, and even do it provided it does not actually stop me getting what I want. I compromise a lot and hide my frustration. So we get something worthwhile done in the end. It's not perfect but it's a lot better than nothing. Give it a go. If you can make a group of old biddies like you then you have gained a useful skill.'

'If you do go, Susan, make yourself look ordinary.' My dad was back on his earlier hobby-horse. 'Don't wear clothes that scream "I'm not like you!" That way you are acting like an enemy and you can't grumble if you get treated as one. You could do worse than to borrow a skirt and blouse from your mother. They may be a bit old-fashioned for you, but at least they have quality.'

'Well, thank you so much, Frank!'

I went. The day before, I rang up Maude Travis, who runs the group. She is an official of the Ornithological Society and her name was on the poster. I told her about the project I had done. She sounded very welcoming. She said it would be great to have somebody younger at the meeting. Before she rang off she told me that I might not be the only new person. We might be joined by a visitor to the district called Evelyn Mzambe, which sounded African.

I got there five minutes before the meeting was to start – not a romantic place – the old wooden hall beside our church. Mrs Travis was already on the platform with a tall skinny woman in a bright red dress. Perhaps the speaker? Mrs Travis waved to me and made signs that said 'Take a seat! Anywhere!'

There were empty seats about four rows from the front, and the woman near the end had to be Evelyn Mzambe. She was obviously African, a true ebony colour. What I had not expected was that she was a real doll. Her clothes were not fancy, but everything was of the very best quality. I guessed her to be in her middle twenties. As I took the seat beside her she smiled at me and said, 'Good evening' in a voice that was very much like mine. I thought of the two black girls in my form whose speech still showed an overseas childhood. This woman was different. She must have been born here, I thought, or lived here many years.

Maude Travis was on her feet. I soon saw that one of her strengths was being direct and clear without sounding

173

abrupt. 'Before we start, I am pleased to tell you that we have two new people here today. They might even join us if we're nice to them. Susan Halliday and Evelyn Mzambe both got to hear about us through that advertisement we put up in local pubs. I will ask each of them to introduce themselves briefly.'

I was shocked when Evelyn nudged me and muttered, 'You go first!' Was this smart person human enough to be nervous? I pulled myself together and stood up.

'I am Susan Halliday and I have just finished a sixth-form project. Most of the subjects suggested seemed rather dull, but there was one that was about birds. It suited me because our house has woods close by and I can see an awful lot from my two bedroom windows. And my dad lent me a pair of big binoculars. I found it really, really interesting and I just want to know more. I think it's the variety that I love. So many, many different types, all with their different habits and songs.'

It did not take me long at all. Evelyn followed.

'I am Evelyn Mzambe. I am afraid I won't be a permanent addition to your group because I don't live here. I'm employed on a project that brings me here three days a week and I stop in the Station Hotel at Charing. The evenings are pretty dull and I saw your notice in a pub at lunchtime. I have always been interested in birds so here I am. When I was at school in Africa we never had nature projects like Susan spoke about, but birds were everywhere. We got to know how they lived by the way they interacted with our lives – like the tick birds that eat the ticks off the backs of our cattle, and the Flamingos which ruin the fishing. When I came to England and woke up in the early morning I was amazed by your song birds. I wondered how they all lived. Some "birding" (if that's what you call it) will fill in my spare time nicely.'

'Thank you both very much,' said Mrs Travis. 'Now to

the feature of our evening. Here's Jane Gollix who gave us a lot of laughs last year with her talk "Is the Kingfisher too fat?" I remember she told us that he's not fat really, but just looks stocky when he is perched. She has a different title this evening "Is the cuckoo always evil?" Remember, Jane has rules of her own: because we are a small group of enthusiasts we can break in if we want to. In fact Jane rather likes it. She feels it shows that she's not boring us. Jane!'

Jane talked for about twenty minutes. I was really surprised to find that I followed everything she said. I am used to school lessons that are always messy and disorganised. Of course, Jane had an audience who had come along because they wanted to hear her, and there were no troublemakers. But she had planned her talk well, she spoke with confidence and she had first-hand experience. Her jokes were never feeble and never long-winded. Most of all, her equipment, pictures, Power-Point presentation and so on, worked smoothly. The techies at school could learn from her.

Jane Gollix pointed out that every living creature plays some constructive part in nature and the cuckoo is no different. Amongst other things, it eats large furry cater-pillars, including poisonous ones. Apparently its digestive system has chemicals in it that nullify the poison. If there were no cuckoos then there would be far more caterpillars and more of our crops would be destroyed. An interesting fact is that cuckoos are in decline, and nobody is quite sure why. It might be because some of the birds in whose nests they lay their eggs are also in decline, but that does not stand up because other types of their favoured victims are doing very well. Some experts say the cuckoos may be suffering because of hard times in the place they go to for the winter, but nobody is yet certain exactly where that is.

Jane asked whether we could think of any other cases that were like the cuckoo and the caterpillars. After a moment of silence, Evelyn Mzambe spoke up.

'I suppose this is much the same. Along the rivers in my country the government tried to protect crocodiles. You see, crocodiles eat the predator fish that prey on the fish humans eat. So fewer crocodiles means more predator fish and more predator fish means fewer fish for the people. In our case the fishermen were in favour of the law, but villagers living close to the river were furious because the crocodiles began to take their goats in the night. More crocodiles meant fewer goats. There was also the fact that if you can kill a crocodile it's very good to eat.'

'That's a finely balanced clash of interests,' said Jane. 'What happened in the end?'

'The law was unenforceable. The government abandoned its efforts to control the situation, though so far as I know crocodiles are still nominally protected.'

Jane spoke a bit more about the cuckoo, making comparisons with other parasitic species. In question time, too, I thought that Jane was excellent. She made everybody feel that the question they had put was intelligent and penetrating. A thought flashed through my mind about 'social skill' as described by one teacher. Perhaps this was it.

Afterwards we had buns, wine and coffee while we chatted around. Once again I was pleasantly surprised. The coffee was drinkable and the wine positively good and nobody treated me like a poor relation. Nobody said 'Don't you think you have had enough?' Several of them even remembered my name. One or two picked up on what I had said about my house being surrounded by woods and asked if I had seen particular birds there. Early on I got talking with Evelyn Mzambe and she was hilarious about her stay at the Station Hotel. I know the place, because it's kept by Jeremy Hatch, and his daughter Penny is in the sixth form with me. It is one of those hotels built in the early days of the railways when a train journey was a huge adventure and every single station had a Station Hotel beside it. Ours still survives. Penny's parents don't have a lot of overnight guests and they have annexed several of the guest rooms for their own use. But a few travellers and sales representatives still use the place, and summer tourists of the type that rate themselves above the B&B level. So when Evelyn booked by phone they thought nothing of it. The arrival of a smart professional black woman must have surprised them. They did not quite know how to treat her. She speaks upper-class English and looks terrific, and her transport was not the Mondeo or Granada of your average sales rep. She also had luggage by Gucchi. Evelyn said that they tried in the politest way to find out whether she wanted any special type of meals. They were disappointed when she said, 'Provided you have bacon and eggs for breakfast I shall be very happy.' They put her in the best of the available rooms and put in a television – which the Station Hotel does not normally provide. By asking a few questions (like 'Did the batteries keep falling out of the remote control?') I established that it was the set from their sitting room, which I have often watched. Penny will have missed one or two soap operas.

I said that Penny was a friend of mine and helped around the hotel after her homework was done. 'In the sixth form with you?' Evelyn exclaimed. 'Your friend Penny is out of this world. I love her! She came in to check the room over just at the moment I had knocked my make-up case off the dressing table and our first meeting was at floor level picking up little bottles and tubes. She could not stop herself saying, 'What's this, miss?' and I was happy enough to explain. My day had gone well and she was fun to talk to. One thing led to another and we got onto hair styles. What would she look like with dreadlocks? Could it be done? Could she have her hair in tight little knots? Obviously she asked that because I'm black and lots of black people follow that fashion. And some of the bottles she picked up off the floor had those pictures on them.'

'But your hair's straight, Evelyn.'

'It is now, but I had tight little bunches for a time last year and there were things in my make-up case with those pictures on the labels. I'm not sure now why I tried it – for the novelty, maybe.'

'Honestly, Evelyn, if Penny tries dreadlocks or bunches there will be a riot. If her dad doesn't kill her then the sixth form will laugh themselves sick and the Head Mistress will throw her out.'

'I don't think she'll try it. I told her the idea was far out. Fashion is all about having enough people doing the thing to give it credibility. Just one person doing it alone looks daft. And dreadlocks on a white person are so wildly unusual that it looks mad.'

'Evelyn, about her not trying it: with Penny you can never be sure. She has done some pretty weird things before. I can't wait to see how she turns up next week.'

Then Evelyn really did make me laugh. 'Susan, if you think there's any chance of Penny trying the idea, then I suggest that you and two other friends do it as well. One person trying to set a fashion is crazy. If it's four in a class of twelve then you maybe have a chance. Give it a go! Provided you try it in the next two weeks, I'll help you. I'll probably do it a great deal better than four teenagers will. People say "there's safety in numbers". The Head Mistress would find it hard to throw four of you out.'

We were interrupted when Mrs Travis called for silence and announced that Jane Gollix was going to join up with herself and Mrs Brewen for an early-morning visit to the Naboth Corner hide on the edge of Romney Marsh. 'Mavis and I were going together, but Jane has just told me that one of her engagements tomorrow has been cancelled and that she would quite like to come with us. It would be a shame to have her expertise shared by two people only. Would anyone else like to come?'

Immediately Evelyn raised her hand. 'Can we be back in time for me to keep an eleven o'clock appointment?'

'Certainly. We need to be in position by six a.m., and unless one gets a lot of unusual sightings a stay of three hours is as much as most people manage. We are bound to leave the place before ten o'clock.'

'Count me in then. Susan, why don't you come too? We are bound to learn a lot with a real expert beside us. And we might even see some exotic plumage that gave us ideas for your Afro hair-style! Come on! Say yes! I don't suppose I shall have another chance to be a real twitcher (sorry – "birder") and I just love new experiences.'

Maybe I was a bit overwhelmed by this woman being so nice to me and apparently wanting my company. Why, otherwise, would I give up my usual policy of lying in bed till until my mum lost her temper? I would have to get up at half-past-four. Could it be done? Did sensible people ever rise at that hour? But I agreed. I was impressed by Evelyn, and in the next ten days I did several out-of-character things so as to enjoy her company and her approval

So at 5 a.m. next morning I stumbled out of the house in response to a horn blast from Evelyn. She was driving a bright yellow mini. The arrangement had been that two people, Mrs Brewen and Miss Farthing, should go with Mrs Travis and that Evelyn and I should go independently. I was supposed to navigate to the edge of the marsh, and then Evelyn would study the site map.

179

There was no trouble for the first 40 minutes. Evelyn had brought some coffee with her and in ten minutes I had more or less got over the early rising. In fact I found the world before 6 o'clock to be a much better place than I expected. It felt clean and fresh. Believe it or not, there are still live cocks and hens in farmyards (as well as chicken farms stinking of ammonia) and the cocks really do crow. There was little traffic, the sun was low in the sky giving things an appearance I had never seen before. Wildlife was all around us, including a few foxes. I saw a badger, too. I learnt that the local variety of pheasant has been born with a death wish. You read of Islamic fanatics trying to get into paradise by acting as suicide bombers: the pheasants seem to imagine that the only way to get in is through being slain on the road.

I said 40 minutes, didn't I? It was just about that time into the journey when my mobile rang. I had been expecting nothing, and it took me a moment to realise that the fancy tune was coming from my handbag. Who was it? Answer, Mrs Travis. 'My dear, I'm terribly sorry, but we have been in a minor accident. No, it's not serious. Nobody is hurt. But there's damage to the car that makes it stupid to continue. You two go on and enjoy yourselves. It's taken me ages to get through because I had to ring your home to get your mobile number. I don't think your mum is very pleased with me for waking her up.'

The conversation took a bit longer, of course. I had to make all the usual sympathetic noises about the accident, and Mrs Travis had to explain that she had rung the warden to tell him that her party would now be two people only and to give him our names.

Evelyn was unworried. In fact she seemed quite pleased. 'This way we can do exactly what we like. Nobody to think us idiots because we call a wren a shrike or a peacock a plover. Nobody we have to be polite to. Nobody we have to make excuses to if we want to leave early. I like it! Give me that flask of coffee, and give me that little silver flask that you'll find in the glove compartment.'

Romney Marsh got Evelyn quite excited. 'How wide it all looks! The flatness means you can see for miles in every direction! And almost no humans! You don't find many places in England where nature has the world to herself. If it were not so green it would be a bit like the land around my village. What's it like in winter? Does it get so fog-bound that you get lost?'

I told her what I knew about the marsh, including the stories of smugglers that had excited me in childhood. About the fog, I told her that when I was young, reading *Winnie the Pooh* I had imagined the attempt to unbounce Tigger as taking place on Romney Marsh.

Shortly afterwards I found myself in a surprisingly comfortable hide, savouring coffee that must have been at least 50 per cent whisky.

I enjoyed it. I can't say that Evelyn treated me fully as an equal because in lots of ways she was far more competent and experienced than I. But in things that she did not know about – like birds and the local countryside – she seemed to think that my opinion was quite likely to be right. There were a few times when she identified a bird wrongly and I was able to put her right. She accepted what I said and thanked me for it. It did my ego no end of good.

About 9 o'clock a warden came along on his normal tour of the reserve and stopped with us for half an hour. It was funny, because he was slightly put off by the bright yellow pullover Evelyn was wearing. He said something like 'Are you watching the birds, or the other way round?' It seems that birds are actually more sensitive to movement than colour, but of course bright colours make your movements more visible. True birders apparently favour 'camouflage' colours. I was in fashion, because I had grabbed the first garment that came to hand when I crawled out of bed: my brother's black and dark blue rugby shirt.

I was quicker than Evelyn at spotting birds, but she made much more out of what she observed, forever pointing out what a bird was doing and guessing at reasons. 'That yellowhammer you noticed, Susan, it's been down into that ditch over to the right five times now. It must have found a food source, or nest-building material.'

Suddenly the warden told us to keep silent, and focused his glasses on something away to our right. He studied it for a full minute and then gave me the glasses with whispered instructions. 'Just to the right of that gorse bush beyond the oak tree. Sitting on the lowest strand of the wire fence. See it?' Yes, I saw it. It was a medium-sized bird, somewhere between a blackbird and a magpie. It was grey, with black and white patches and it perched in an upright manner as if posing for the camera. It frequently dropped from its perch, flitting downwards and then returning to the same or a different position. Presumably it had spotted something to eat.

'What is it?' I asked.

'Hush. Just a moment.' And he passed the glasses to Evelyn who watched for a short time and then exclaimed 'Gone!'

'Lucky people! You've just seen a rare visitor. A Great Grey Shrike. I seldom see more than one each year.' He delved into the back pocket of his jacket and brought out a reference book. The page he turned up certainly had a picture much like what we had been looking at, but I did not have a clear enough recollection to be sure. Evelyn was more confident 'Yes. That was it! The upright way it sat was quite distinctive.'

'Give me the book for a moment,' I asked. The more I looked at it the more I thought that I had seen it before.

'This may seem crazy, but I'm sure I have seen that bird in the woods near my house. Is that possible? I mean, Pluckley is 15 miles away.'

'I can't say it's impossible,' the warden answered me. 'It is most unlikely that a Great Grey Shrike would be nesting there, but almost anything can happen during migration if the wind patterns are unusual. That's especially true with easterly winds, and we have had those frequently in the past weeks. Of course, you may have seen a related species.' He showed me some pictures, but none of them were a close fit with my recollection. Still, he was the expert. I was going to agree that I must be wrong when Evelyn joined in.

'But is it impossible? I mean, can birds get blown off course, or find some food source by accident? It would be quite exciting for Susan if she confirmed some novel feature of bird behaviour. She might get mentioned in a bird magazine.'

'I can't rule it out. When you are watching, try to have a good camera available because serious bird magazines always ask for a picture.'

Why did Evelyn get so excited about it? Whether I had seen a rare bird in the woods beside my house was no big deal. I found it interesting, but I was not about to make a huge noise about it or call in local experts. 'Susan, it ties up with other interests I have. I am fascinated by the way one thing causes another. If a bird turns up at your home when that's quite the wrong place for it, I want to know why. What made it happen? Did whatever make it happen make other things happen too? I just love finding out how something that seems quite unimportant on its own can have big spin-off effects – apparently unconnected. In my country, for instance, the course of a stream can change from one year to the next. In the dry season there might be no water at all so you don't go near it, and then when the rains come you find that half a mile of the stream has shifted a hundred yards to the west. You never know why for certain. It might be that migrating animals have lowered the ground by a few inches at one point, and maybe kicked up some stones at the side. Then, when the storms come and water rushes down in spate it just goes left instead of right and the stream has a new channel. Don't ask me why I have this interest. I've been like that all my life.'

'At my school, Evelyn, Miss Shargot would love you and Mr Fell would loathe you. She is always telling us to be curious and ask questions. He is a go-by-the book body: learn the right answer and put it down in the exams.'

'I know what you mean, Susan. You are lucky if you have even one Miss Shargot. There are far too many of the other sort. Look, could we spend a few hours together at your house looking for that bird? I mean, tomorrow is Sunday so you won't be at school and I don't have anything I can't get out of. Of course, if you have something planned then forget it, but I would love to have a look at where you saw that bird and figure out any reason why it might have shown up there. How do you feel?'

She asked, naturally, whether my parents would mind. I said that my father was away on business for a few weeks and that my mother would welcome any activity with an educational value.

So I spent that Sunday morning, and the next one too, earnestly studying the woods from our upstairs window with Evelyn Mzambe. She was interested in all sorts of things as well as the birds we were set up to watch. Our house has farmland beyond two of the boundaries and she noticed all sorts of things about it that had never meant anything to me. She could see which way the land drained, and how the hedges were made up of different types of shrub, and why there were blackberries in one corner and none in another. She was fascinated by the fact that we have cattle grids. In her part of the world cattle are never confined at all. Everybody knows who owns which cow and they roam freely.

We certainly found the bird life more interesting as a result of our visit to Romney Marsh. We knew what to look for and where to look. Together, we identified more species than either of us would have done on our own. Each new sighting was a small thrill. The big moment was sighting, late on in our second session, the bird that had been pointed out to us in the hide. It really did look identical to the one in the book.

Evelyn was also extremely interested in Corner Wood Hall, the place Brad Pullinger bought recently. I pointed it out to her because you get a fine view of it from one of our higher windows and you can pick out all the details with a decent telescope. When Pullinger bought the place none of us knew anything about him and I used to spy on his comings and goings. You also get a good view of the ruined keep that is part of the property. That's a story in itself, and Evelyn was keen to hear all the details.

Records show that some sort of fortified structure existed as early as 1450, when it was the scene of a conflict between two local noblemen and got badly knocked about. A sketch exists in the county archives in which all the conventional features of a castle appear, though the building is small by comparison with others. In the later fifteenth century the owners ceased to live there and built the first part of Corner Wood Hall to give themselves more comfort and fewer draughts. The place was abandoned and neglected. Local people looted the stone to build their own houses, and it can be seen today in the foundations and lower storeys of houses and barns nearby. Then, in 1570, the owners had military ambitions again and the earl, or duke or whatever decided to renovate and restore and improve the ruin. In those days you had to get permission from the king (it was a queen then, of course) to build a castle. This earl was a bit over-confident and started building more or less at the same time he started his petition to the queen. Unlike modern builders, his lot worked fast, being seriously scared of the earl, and the queen was desperately slow. At the same time, the earl's status at court began to slide. When the queen finally got around to considering the petition there were rumours that the earl had jumped the gun. Elizabeth sent people to take a look, and found out that the castle was half-built. It had a moat, and most of the keep was done, and a good deal of the outer wall. Elizabeth was furious and said, 'Petition denied! And you had better start destroying whatever exists already!'

It was the Elizabethan equivalent of modern cases where somebody makes alterations to his house without getting planning permission. A neighbour sneaks to the council and they demand that your extension, or loft conversion be destroyed. Nothing changes.

That's not quite the end of the story: obviously not, because the keep is still standing. The earl took a leaf out of Elizabeth's book on delaying tactics and put off any destructive work as long as possible. He wrote letters full of fine phrases like 'Orders have been given' and 'Labour has been scheduled' and 'Demolition is expected to be completed by such-and-such a date'. But he actually did nothing. Finally some people arrived from London to check on progress. The earl hired workers the day before and the visitors saw stones being rapidly thrown to the ground to join a pile already there. What the visitors did not know was that most of the pile was original material intended for further construction work and left behind when that work ceased. Little of it was the result of demolition. They thought, 'He must have done a lot of pulling down to create that pile'. They were also lavishly entertained. Presumably they reported something like 'Work is proceeding apace' and the earl relaxed for a time. In the end both queen and earl died before the thing was more than one-quarter destroyed.

Since then, the structure has quietly deteriorated. It is a mix of the original stonework from the fourteenth and fifteenth centuries plus such improvements as were made by the earl and not thrown down to please the inspectors. In appearance it is a small-scale ruined castle with crumbling stonework, plants growing out of the walls, and large areas of stagnant water in what was once a moat.

Evelyn spent a long time looking at it through the telescope. 'We don't have bits of history like that in my country. Has the present owner, Pullinger, been there long?'

'No. Before him the owner was an idiot called Laythorpe who actually took an interest in the place. He tried to make a tourist attraction out of it. He made up wild stories about its history, and set up notices at every point of interest, and had fancy lighting effects after dark, and made a little museum showing details of mediaeval life. He paid a local historian to research the place. Her name was Gwen Charmount. She did the job as a freelance to help financially while she was in college and she was really very good. I think she now works for the council. Laythorne read her report and produced his own glossy version. He ignored all the dull bits and created fantastic stories of his own whenever there was the slightest hint of excitement.'

'He must have been an imaginative fellow, then,' said Evelyn. 'It's not easy to make up a false history. He must have been in the same class as Geoffrey of Monmouth.'

'I've never heard of your Geoffrey fellow, but yes, it was not at all bad. I went over The Keep once when I was 13, and looked at all the exhibits and read the pamphlet. I remember it quite well. There was a lot of recorded sound, and you heard the scream of an attacker as he was thrown backwards from the parapet, and a better scream still from the unfaithful wife as she was chucked from the window of the solarium. There was a good deal of "Bring me flesh and bring me wine" and the clash of steel on steel, and the lighting went blood red when people got chopped in battle. He had a few actors hamming it up with swords and axes. I enjoyed it. My parents told me it was a load of lies and none of it had ever happened anywhere near Pluckley, but that did not bother me too much. I've always been good at imagining things. I remember a lovely scene with a knight kneeling at the feet of a lady and proposing marriage. The knight had a lot of flowery language, but it was spoiled for me because the girl responded in a strong local accent. She was one of the girls who work at the stables on Charing Heath. You can see the "Proposal Chair", as Laythorpe called it, through the scope.' Evelyn followed my advice and stared at it for several minutes. 'I hope the girl had a few cushions, or the knight got to the point quickly. Do you know how cold stone gets in the late evening? It really crawls up your spine!'

I went on, 'There was a guide book about the locality, too. The writer's family had lived here for centuries. He was short of money and was happy to churn out lies for Laythorpe. His name was Huntshill. He put some pictures in the book showing what the place looked like when the whole thing was standing. Quite interesting, it was.'

Evelyn took another look through the telescope. 'It's hard now to see just what all the architectural features were. You certainly need imagination to picture a romantic assignation at that Proposal Chair place. But I'm glad you told me. It's a good story.

'Still, I can't stay too long taking time off from work. I'll have to leave soon. But I'm going to write to one of the bird societies about the one we saw here. I'll let you know what reply I get.'

Evelyn was as good as her word. Between us we made a drawing of the bird at my place and sent it off. Two weeks later Evelyn sent me a copy of the reply. It said that our drawing was a good one, and that our identification was probably correct. It offered one or two explanations for the bird being so far inland and asked us to write in again if we saw it next year. Sadly, I never spotted it again.

I have not seen Evelyn since. That is a pity, because a few weeks later there were some extraordinary events at The Keep. She would have been interested.

Goodbye, then, to the Evelyn Mzambe personality – though I had enjoyed the experience. Welcome back, Nshila Ileloka, soliloquising about progress in my Eastcheap fastness.

Yet again, I have had to work hard for my information. But it was fun, too. When you meet young people like Susan you feel that there is still hope for the country. She is intelligent and amusing and in a year's time she will be a very attractive woman.

I have learnt a lot about The Keep and seen it clearly through the telescope. It is quite high, structurally unsafe, slippery in places and adequately distant from any dwelling. There are remnants of a moat, filled up with stagnant water. Pullinger might:

- Be physically attacked out of sight of any observers.
- Be crushed by a huge falling stone.
- Fall from a great height onto loose stones below.
- Fall into the stagnant water of the moat and be drowned.

It is looking like the best location for the hit. As far as immediate action is concerned, I am going to make some contacts inside Pullmax Industries. I must find some way in which Priscilla can benefit from the coming death.

Chapter Fourteen

The Open University Summer School

'Professor, I am pleased to be here. I am sure I shall enjoy it, and learn a lot. But I am in the dark about why I was chosen. I have a modest academic record, I am quite junior in my company, and the company is hardly a blue chip enterprise. How did Pullmax Industries come to your notice and how did the name of Michael Middleton come out of the hat?'

'People do sometimes find it confusing. We like to add value to the summer schools by bringing in guests from industry or commerce to offer a realistic perspective about what happens on the ground. We try to get a spread. We look for people from government, and the public sector, and various branches of industry, and the big utilities, and commerce, and even charities. We like to get people from different cultures with different work ethics.'

'If you categorise sources in that way, then I suppose Pullmax Industries has a certain value. But some critics would see us as a dodgy outfit. We get a bad press from time to time. My invitation has come at quite short notice, too.'

'I'm sorry about the short notice, but we are sometimes let down through cancellations, and that was the case here. Somebody suggested trying Pullmax, and we were indeed a little concerned about the dodgy reputation. But there is a strong argument that the reputation was a plus factor, given our objectives. We don't want our students to be starry-eyed about industry and think that every British company is an honourable outfit, without skeletons in the cupboard. There are plenty who win contracts by discreet bribery, and plenty that sell gun barrels to dictators labelled as "plumber's piping". You can take it from me that dodgy things go on in even the highest-rated companies. It would do our students no harm to debate these issues. Of course, we don't ask you to incriminate yourself.'

The professor managed a sickly apologetic laugh.

'I can see sense in that argument, but why me?'

'The truth is that these things are always a compromise. We first of all ask whether an organisation would help us in principle. Then we look at the promises we have got already and try to think what sort of department we would like additional people to come from. Then we go back to the organisation and say, for instance, "Have you got anyone in credit control that you could let us have?" It then comes down to individuals, and to practical considerations like who is away on holiday and who is available. I can't swear that you are the very best person that Pullmax could have sent us, but you meet the requirements and we are pleased to have you. In fact, you work in the asset management section and that suits us pretty well.'

'I understand now, Professor, but please don't think that I am personally committed to anything dodgy that Pullmax gets into. I don't have much influence and I largely take orders. Don't cast me as a representative of practices to be avoided!'

'Of course not. There will be a wide range of opinions expressed and nobody will suffer from stereotyping. When I say that, I must contradict myself straight away because the syndicate you will be in has Dr Hackneath as the leader. It won't take you long to nail her as the stereotype of an academic. She gets up a few noses, but the discussion in her groups is dynamite.'

'I don't think I know many people like that. It will be a memorable experience.'

'You will surely get that, since Dr Hackneath will be assisted for part of the time by an ex-student who got her MBA three years ago. She is an African called Nshila Ileloka. Her story reads like a fairytale – born in a remote village in darkest Africa, chosen to go to a multi-racial secondary school, offered a scholarship to LSE and then getting an MBA from us on top of it. Nshila is quite special. There are rumours that she is the daughter of a witchdoctor and can make rain come down out of nowhere.'

'Sounds exciting. But I hope she won't turn me into a toad, or anything. Mr Pullinger expects me back in the same shape.'

'Toads are not her style. She would go for something more elegant, like a cheetah.'

'Thanks very much.'

'In fact your paths may have crossed already. She was in on the decision to approach Pullmax and even identified asset management as a possible section to give us the right balance of experience. I think she was taken with the fact that you are involved in re-locating bought-up assets. Is it not something you do?'

'That's right. We make several purchases a year, usually of quite small companies. They all have different assets. In some cases it is obvious whether we should sell them again or integrate them with an existing Pullmax company. In other cases it takes a long time to decide their best use.'

*   *   *

193

Work in the Hackneath/Ileloka syndicate was exciting. The diverse backgrounds and lively personalities of the members meant that they never agreed about anything but thrived on the arguments. Divisions were most acute in regard to decision-making at middle and junior levels. Members from large organisations were in favour of formal structures that placed limits on freedom of action. 'If people have limited decision-making scope there will be fewer mistakes,' they said, 'and fewer variations from company policy.' Their opponents saw it as more important to encourage initiative and personal growth by allowing more freedom. Michael Middleton realised that, if they knew the truth, such people would see his subservience at work as feeble in the extreme. They would want him to challenge the system by taking initiatives of his own and discovering what happened. The most extreme views came from a member who had joined as a 'wild card' at the request of the professor. He ran what he called a 'virtual organisation' employing only himself and his wife. They spent their time entirely on creative work and used contractors to convert their ideas into something saleable. His line was 'Ask nobody. Make up your own mind. Go ahead and do it.'

The member causing the most aggressive discussion was a self-styled entrepreneur who paid no attention at all to values other than money. His aim was to make large amounts of it, and he examined all options by their likely financial yield. He did not see it as any part of his job to consider the legality or social value of a business. That was for other people. If the government decided that something was illegal then they could pass a law against it and he would be forced to stop. If the public did not like what he was doing, then nobody was forcing them to buy, and they could watch his company go bankrupt. His only role in society, as he saw it, was to make money.

The students found Nshila Ileloka to be terrific value. In formal sessions she was scrupulous about sticking to the subject and offering the conventional wisdom of the day. She never prevented group members from arguing and speculating but always emphasised that much of it was deviant. She said, more than once, 'This course is intended to encourage original thought, and I love to watch it. But you have to take a final exam. If you fill your papers with stuff that decries the conventional wisdom then you may be cutting your own throats.' Over this, she was at odds with Dr Hackneath who did not believe that she herself or any other professional academic could fail to be detached and objective. She resented the idea that she had expectations to which she would require students to conform. The male members of the syndicate were amused by the sharp exchanges between the two.

Before the summer school ended, members knew a good deal about each other and all were aware that Nshila had links to what she chose to describe as para-psychology. She agreed to spend an evening exploring the subject with a small group who were seriously interested. But the first question she had to field was meteorological.

'Nshila, the common rumour about you is that African witchdoctors can make it rain, and that you have enough knowledge to work it. Have you ever really made it rain?'

'I always give the same answer. I have tried several times, and mostly it has rained after my attempts. But did I cause it, or was it going to rain anyway? Much of what you hear is public relations work, not fact. The most famous rain-making story of all time is in the Bible – Elijah and the Priests of Baal on Mount Carmel. The people, under King Ahab, had forsaken the true God – Jehovah – to follow Baal, and God had sent a prolonged drought to punish them. Elijah set up a challenge match to prove which was the true God. The challenge was to

195

send down fire from heaven to consume a sacrifice. The priests of Baal tried for most of the day – mocked all the time by Elijah – and failed. Then Elijah called on Jehovah, fire arrived instantly, and the sacrifice burnt up. The people were convinced, they swung over onto Elijah's side, and when he ordered them to kill all the prophets of Baal straight away they did just that. Then Elijah started the rain-making. Here's how it goes:

> Elijah went up to the top of Carmel; and he cast himself down upon the earth, and put his head between his knees. And said to his servant, 'Go up now, look toward the sea.' And he went up, and looked, and said, 'There is nothing.' And he said, 'Go again seven times.' And it came to pass at the seventh time, that he said, 'Behold, there ariseth a little cloud out of the sea, like a man's hand.' And he said, 'Go up, say unto Ahab, Prepare thy chariot, and get thee down, that the rain stop thee not.' And it came to pass in the meanwhile, that the heaven was black with clouds and wind, and there was a great rain.

'The Bible is all about the supremacy of Jehovah – the only true God – so Elijah is the good guy. But if the Priests of Baal had lived to write the story, it would have said that their efforts had set a spark smouldering deep in the woodpile and Elijah had cashed in on a process already in motion. As to the rain, it was coming anyway and Elijah's dramatics had nothing to do with it.'

'Tell us about one of your own attempts.'

'Years ago, at school, I had a boyfriend who was mad keen on cricket. There was a tournament at the school with three other teams visiting us. On the first day we looked like losing our match and my friend insisted that I should try to make it rain before his side were all out, and so get one point for a draw. The team they were to play the next day was known to be weak and we expected to get two points for a win. I cast all the right spells and there was torrential rain when we were 145 for eight wickets, chasing 220. We got the draw. But the rain did not stop for twenty-four hours and the match that we expected to win was drawn also. I got rain, but my clients did not get what they wanted.'

Moving to other aspects, Nshila again entered some modest disclaimers.

'You have to start from the fact that humans have acquired a vast stock of knowledge down the centuries. But that does not tell us anything about the amount of knowledge still behind the curtain. What Hamlet said is still true: "There are more things in heaven and earth than are dreamt of in your philosophy". Take the way Europeans explored Australia. They came up against these massive deserts and thought "These are dead places. Nothing could live there". They thought like that because their minds were dwelling on plants, birds and animals with which they were familiar. Such species could not, indeed, live in the deserts. But we now know that there are many species of animal that have adapted to that sort of life and can survive quite happily.

'It is like that in the field I am exploring – and I say exploring because I am still not much more than a novice. An awful lot of things that appear mysterious are only perceived as such because we have tunnel-vision. Some of them cease to be magic once they are explained. So what does "magic" mean? You can argue that it means only something that has not been explained to you. I'll start by using nothing more than ordinary human intelligence and then revealing the mystery. Perhaps we can consider the old crystal ball, which must be familiar to you from fairgrounds.'

Nshila produced her crystal ball, set it on a black cloth on a table and reduced the lights. 'All the small things add up. They create an atmosphere in which you are expecting something unusual. If I told you something about your future when we were sitting at a bar it would go in one ear and out the other. If I tell you the same thing in a fortune-teller's setting, your attention is focused. Who's first?'

Corinne Cruikshank volunteered. The first things she was told were obvious. 'I see you sitting at a desk in a large hall. You seem to be taking an examination. You scratch your head. You seem worried.' Everybody laughed. Nshila moved on. 'I see a train journey that is noisy and uncomfortable. It is somehow linked to Scotland ... or it may be Ireland. You are going to experience a loss, and find it restored in an unusual manner. I see you testing strange paths and finding frustration. There are five years in which I can see nothing, for your life is overshadowed by another. I can see you struggling with a weight problem and finally defeating it.'

What Nshila actually said was longer than this. It was interspersed with exclamations, wordless peering into the depths of the ball, sharp glances at Corinne and thoughtful pauses. Then the discussion. 'Everything I said was based on what I know of Corinne and what she has told me. I guessed at the sort of things that might happen to her, based on things that have already happened, and her reaction to them, and what might logically happen to a person like her. I wrapped this up in vague words that might apply to a whole lot of different happenings. Can you point out some examples?'

Ken Dodson spoke up. 'The bit about train journeys is clear enough. Corinne comes from Scotland and travels quite often from Glasgow to Euston. Those trains are always full of loud-mouthed people consuming six-packs of lager one after the other. Other passengers frequently have an unpleasant journey.'

'Right. Anything else?'

Penny Langton had a comment. 'The bit about losing and finding. That is such a common experience that it has to come true some time, and the thing lost could be absolutely anything. It could be a boyfriend or it could be a bag of sweets.'

'Right again! There is a long list of sentences like that which the fortune-teller can fall back on and be completely safe. But did you notice the suitability for Corinne? She is a bit careless, and frequently loses things, and makes a good deal of fuss while they are lost. Do you remember how we were all searching for a charm, a week ago, that had fallen off her bracelet? The cleaner found it under her bed.'

Ken intervened again. 'All that makes sense, but you also said other things for which I can't see an explanation.'

'That is because a key quality for fortune-telling is knowledge, and knowledge comes from observation and sensitivity. People are offering information about themselves all the time by their appearance, by what they say, by what they don't say and by the manner in which they handle problems. But most of the time we are thinking about ourselves rather than the other person and we don't pick up the signals or see their meaning. Can you see why I said something about a weight problem? Corinne is slender, and even under-weight for her height. How can I justify what I said?'

Corinne herself answered. 'I know that. We first met when we standing at the service counter in the restaurant and you took a large helping of treacle pudding. I remember telling you "I can't go for that one. It's the sort of thing that did for my sister's waistline, and my aunt's, too." You must have deduced that the women of my family tend to put on weight as they get older. You are right.'

'Come to think of it, I heard that!' Bert Bingham joined in. 'I was behind you, and it comes back to me now. But I never gave it a thought between then and now!'

'That's because it was of no concern to you. But I have become quite skilled in listening, and observing and interpreting and remembering. So I can build informed guesses that you probably can't do for each other.

'People who use the crystal ball don't claim to influence the future or cause anything to happen to the subject that would not happen anyway. They pretend only to reveal things that are already scheduled. But in reality they may exert an influence if the subject takes them seriously. Because I have warned Corinne about the weight problem it just might be that she takes extra care about her diet. That would be an action initiated by her rather than me, but you could argue that I made it more likely to happen. So perhaps the fortune teller can affect the issue by investing the prophesy with drama.

'The same goes for the tarot cards. They have more mystery than the crystal ball because of their antiquity, and the emotive names, and the variety of meanings with which they have been invested. Their strangeness is increased by having something "normal" – the ordinary suits – with which to contrast them. You have the feeling that there must be something a bit weird about Wands and Cups and Swords and Coins. Likewise the "character" cards have such emotive names – The Fool, The Magician, The Hanged Man, The Chariot, and so on. Think back to what I told you about things unknown. Your intellect tells you that the hidden power to which these cards relate is a load of rubbish. But you don't know that for certain. You can't prove it. So part of your mind says that they might link back to forgotten knowledge. You might stumble by accident through a door into the unknown. That is all a little exciting. So you are more willing to suspend disbelief.

'The twenty-two cards called the Major Arcana have the same titles in different packs, but allow great variety in their design. Indeed, occultists who use the tarot often make up their own personal cards. They are all pictures, and there is a broad general agreement about the meanings attached to them, but when it comes to explaining those meanings there is huge freedom of interpretation. I, and most practitioners, match my interpretation to the person who consults me. Let's look at this card called THE LOVERS.'

In Nshila's pack THE LOVERS had boy and girl in mediaeval dress, the colours being blue, red and gold. The boy is obviously making the running, holding the girl's hand and gazing at her. The girl is looking bashfully at the ground. Above them is a Cupid on a cloud, aiming his arrow. If the arrow was released it would hit the girl's head but would not touch the boy. The cloud has heavy shading on its lower edge. Watching the two is a much older man. He appears to be less smart then they are. He has a plain blue pillbox-type hat and a worn brown cloak. His hand rests on a long white staff. His expression might be described as quizzical or patronising or approving or merely watchful.

Nshila went on, 'One of the common explanatory texts gives these meanings for THE LOVERS: "Harmony/intuitive hard choice/struggle between two paths/second sight". Given those words, and the picture, you will see that I have a wide choice as to how I relate it to my client. Jim Parkman has told us all often enough that he is highly ambitious and even admits to being a bit ruthless. So if Jim is my client, and the cards that fall to him include THE LOVERS, here's what I will tell him:

'This is all about your relationships with girls, Jim. I think you will have to make a very hard decision between the dictates of your heart and your head. Remember that being loved is not enough if you don't love deeply yourself. I think that some girl will love you a lot, but that you have aspirations that may conflict. I think the watcher here is some mentor from your past who expects you to achieve great worldly success. He is looking indulgently at your youthful flirtation and hoping that it will pass.

'But if my client was not Jim, I would come up with quite a different story.'

'Try doing it for me,' Michael Middleton asked, 'I find it quite interesting.'

Nshila looked at him carefully. 'Michael, I get some rather weird vibrations when you ask that. I don't know why, but I am not sure I could keep it to a non-serious demonstration with you. There's something about you that makes me uneasy.'

'I don't mind that at all. My life is not so exciting that I am going to turn up my nose at a bit of mystery. Go on, Nshila. I'm not scared.'

'All right. But let's use a different set of cards. Take this deck, Michael, and deal yourself eight off the top. Put them face down and then turn them up one by one in front of me.'

In a few moments, everybody was looking at:

- The Eight of Cups
- The Three of Cups
- The Page of Wands
- The Ace of Swords
- The Page of Swords
- Justice
- The Hanged Man
- The Wheel of Fortune

'Wow,' said Nshila. For a moment nobody else spoke, waiting for her to go on.

'I see some sort of psychological turning point for you, Michael. You have been behaving in a way that is against your true nature. It's bugging you, and you are looking for a better way to handle things. It is going to come to a head in a way that causes you to reject previous habits and go boldly for the things that seem to you to be right. It is going to be a big effort for you, fraught with danger. If you choose well, you will feel you have made a big personal break-through.

'Does that connect with you in any way, Michael? It was quite hard for me. This hand is definitely scary.'

'Well, it's true that much of my work goes against my personal inclinations, but I have never questioned it because I assumed there were reasons behind it that I didn't know about. Is there a suggestion that I am going to stage some sort of revolt?'

'It might happen. The meaning of the cards is affected by the character of the subject. What sort of person are you, Michael? Are you one of those who suffer a poor situation for ever, or one of those who protests immediately? Or are you a slow-burner type who lets things rumble on until an incident drives you over the edge?'

'Your third category fits me best. The illustration makes me see a connection to the work of asset assignment. There are times when I have to take actions that seem misguided and even wrong. Lately they have been worrying me more and more.'

'What do you mean by "asset assignment"?'

'You probably know that Pullmax has a reputation for asset-stripping: buying up weak companies for a low price and selling off the component parts separately at a profit. You can get very good money for those assets if you can find a buyer to whom they appear valuable: that's to say, a business to which those assets are complementary. For instance, let's say you buy a local business that used to have lots of overseas customers and acquired a small hotel for entertaining guests. Then you find a hotel chain that has no presence in that area but would like to move in. The hotel chain has no interest in buying the original business, but if it can get the hotel on its own then you have a profitable deal.'

'Do you have to handle buying and selling at that level, Michael?'

'Subject to guidelines, yes. But sometimes I get direct instructions from above that seem to make nonsense of those guidelines. I get a bit confused at times.'

'Can you explain a bit more?'

'Some of the things that I am told to do are illogical. Things get assigned to companies that are quite in-appropriate and can't make use of them. And others are left in limbo. That's bad. The asset may be one in which business is still going on and employees are at work. They exist in uncertainty and ignorance with no idea what is going to happen to their jobs. And I think that in some cases there are pretty devious financial objectives. If an asset has no particular value to the company that nominally owns it then I think it gets written down in the books for tax purposes. If it gets passed on to a place where it can be used, then it magically goes up in value. I don't understand the financial angles well, but the thing smells rather.'

'That links up, Michael, for the Wheel of Fortune was here with the other cards. It might mean that you have the power to determine wealth or poverty for people. Are you on your own in this? How about your boss?'

'He is the one who gives me the directions. But now I think it over, he may have been hinting that I should make more decisions myself. He has never said it directly, but sometimes I have heard him repeating maxims and mantra along those lines.'

'Like what?'

'One of his favourites is that "Rules are for the obedience of fools and the guidance of wise men".'

'Maybe, then, the change of behaviour hinted at by the cards has to do with being more assertive, and deciding things according to your own sense of value.'

'It's a thought, Nshila. Maybe this OU Summer School has taught me to be braver.'

Everybody laughed, but Nshila looked tired and upset, and showed no more tricks that evening.

Chapter Fifteen

An Outline Plan Emerges

Did I make a mistake in getting too concerned about Priscilla, and the hope of enriching her through Pullinger's death? I certainly spent a lot of time making the necessary contact with Michael Middleton and putting the right suggestions into his sub-conscious mind. It delayed the hit, and delaying the hit could have meant that Mrs MacAllister died first and the living Pullinger scooped all her money. On the other hand, I had plenty of time to brood on the place of death, and the method, and I took no risks through hasty action

Anyway, I had made the choice and it was history. Picture me in Eastcheap once again, thinking further about place and method.

Killing him at Blackheath I had discounted already and Billericay presented the major difficulty of getting him there. The Keep at Corner Wood Hall was the strong favourite. But I still didn't know it well enough to make detailed plans. How could I judge the suitability? I was pondering the options when the buzzer sounded. I spoke into the intercom to find out who wanted me and what for. Back came the reply, suitably garbled by electronics and the inability of the speaker to master simple English. Translated, it meant 'Measurements Limited, madam. We are contractors employed by the electricity board to replace your old electricity meter with a modern one.' Typical. A quasi-government busybody wanting entrance to my property to replace something that works well with something that probably won't! Till then I had had one of those lovely old things that had about six dials on it and you had to see whether the one measuring 'tens of units' was saying 9 plus something or 1 minus something before you could be sure whether the one measuring 'hundreds of units' was saying 0 or 1. I just love the way things like that trigger each other – the cause/effect relationship is so neat. When railway stations had those clocks that showed numbers for all the minutes and seconds – like 09:17:48 – I used to watch till it said 09:59:59 and at the final second everything changed at once to say 10:00:00.

How does that digression connect with my assignment? Easy. The intrusion convinced me that I should be a government busybody for a day. So, a few days later I was accosting Pullinger's housekeeper on the steps of Corner Wood Hall.

'Health and Safety Executive, madam. External Public Structures Division.' I flash my identification card at her. And I do mean 'flash' because although it is colourful and imaginative and carries my picture it is not produced to a particularly high standard. It works, of course, because they all do. Very few people, shown a glimpse of a police warrant card, say 'Let me have a closer look at that, please!'

'Madam, I have to carry out an inspection of The Keep to make sure that it conforms fully with current regulations.'

'But nobody ever goes to The Keep? Why on earth do you need to see it? And it's private property anyway. Surely there must be some mistake.'

I do some business with my briefcase and a file. 'I don't think so. I have the Certificate of Registration here, dated about seven years ago. 'Access to visitors between Eleven Hundred Hours and Sixteen Hundred Hours, three days a week from April to October'. That brings it into class B5 – more than 400 hours and less than 800 hours – causing the regulations of Section 7 (d) (iii) to apply. Now, if one of your days had been Sunday then only two days would have been counted and the regulations would not apply. But your declaration says Tuesday, Wednesdays and Fridays.'

'But this is crazy. The Keep may have been open to the public at some time in the past but Mr Pullinger has never let people into it. He likes his privacy. You are wasting your time here.'

'Can I know your name?'

'Mrs Cornton.'

'I am Sarah Kovango. Look, Mrs Cornton, I don't make these regulations and I don't have the power to alter them. My schedule is sent down from Head Office and it says that today I have to do The Keep at Corner Wood Hall. Are you going to let me do it? You ought to know that the owner has a duty of care towards any members of the public entering on the property and that somebody who was injured could sue for damages if the site had not been passed. I assure you that I shan't do any damage. If my report requires special safety installations or significant structural alterations then Mr Pullinger will be notified formally and there will be an appropriate right of appeal. Today is just a first assessment.'

'I suppose you're the Government, so I can't stop you. But I shall certainly let Mr Pullinger know, and if you have pulled the wool over my eyes, then he is a man who can cause a lot of trouble.'

'That's all right, I promise you. There's something else, too. If it seems to me that there is any error, and The Keep should not be on our list, then I am allowed to recommend striking it off. That should please Mr Pullinger.'

There I was then, quite alone in The Keep (more substantial than I had thought) looking to see in what way it might be a danger to a visitor, and whether I could make it fatal to the owner.

In the Health and Safety Executive they learn all about common causes of accidents. High on the list comes the heading 'Slips, Trips and Falls'. It is astonishing how many man-days are lost through people slipping on polished floors, or a slope, or spillage, or falling over an old broom. The Keep was full of places where this could happen. It also had lookout points where the coping was low or damaged and a person might fall over. If he did fall over, he might land on the boulders which I could see, and break his skull, or fall into the foul-smelling water of the moat and drown. I noticed places, too, where a person would be standing fully exposed and an excellent target for a sniper. My romantic mind flew back to literature classes at St Albans and the wonderful story in *Kidnapped* where David Balfour is despatched up the ruinous staircase by his uncle, in the hope that he will fall over the edge at the top. I laughed to think of Pullinger climbing up his ruin in the darkness and disappearing with a scream into the foulness of the moat. The Keep also provided numerous hiding places, from which I could emerge as he went past and knife him. Or I might be able to scratch his face with thorns or brambles dipped in poison. But the trouble with those last two ideas is that they clearly say 'foul play'. I preferred an accident.

Unfortunately, I needed certainty. I had to make sure that Pullinger had the accident in a certain way at a certain place in a certain manner so that his next resting place was the morgue rather than a hospital. I had to know straight away that the plan had worked. And if I were to choose The Keep as the location then I had to get him there. How was I going to do that?

When you are planning this sort of thing you play out alternative scenarios in your mind and examine each to see whether it will work. Suppose that I stuck with my Health and Safety role. It would be easy enough to demand that the owner of the structure accompany me round The Keep so that I could personally indicate the danger areas. I could pick a time when there would be no observers and simply push him over the edge. I might get us both leaning on a parapet and say, 'You realise, Mr Pullinger, don't you, that either of us could easily fall over this inadequate barrier,' and PUSH. The two of us being alone, I would have plenty of time to make sure that he was dead. The trouble, of course, is that I am not part of the Health and Safety Executive at all. I would be blown the moment the police started checking on me.

I really needed to lure him to The Keep alone, and at a specific time, I myself being out of sight but yet close enough to allow physical action. I used that very word 'lure' in my mind, and the answer to my first problem appeared out of nowhere. An assignation. Pullinger saw himself as God's ultimate gift to women, and if it was suggested to him that an exciting prize would be waiting for him at a particular place and time then he would be psychologically compelled to meet the challenge.

How could I make the suggestion? I had to involve a woman of the right appearance and attitude but I could not allow her to know about it. Nor did I want Pullinger ringing her up asking: 'Do you really mean it?' Well, I remember some comments about Pullinger from the talk in the Plantagenet Arms and I know the type of lure he would fall for. Somebody like Polly Basing. As to throwing out the lure without risk, Zach Kawero might be able to help me.

211

How should I do the deed? I am not expert with a rifle, and even if I were I would still have difficulty in obtaining, concealing and disposing of the weapon. If I were as good as the Boy David with a catapult, I could plant a stone in the middle of his forehead, but you need an awful lot of skill, and there is still evidence of murder. From my Open University days I recalled the slogan 'Keep It Simple and Straightforward', or 'Kiss'. (Some versions have 'Keep it simple, stupid!') I needed something basic that was easy to carry out and could be judged an accident. I examined the area round the 'Proposal Chair' carefully. Two things in particular seemed useful. The area was well covered in long grass. This seemed strange in view of the fact that it must have been an upper floor of The Keep. Presumably the winds had blown in enough soil over the years to allow seeds to germinate. And Laythorpe, the imaginative previous owner, might have improved it – trying for a 'green sward' effect. The second point was that the Proposal Chair itself was adjacent to an opening in the wall that began at floor level. There might have been a window there in the beginning, or an arrow slit, but the stonework had now been so broken down that it was effectively a doorway. It looked as if I could attach a rope at some strategic point, let it out over the edge, and bring the Proposal Chair and anyone sitting on it crashing onto the rocks, or into the moat.

The idea didn't seem quite right. Too many uncertainties existed, like would he actually sit on the chair, and would I be able to see when (if) he did so, and would I have the strength to bring the whole lot down? Perhaps it was the rural environment that brought Mike Fanshawe to my mind. He once took me to his ancestral home, and his grandfather talked about his own schooldays. Apparently, in the woods close to the school was a wonderful old craftsman who made cups and bowls out of wood on a 'natural' lathe. This contraption was composed of a live sapling, from which a strap passed downwards, round a spindle, and was secured to a pedal on the floor. When the pedal was pressed down, the strap caused the spindle to rotate and the sapling to bend down. When the pedal was released, the sapling sprang back to the erect position, causing the spindle to rotate the other way. The wood being worked on was attached to the spindle, and the craftsman cut it with his tools as it rotated. Mike dug out some of the pieces this man had made. They were marvellous. The idea really grabbed me. Was there anything natural in the area that I could manipulate so that, springing free on my signal, it would smash Pullinger through the doorway?

I found nothing suitable. But I followed the idea forwards and came up with a more technical, but related method. It would work. An elegant concept based on nothing more than a colossal mousetrap and a mobile phone. It would mean a bit more work for Zach Kawero and I would need somebody with contacts in the engineering world. Perhaps Mike himself would be able to fix it. Great! They teach you planning at Business School! I took some careful measurements and left. I would be able to set the trap on the day itself, watch it work, and clear up the evidence afterwards.

Finally, could I somehow make this death 'ignominious' like my client wanted? If the reason for his coming to The Keep was an assignation with a woman then there were obvious ways to shame him. But they would probably involve a real woman and lead to further enquiries. Not a good idea. But the mousetrap? It's surely ignominious to be killed in a mousetrap? If it were bigger, could it be called a rat trap?

Chapter Sixteen

Mike Fanshawe's Narrative

Nshila Ileloka has given me two wooden clothes pegs and asked me to get some fancy metal springs made by my contacts in the engineering world. It won't be difficult, of course. The man who makes special parts for my old Lagonda can do it easily. But why? What for? Inside each clothes peg is a spring. You press the two halves of the peg together at one end, and the other end opens up. When you release your grip that other end is closed by the power of the spring. Simple. She wants two springs made like this, but about ten times larger! I asked her what it was all about and she told me I did not want to know. So I shut up. Our relationship is based on mutual respect.

It is an unusual relationship. You seldom find a friendship between a healthy young man and a smart, striking woman that is almost devoid of a sexual element. Ours is. It is intellectual and psychological, each of us meeting some need in the other. What I get out of it is the joy of her top-class mind and her absolute freedom from prejudice – racial or religious or class or political. I also have social benefits. I remember a quote from a minor poet: 'What lasting joys a man attend that has a polished female friend'. It's true. You can rely on her to be dignified and polite and intelligent. And I have immense admiration for

215

what she has achieved in life. What she gets out of our friendship is, I think, the re-assurance of meeting somebody perfectly adjusted to his position in life and unaffected by doubt. She has quite serious internal conflicts from time to time, when she is uncertain about who she is and what she should do. Not surprising, given the road she has travelled. She finds my simplicity and certainty a comfort. I am an unconscious psychological relaxant. Being rich helps, of course.

Does my appearance help as well? Many women find me attractive, and it annoys me just a little that the physical assets buy me nothing extra in Nshila's eyes. Knowing that I am descended from a long line of aristocrats, you would expect me to be the traditional chinless wonder with swept-back straw-coloured hair and a braying laugh. Not so. I am just under six feet tall with a good strong body and a face resembling a friendly bulldog. Fair-haired – yes, I am that – but it sticks up all over like a badly made bottle brush. Women want to re-order it somehow. My voice is deep, and when I laugh you get a dull rumble rather than a bray. But it's all lost on Nshila – she seems to value my serenity much more highly.

It is surprising, perhaps, that I am so well-adjusted. Many sons of rich parents develop a guilt complex and try to give it all away, or join the Communist party and fund a revolution somewhere. I learnt early on that generous use of the goodies showered upon me brought far more happiness than being status-conscious and stand-offish. I am rich, and I enjoy it, and I spread it around. Nothing in my philosophy has changed since the groom's son rode my new mountain bike under the tractor. I was very worried about Jim's injuries, but the bike was nothing. My dad bought me a new one next day. As an adult, I have watched the government spending the nation's money and decided that I am a much better distributor of wealth.

Anyway, I didn't ask to be born with a silver spoon in my mouth. Since it happened, I'm going to enjoy it.

I am intelligent and well-educated. The mind comes from the genes, I suppose, but the education was purchased. They put my name down for Eton the day I was born, and whatever its detractors may say, Eton educates you well. So does Balliol, and if you work hard you can get a First Class Degree. I did. After that, the City of London, first in a broker's office and now as a trader on the stock exchange. I am one of those people who earn a big bonus in a bad year and an obscene one in a good year. Do I need to work? No. But I enjoy it. I love some of the people and I find the excitement of trading in megabucks a colossal thrill.

I met Nshila on a train. I remember the day very well because the evening papers featured the death of a serial rapist who had been acquitted a few years ago on a technicality and was suspected of having resumed his trade. It seemed that he had injected himself with what he believed to be heroin. Unknown to him, somebody had filled the syringe with a deadly poison. Exit the rapist. Nshila had a copy of the same paper and we got talking about the case. The talk flowed on naturally to other subjects. At some point she mentioned that she seldom travelled First Class, but that she had just completed a major business assignment and felt she deserved a treat.

Most casual conversations on trains lead nowhere. Why was ours different? We made the usual enquiries about destinations, finding out that she was going to Bristol to change for Keynsham and I had a car at Bristol Parkway in which I would drive home to Upton Cheyney. The destinations are close. I almost offered to drive her to Keynsham, but decided it would look too pushy. I changed my mind a few minutes later when the conversation turned to motor cars generally. Living in London, she said, the

217

most practical vehicle would be a Mini, but she had been tempted into going for a BMW. She also confessed to a passion for vintage cars of the years between the wars. That morning I had driven to Bristol Parkway in my 1926 2-litre Lagonda, instead of the Ferrari. So then I did offer her a lift. She accepted.

Our friendship has lasted. We meet regularly, but not frequently. When she calls me, it seems to be my company that she wants most. It does not matter what we do or where we go. It has been cricket at Lords or horse racing, or an agricultural show or a walk along the Pennine Way. Once she said, 'Take me to the most desolate place you know!' We ended up at a place called Gedney Drove End on the edge of The Wash, with the tide out. We have never had a sexual relationship. I think we both gain tremendously from what we have, and don't want to enter the turbulent waters that sex often brings. Yes, I find her sexually attractive, but I make no moves. I'm not sure how she sees it. I think she knows a great deal about me because I am not at all reticent. What I know about her is far more limited. I'm sure she has depths that she doesn't disclose. I'm not worried.

When I call her it is most often because I have to go to a party where there will be an excess of city types. We have our fair share of ignorant conceited pigs and many of them have wives or girlfriends to match. Dress-wise, it is a competition to see who can wear least clothing. The conversation is all about who spent most money most wastefully. Nshila doesn't enjoy those events particularly, but comes to help me endure them. When offended by one of the more stupid remarks, she fires off the harshest reply imaginable and I get huge enjoyment from seeing an oaf deflated. After such events I hear her described alternately as 'terrific' and 'vicious', but when I go to a party without her they all seem disappointed.

218

Just once she came to a ball in my family home at Upton Cheyney. She was nervous about it, fearing that our county types would be racially prejudiced. I was able to say that the local Master of Foxhounds was as black as she was. They danced together, but her scarlet ball gown clashed disastrously with his hunting-pink dinner jacket.

Getting those springs for her will be easy.

Chapter Seventeen

Zach Kawero: His Part in the Plan

Nshila rang me one morning and told me to meet her at a West End hotel in twenty minutes. That was just about possible if I dropped everything I was doing, found a taxi easily and met no traffic jams. I did drop everything. I didn't find a taxi quickly. There were two traffic jams. 'You're late, Zach!'

Luckily she was in good humour: sharp, positive and direct, the way she gets when she has solved a problem in her mind and wants you to leap into action.

She has given me three assignments, which seem to be related. A lot of work is involved. I welcome jobs from Nshila because she pays well, but doing all she now wanted to the required standard looked tough. She offers plenty of carrot, but you're never allowed to forget that there's a stick around somewhere. She expects the best, without asking how hard it is to achieve. She once employed a sixth-form schoolboy to do a job. He made a real mess of it and she went totally ballistic. 'Right. You're going to have spots all over your face for the next month!' Like me, he was from Central Africa and had a healthy fear of witchcraft. He had a date coming up with the alpha female in his school and serious acne would kill it dead. He begged her not to do it. She was still mad as a hornet. 'Would you like to be whipped instead, careless schoolboy that you are?' 'Anything, Nshila, but not spots and boils.'

For a moment I thought she would actually find a way to carry out her threat. Then she realised the impracticality of it, and just slapped him twice across the face, very hard.

She hurt him, and I could see that she enjoyed it. Later, she confessed that she has a sadistic streak that she struggles to control. But she paid the schoolboy the full agreed price, despite the uselessness of his work.

For the first assignment she gave me a photograph of a beautiful woman sitting on a garden bench, facing the camera. I judged her to be about thirty years old and on the back was the name Polly Basing. She also gave me a photograph showing a window embrasure in what looked like a ruined castle. It had a grass floor, despite the window being obviously far above ground level. Beside the window was a stone seat.

I was told to use one of the sophisticated photo-enhancement computer programs and put the woman on the stone seat in the castle instead of on the garden seat. When I had done that, I was supposed to create several different images in which the body language of the woman became increasingly provocative. In the first one, Nshila said, the woman must look friendly but neutral. She must then show subtle changes in each image till, in the last one, she was offering an open and irresistible sexual temptation. Nshila suggested things like more buttons undone, the dress pulled lower, and more leg showing. I was told I could change the colours and details of the dress, and even facial expression provided it was obviously the same woman. I had to make sure the lighting suggested an assignation in the evening. Each picture should have words underneath, but Nshila would give me those later on, when she told me how to use the pictures. There was also to be one final picture showing the same woman dressed in a negligee and lying on a grassy bank.

The second assignment was to hack into the Pullmax computer systems and find out all I could about planned take-over moves, and what typically happened to the physical assets of an acquired company. I was told to pay special attention to any traffic involving the work station of an employee named Michael Middleton.

The third assignment was to maximise my own skills at placing messages on particular computer screens. You know about these things from your own experience. You are working away at some task, probably on the Internet, when a message appears out of nowhere asking you to take part in a lottery, or such like, or to buy some marvellous new piece of software at a bargain price. Or the bell rings for incoming mail. You are hoping for a love letter and you find instead an invitation to join a pyramid-selling swindle. Nshila wanted to be quite sure that I could get messages to the right screens, and make them self-destruct after a prescribed time.

I started with what I expected to be the hardest task: the image of Polly Basing. I am skilled with imaging programs, but in this case I found that I was not a good enough artist. Being an artist is about more than wielding a brush. It is also about noticing what you see and interpreting it so well that you can reproduce it. I realised that I had experienced being attracted by a woman, but didn't know what the woman actually did to operate the process. For instance, I might remember that the way she raised her eyebrows at me was provocative, but I could not see it sufficiently well in my mind to get it down on paper – or on my computer screen. All my attempts to show 'degrees of seductive behaviour' were wooden and lifeless.

Finally I hired a model. I found a woman of the right

general appearance and together we put together a series of six configurations of dress and pose and facial expression. She adopted them, I painted them on the screen with my electronic tools, and then we reviewed the outcome together. It was hard work, but the result was terrific. We thought the man chosen to view the pictures would be firmly hooked.

Naturally, this work was done at intervals over two weeks or more. I tackled the other tasks alongside it, and found the third one quite easy. It meant only a small amount of extra learning. The second task, the one concerning Pullmax, meant that I had to report back to Nshila once or twice, because what she intended to do would depend on what I said was possible.

I made my first report sitting in the passenger seat of Nshila's BMW as she drove west down the M4. Mike Fanshawe had persuaded her to meet him in a pub at Lambourn before going to Newbury races. Nshila had decided on a tweed suit and sensible shoes, which made her look older than usual. I was to be dumped at Reading station to make my way back to London.

'Pullmax makes about 15 successful take-overs during a year, and there are about the same number of cases in which they make an offer and are turned down. The targets are all smallish private companies and may be located here or in the USA, or sometimes in South Africa, Australia or New Zealand. Success or failure is determined by the attitude of the shareholders. Sometimes they want to sell their shares and get cash in hand: sometimes they don't. The amount of cash matters, of course. When a take-over is complete, all the shares – and therefore everything the company owns – belongs to Pullmax, which effectively means Brad Pullinger and Eric Holtman. Pullinger, or someone on his staff, looks at the physical assets and decides what to do with them. Suppose, for instance, that they buy a small firm that owns a brewery and ten public houses. Pullmax might sell six public houses to another brewery, turn three into shops, turn one into offices, and knock down the brewery to use as a car park. Suppose also that one of the existing Pullmax companies is in the retail business and another is expanding, and needs extra office space. Ownership of the three pubs deemed suitable for use as shops is transferred to the retail company. Ownership of the pub suitable for becoming offices is transferred to the company needing it. Ownership of the brewery site is sold to the local council.'

'What happens to assets for which there is no obvious use and no immediate sale?'

'They are usually "parked", which means ownership being transferred to an existing company, more or less at random, until somebody gets a bright idea about their future.'

'Who actually makes the decisions, and who does the necessary legal work?'

'Pullinger himself makes more than half. Another quarter are made by a senior manager. The remainder, specially the "parking" decisions, are made by the man you named, Michael Middleton. The decisions are actually carried out by Michael, and he does all the legal work.'

She was silent for a few minutes, concentrating on an aggressive driver who was trying to overtake in the middle lane. She kept perilously close to the car in front so that her enemy had no chance of cutting in. I was scared. After a while the enemy switched to the slow lane to try his luck with somebody else.

'What I want, Zach, is to control the timing of at least one take-over and then control where some of the assets are placed. What can you do about that?'

'The first problem, Nshila, is that we don't know what companies will attract Mr Pullinger, or, if he is attracted

225

to one, when he will make his move. There might be nothing happening for three months or so. I suggest that we make use of companies where he has previously made an offer and been rejected.'

'How will that help?'

'I can hack into the records, and find one or two cases where the sale has been blocked by a few major shareholders refusing to sell, and where the company has since gone downhill and proved disappointing for the shareholders. Then we can send Pullinger an e-mail that appears to come from one such shareholder – or even from an employee – suggesting that a new and improved offer might now be accepted. Pullinger will realise that a target company that previously escaped him is now within reach. There is a good chance that he will make a move.'

'I would like the odds to be more in our favour, Zach. There's no certainty here. I wish we could do it with two or three companies, but I suppose that would be suspicious.'

'Three would be too many, but we might be able to use two. If we can find two companies of the right sort who are reasonably close to each other geographically, then we can invent a third party who happens to be financial adviser to both. It will then appear that he is taking independent action on behalf of two clients.'

'I think that is just about good enough. Bearing in mind that Pullinger may make "normal" offers during the time I am planning for – and that we shall know about them – then I rate our chances as 75 in 100. We can't, of course, do much to influence the acceptance or rejection of the offer. I think I can live with the plan, because it's not the biggest element in my scheme. It's more of an add-on extra that I have become emotionally committed to.'

'I think that's the best we can do, Nshila. About controlling what happens to the assets, I'm sorry to tell you that I have not yet come up with a good answer.'

'It may be enough that you have told me what the procedure is. It depends whether you can promise me to get messages to appear and disappear on Middleton's computer screen.'

'I can do that.'

'Does that mean you are now confident about such messages at any address? If I asked you to send flash messages that would appear and disappear on Peter Grace's screen, in my office, could you do it?'

'Yes.'

We had time in hand, so Nshila stayed on the M4 to Junction Eleven and turned south on the Basingstoke road to find a parking spot in open country. There she went over my ideas in detail to make sure she understood them and believed they would work. She also lit up one of the long, thin cigars that she believes to be good for her image but which offend all non-smokers, like me. I protested. Sometimes she really is over the top. Her response was to finish the cigar and drive me back to Reading station extremely fast.

I can deduce some things about this project of hers, but I would love to know more. As regards the picture, it's obvious that some man is going to be lured to a special location in the expectation of an exciting sexual encounter. Is Polly Basing in on the scheme? If she is, then why this convoluted plot? Maybe she is being used without her knowledge because the target is known to be smitten with her. What's going to happen to the target when he keeps the assignation? Who is the target, anyway? Probably Pullinger.

The stuff about disappearing messages sounds to me like subliminal advertising. She's going to get somebody making the decisions she wants without being aware of her influence. It may not be witchcraft, but it's pretty clever stuff.

There's something else that might be a clue to what is happening, or might not. She is friendly with this city type called Mike Fanshawe, and because of the connection Mike sometimes asks my help on computer projects. She has asked Mike to get two steel springs made. They are not the sort of spring that compresses and expands in a straight line, but the sort that twists. You see things a bit like it making doors swing closed behind you. Or like the spring on a mousetrap, but ten times larger. I asked Mike what it was for, but he said she had refused to tell him. Mike is not at all scared of Nshila because he knows nothing about her witchcraft and simply sees her as a clever girl who operates The Rain Consultancy. He could easily press her for an answer, but he won't. Sometimes I think Mike is a real dumb ox.

Chapter Eighteen

Fleshing out the Plan

Things are falling into place now. I have a plan and it will work. I remember my planning session well. Imagine me in the flat, in casual clothes, enjoying the sublime silence of a deserted City of London on a Sunday morning. Sometimes I spoke to myself in my mind, sometimes I spoke aloud.

The only thing bothering me is that I may be getting too hung up on the side issue of helping Priscilla. I want to do it – no question – but I have been retained to see Pullinger dead and in that I must not fail. It does not bother me that I shall have to pay a lot of money to Zach. The fee is big enough. It does bother me that I might adapt the plan to help Priscilla and thereby lower the chances of a hit on the main target.

I think the schedule has to be worked backwards from the day Pullinger enters paradise – or wherever else he is expected. I need to find dates on which he has no major business events scheduled and a local event around Pluckley will attract him. The seduction picture has to carry a date, telling him when Polly Basing will be there for him. The picture, in one of its variations, has to appear several times on his screen and the first appearance must be sufficiently in advance of the seduction date to allow him to adjust his diary. I have faith in the picture. I think it will do its job. The suggestion is that Polly can't communicate with him openly, but is desperate to meet. No white male with a large ego will be able to resist. But if the seduction date clashes with some appointment that Pullinger can't possibly break, then all our efforts will be wasted.

Things get complicated when we consider the transfer of assets into Braderic Domestic. Getting Pullinger interested in a take-over will need a few weeks, and completing the deal will take a few more. I think eight weeks at least are needed. Say nine to be safe. That's a longer time scale than will be needed to lure Pullinger to the Proposal Chair. Maybe the schedule looks like this:

- WEEK ONE
  Pullmax receives hints that Gregory and Sons and Quorn Quilts Limited are take-over targets. (I have given them names for convenience. We don't know real targets yet.)

- WEEK THREE
  Pullmax makes an offer for one company or the other, or both.

- WEEK FIVE
  One offer is accepted, or the other offer, or both. The first seduction picture appears on the screen of Pullinger's personal computer. The others will be scheduled for intervals of five days.

- WEEK EIGHT
  One or other take-over is completed, and there are new physical assets under the control of the asset management department of Pullmax.

- WEEK NINE
  Ownership of valuable assets is transferred to Braderic Domestic.
  Pullinger exits this world. There must only be a short interval between the asset transfer and the death. Otherwise he might learn what has happened and reverse the transfer.

If it works like that, then I have a firewall between the two halves of the project. The removal of Pullinger can happen even if the asset transfer fails. What have I forgotten? Well, I still haven't done much about making the death 'ignominious' and neither have I mentioned the witchcraft part that will certainly be required. I can do it, of course, and maybe ideas about ignominy will come to me in the process. At worst, the ignominy is non-essential. What my client wants is the corpse.

Thinking along those lines reveals a weakness. I don't have samples of Pullinger's hair and nails. Hair ought to be easy, but when I start thinking seriously about nails it looks tough. Last time I bullied Walter Vokes into doing the job. I realise now that I was demanding a lot, and I wish I had asked him how he did it.

Nail clippings are so small. You can't find them unless you know when and where to look, and people don't cut their nails in public. It has to be done secretly, too, because it is such a strange theft that the victim would be suspicious. I mean, if I rush up to you in the street and grab your handbag, you are very angry about it but you don't sense a mystery. You think: For heaven's sake! Another petty thief after my cash and credit cards. You may not even report it. It's different if you know that somebody has stolen your nail clippings.

I could manage it if the target was unconscious. Being asleep won't do because I would have to grasp a hand or a foot quite firmly to cut a piece of nail off, and the danger of waking would be too great. A tranquillising dart would do the job, or the right dose of a drug: but how do I administer it, unobserved?

Here's the answer. I will hire a couple of low-grade thugs to knock him out in some suitable place like a large, dark car park. Their brief will be to avoid serious damage, merely rendering him unconscious for an hour. I will arrange to be close by, and as soon as he is out they will ring me on my mobile. I will walk in, cut my lock of hair and my piece of fingernail, and disappear. The chances of him noticing that one or two of his nails have been shortened a bit is almost zero. Great idea!

So far in this story I have not made much reference to assassination as a calling or to its social value – which I see as considerable. I have come to see myself more like a gardener than a criminal. A gardener pulls up and destroys weeds so that more desirable types of plant can flourish. That's what Kwaname did, and that's what I do. Looking at it that way, I class some of the known historical assassins as hopeless failures. I mean, what would you think of a gardener who pulled up one noxious weed and never touched another because he had allowed himself to be imprisoned or killed? Yet that's what happened. It happened to John Wilkes Booth who shot Abraham Lincoln. It happened to James Earl Ray who shot Martin Luther King. It happened to Gavrilo Princip who shot the Archduke Franz Ferdinand. It happened to Charlotte Corday who stabbed Marat in his bath. I know that two of those victims were top-class goodies and only Marat deserved to die, but the point I am making is that if you are a one-off assassin you are a professional failure. The best ones are those that we never hear about. They do the job and disappear, sometimes even leaving the world uncertain whether it was assassination or accident or natural causes.

I have often wondered whether the prophet Daniel, in the Christian Bible was one of those. Belshazzar, King of the Chaldeans, gave a big feast in his palace and magical writing appeared on the wall. Nobody could read it, so they sent for the prophet Daniel. Daniel interpreted the words as meaning – freely translated – 'You are finished'. The story concludes: 'In that night was Belshazzar the King of the Chaldeans slain. And Darius the Median took the kingdom.'

Did Daniel orchestrate the whole thing? He obviously set Belshazzar up by putting him in great fear. Did he go back later on with a knife? We don't know. We do know that Daniel went on to become powerful and influential. If he was an assassin, he was a good one.

I do have one heroine, in spite of her being a failure in the sense that her deed became known. It's in the Bible again at Judges, Chapter Four. This tells of a general called Sisera who had a powerful army and was oppressing Israel. He had, the Bible tells us, 'nine hundred chariots of iron' which was an impressive cavalry force in those days. But God decided that Sisera should lose a battle, and the beaten general arrived on foot at a house which he thought was friendly. The wife of the owner was named Jael and she had different loyalties from her husband. Here's how it goes.

> Then Jael, Heber's wife, took a nail of the tent, and took a hammer in her hand, and went softly unto him, and smote the nail into his temple and fastened it into the ground: for he was fast asleep and weary. So he died.

It was not a skilful job at all. You might say it was crude, brutal and unsophisticated. But what determination she showed! What self-control! It was unpleasant, messy and terribly hands-on. Yet Jael was so purposeful. She had made up her mind that it had to be done and that nobody else was going to do it. She closed her mind to all the nastiness and did the necessary. What a girl!

I found an Internet site recently devoted to assassination. A rather odd sentence in it reads: 'Assassination can never be employed with a clear conscience'. (I don't agree). 'Persons who are morally squeamish should not attempt it.' Morally squeamish, Jael was not.

Chapter Nineteen

The Hut on the Churchyard Wall

I changed my focus to consider the witchcraft element. At the same time I remembered the things I wanted from Zach and wondered where the boundaries of witchcraft and science lie. For many people, the sudden appearance and disappearance of strange pictures on a computer screen would be magic. Yet so far as Zach and other hackers are concerned it is a totally logical process using the known properties of natural elements. One man's science is another man's magic.

What about subliminal advertising? I had never tried this before. Can a message be flashed on a screen so fast that the conscious mind fails to notice it but the sub-conscious mind is influenced? Theory says 'Yes'. By that means I intended to influence Michael Middleton to assign assets to Braderic Domestic. I had, of course, already prepared him to be bolder in the exercise of his personal judgement. Is this witchcraft? Are the mental processes involved well enough understood for anybody to describe the process as logical? I don't know. What relationship is there with hypnosis, which certainly works to some degree in some circumstances?

Because this subliminal business was new to me, I decided to try a parallel experiment. Zach had said that he could put subliminal messages on Peter Grace's screen.

I knew that Peter was accustomed to eat a huge amount of chocolate but never touched the thing called Peppermint Cream. Getting him addicted to the product by subliminal advertising would prove the case and do Peter no harm.

You know by now that I favour out-of-town locations for the witchcraft element. Eastcheap is no good. Visitors may come round, or some government official wanting to inspect things, or a repairman coming to mend the cooker. I cast minor spells in Eastcheap and practice tarot readings, but only things demanding small and easily hidden equipment. For the bigger stuff I like to find special locations, furnishing and using them once only. Perhaps because of my childhood memories I prefer old, scruffy buildings in rural areas. They are not difficult to find. All the changes in agricultural practice have left unused huts, sheds, barns and outbuildings all over the country. I once used a tree house on a large estate. It had been, at one time, the treasured refuge of young children and I found enamelled plates, an empty beer bottle and a very large teddy bear. He was mouldy. This time I found a shed in a churchyard.

Things did not go exactly as I intended. To make matters clear I will have to unveil my plan in more detail. First, have you ever seen an old-fashioned mousetrap? Most modern houses are mouse-free, and if any invasion takes place then poison is the normal answer. It was not like that in older buildings, and especially in streets of older houses such as described in *The Tailor of Gloucester*. Would you believe that I read *The Tailor of Gloucester* in my primary school out there in the bush? Goodness knows how the book arrived there, but it did, and we read and enjoyed it. Here's the bit I mean:

... behind the wooden wainscots of all the old houses in Gloucester, there are little mouse staircases, and

236

secret trapdoors; and the mice run from house to house through these long narrow passages; they can run all over the town without going into the streets.

People who did not like mice had mousetraps then. It was a piece of flat wood a little smaller than a postcard. Imagine a postcard-sized piece of wood in front of you, placed portrait-wise. Now imagine a piece of strong metal wire that's bent into a rectangular frame and lies on one half of the wood. Where it lies across the middle of the wood it is held by brackets so that it is hinged along that central line. There are two strong springs at the centre to keep the metal frame firmly against the top half of the wood. If you raise the outer edge of the wire frame and pull it back through the vertical position to lie on the other half, you are pulling against the spring. Hold it there by some sort of catch, and the trap is set. If the catch is released, the metal frame will flash through 180 degrees and slam down onto the other side, killing any small creature in the way.

My Pullinger trap was going to be half a mousetrap and measured in feet instead of inches. That makes the 'postcard' about six foot by two-and-a-half and the metal frame about three foot by two-and-a-half. Imagine such a thing set half in and half out of an opening in a high wall. That sounds ridiculous, I know, but the point is that I don't need the half that sticks out, and I don't even need the wood. All I need is the metal frame and the springs. The hinged side of the frame can be held to the ground with something like a croquet hoop or the staples you use these days for tent pegs. When the trap is not set, the metal rectangle will be sticking out into space, but except for a few moments when the deed has been done that will never be the case. When it is set, it will lie with one edge concealed in the grass exactly on the lip of the opening and the rest, equally concealed, behind it. Once I have lured Pullinger into position in the doorway, I can release the catch by a radio signal. The top end of the metal rectangle will strike him in the small of the back with enough force to propel him into space.

After developing this concept I asked myself: Is it simple enough? Can I think of anything easier? The short answer was 'Yes'. Once you are working on the concept of knocking the victim forward, you can't ignore the old method of the swinging sandbag. I could hang a string bag full of rocks from the top of the doorway and draw it back on a rope so that it was well behind the doorway and above it. When triggered, it would be certain to swing through the opening. Geometry would ensure it.

I went for the mousetrap idea. The swinging weight was simpler, but not by a great margin and the mousetrap was so unlikely. What investigating officer was ever going to come up with the idea of the victim being killed by a mousetrap?

So I went off to my chosen witchcraft location with a normal-sized mousetrap, and a model of Pullinger to match it, and the materials for a much larger model as well. The small one was to act out the mousetrap scenario and the larger one to ensure the fatal outcome. My churchyard shed had been used as a store for garden equipment but was now empty. Perhaps the care of the churchyard had been contracted out. It was at the very edge of the churchyard where the level was higher than the road and the back of the hut was like an upward extension of the retaining wall. If you pushed a stone through one of the many holes in the wall of the hut, it fell into the lane below. The holes were worst at floor level. One was several inches high, and equally wide.

I did some horoscope research to decide which date would be most favourable and took possession of the hut half-an-hour after midnight. I hung various impedimenta on the walls, created a hot, smoky and scented atmosphere, and started work.

An image must have marked similarity to the target person. It does not have to be exact, but there must be at least one obvious characteristic that the image and the real person share. It's like a cartoon. The cartoonist picks a distinctive feature, exaggerates that, and does not worry too much about the rest. When you see the result you know immediately who it is meant to be. I have just said that the rest of it does not matter too much. That's true in a sense, but it must contain nothing that contradicts the primary similarity. For instance, if your subject had huge ears and was otherwise of normal size and stature, it would be wrong to have an image that had huge ears and was also monstrously fat. Somebody would die, probably a fat man with huge ears, but it would not be your target. I knew from overhearing Millie and Priscilla in the tea room, that Pullinger had a huge scar on his forehead and remarkably large hands.

I had a minor problem over image size, because I wanted Pullinger to smash his skull when he fell from the gap beside the Proposal Chair and save me the aggravation of finishing him off. So I planned to make the head out of an egg and let it smash on the floor. The head accounts for about one ninth of the height of a human and if your image is to be in the right proportions you will find it needs to be about twenty inches long. It won't go in your handbag. The smaller image, of course, the one to use with the mousetrap, went in easily.

I put the larger image together on site. I really wanted this thing to work, so I talked to both images while I was doing it to make the identity quite clear. 'Now your legs, Mr Pullinger,' I said. 'The right one seems a tiny bit shorter than the left. We must correct that. We don't want to hit some local worthy who happens to have a limp, do we?' The job took some time, and the atmosphere made me hot and sticky and a trifle light-headed. There were moments when I was mentally back in the hut under the baobab tree and could almost feel Kwaname standing beside me. 'Do it carefully, Nshila. Don't go too fast. We have plenty of time.' I got the spells in place just before fate struck.

As I was placing the small image in position on the mousetrap, I remembered that Pullinger had a son! I had quite forgotten Angus, presumably asleep in the safety of Garden Lodge. Was it possible that the spirits would get the wrong message and decide that Angus was the target? Would he get shoved off the trapeze in the school gymnasium and break some bones? What an awful thought! After all, I was making two images, and one of the dimmer spirits might think this was a father-and-son operation: a sort of dynastic kill. What could I do? I deepened the scar on the face of the smaller image, and flattened the hands a bit so that they looked even larger, and scratched the name 'Brad' on the back. That was the best I could manage.

I put him in position on the mousetrap and sprung it. Now, I had not bothered to replicate the exact situation and was using an ordinary unmodified trap. The wire sprang up exactly as planned and smote Pullinger hard in the small of the back and threw him forward. The trouble was that the speed of the wire did not throw him fast enough to escape the downward force once the wire had passed its highest point. He ended up with his feet caught underneath the wire and the rest of his body hanging over the edge of the wood. I did not see how this could happen in reality, but it still worried me.

I turned my attention to the larger model, intended to ensure that the fall was fatal. I had another shock.

The church clock struck twice. It was particularly loud

in the silence of the night and I had not been expecting it. Various birds were disturbed by the noise, and a large owl flew in through a gap under the roof. For all I know the hut was his normal home and he saw me as an intruder. For whatever reason, he flapped around aggressively before settling in his corner. I was startled and must have made a series of nervous movements. One of them knocked the image off the work bench and Pullinger fell through the largest of the holes in the wall. He disappeared into the lane below.

Just as he fell, some yob in a fast car shot by underneath with rock music blaring from the speakers. My image cleared the back of the car by inches and I was really mad at myself. 'How stupid can you get, Nshila?'

I recovered the image, finding that the fall had smashed it thoroughly. But would the accident affect things? It was smashed, but I had not personally smashed it. What would happen? Well, I had no time to carry out the whole thing over again so I convinced myself that everything would work as planned. I sat for a while outside the shed to get over the trauma I had endured. I left the door fully open so that the smell of my activities would be lost. It was one of those rare nights, in Europe, when one could see the stars clearly and it was all very peaceful. I dreamt briefly of being back in the village, but it was not bright enough, and I could not smell the sun-baked earth or hear lions in the distance. Nor was there the deafening noise of the crickets. Looking around the churchyard I saw an iron basket in which people throw the dead flowers that they have removed from graves. It seemed an excellent place to get rid of the images, so I broke them into small bits and buried them deep under the vegetation. Possibly a refuse collector would wonder what a broken raw egg was doing amongst dead flowers from churchyard graves. Let him wonder.

I was back in Eastcheap by 8.30 a.m. feeling tired and dirty and much in need of a long hot bath with plenty of bath oil. I reflected that most elements of the plan were now in place. And yet, could I do anything more to reinforce the Priscilla benefit strategy? Perhaps. During the next week I arranged two telephone calls to Michael Middleton. The caller pretended to be Priscilla and asked for information about the worth of the company. She put on her most charming manner and implied that she had received an offer for her shares and wanted to know what to do. This caused Michael, I hoped, to perceive Priscilla as a charming person who was also rather needy. She also asked him how to go about transferring shares into the name of her son Angus.

Chapter Twenty

The Deed

The day dawned. In the morning I watched every news programme. Why? Well, I have told you often enough that I don't know for sure whether or how or why the witchdoctoring works. Suppose my activities in the churchyard shed had done the business already? Perhaps Pullinger had fallen down his cellar steps when he went to get his Chateau Excelsis 1911. The environs of Corner Wood Hall might even now be swarming with police investigators.

If I had heard of it, would I have been disappointed? Mixed emotions, probably. I was all psyched up to do the deed and finding it unnecessary would have been a let-down. But I would also have been pleased with the extra evidence of my witchdoctoring success and grateful for the removal of risk. Something similar happened to me once before, in a minor way. I had been asked to make sure that a horse failed to turn up for a race. I think it was at Doncaster. I had cast a variety of spells to block the relevant roads and planted a bug on the horsebox so that I could follow its progress. The plot on my receiver never moved at all and I was close to panic. I was all set to apologise profusely to the client and waive my fee when he rang me himself, full of gratitude and praise. Apparently some vandals had slashed the tyres of the horsebox in the stable yard. It had never started out.

When I spoke about being worried whether a spell would work, you may have wondered if I sometimes fail. After all, I have emphasised the uncertainty of the craft often enough. The answer is 'Yes'. I will tell you about one of them. A girl in my year at LSE was extremely clever, knew it, and was constantly attempting to make other people look stupid. In seminars, she always managed to suggest that objections to her views must come from morons who ignored the facts and failed to use their brains. She poured scorn on everybody else, and since she was intellectually very good, it often worked. She was what I call a brain bully. She was well hated by the majority, and adored by a small group of dumber students who accepted her leadership. She was proud of her long blonde hair, and I tried a baldness spell. I knew the technique quite well because Kwaname had used it three times in my presence. It was a limited spell, involving no likelihood of serious injury or death. It was meant to make all her hair fall out and cause a few years of misery till it grew again.

What happened? On a very hot day her hair got caught in a large electric fan somebody had brought into the lecture room. She was screaming in pain, and right at that moment a power cut occurred. I mean a general power cut, with all the lights going off and the lecturer's presentation slides going black. It was not a matter of somebody pulling the plug from the wall to save her. It was near enough to an act of God. Her hair was untangled from the fan and she lost only a few strands. Why did that happen? Maybe my spell was not specific enough. Maybe my spell had no effect at all and the whole fan incident was a chance event that would have happened anyway. I did not know then, and I don't know now. It was a good thing I had told nobody what I was going to do.

Back now to the morning of my date with Pullinger. Radio never mentioned him, nor television, and early in the afternoon I drove to Pluckley, concealed the car in a remote wood and walked in my combat suit to a point below The Keep. I saw nobody and nobody saw me. Carrying my frame trap, the steel springs that Mike had produced, and a clever electronic signal device I climbed to the Proposal Chair.

Going to the edge of the doorway into space, I cleared a narrow strip of earth and laid the hinged end of my frame, with the springs, in a shallow trough. I fixed it securely into place with croquet hoops and covered it all up. The 'striking' edge of my frame was now lying outside the wall and the springs were under no tension. The problem now was to haul the 'striking' edge back through 180 degrees into the 'set' position. It proved much harder than I had anticipated. I had to tie a rope round the outlying edge of the frame, pass this over a rock, and pull with all my weight before I even got that edge to the upright position. Then I found I could not get it down through the extra 90 degrees, and I was almost catapulted through the opening myself. Finally I found a plank of wood, balanced some stones on it, and used that contraption to give me extra downward thrust. At last the catch clicked over the frame. I was shaking and sweating. Anyway, I thought, the springs are fully strong enough to do the job. The power would surely throw a body over the edge. I covered all the remaining exposed parts with grass. I could still just see where the trap lay, but it was unlikely to catch the unsuspecting eye. When the electronic box received my remote signal, the catch would be released and the trap would operate.

I then placed a mobile telephone on the Proposal Chair and left. Three hours remained before Pullinger was due to arrive, but it's good to have time in hand for emergencies.

245

However, time for reflection can be a pain. You know how, as soon as you have done something, you think of a way you could have done it better, but it's too late? It crossed my mind then that I might have fixed poisoned needles onto the edge of my frame so that they pierced the back of Pullinger's jacket when the edge struck. Or I might even have used piano wire instead and taken his head off! I dismissed these thoughts quickly enough because they would have looked less like accidents.

Shortly before the assignation time I was sitting in a tree and able to see what was going on while remaining concealed. I had my field glasses, and my mobile phone and the radio transmitter to release the catch of my trap. As you can imagine, I was apprehensive.

It began. I saw Pullinger emerge from Corner Wood Hall, and he was carrying a bottle of champagne. He did not go to his garage. He did not walk down the drive. He walked directly towards The Keep. It was wildly exciting to watch the prey accepting the lure. I lost sight of him while he was climbing the stairs, but saw him emerge into the green area at the top. Time for the next step. On my own mobile phone I dialled the number of the phone left on the Proposal Chair and watched his startled movement as it rang. I saw him recognise the signal, pick up the phone, and press the answer button. He stared at the screen. I knew what he was seeing because I had engineered it. He was seeing the picture of Polly Basing reclining on a green bank in her negligee and he was reading the text message 'Look over the edge'. He was expecting the final acts of enticement and consummation. He was seconds away from taking up the required position in the doorway and getting my mousetrap in his back! I have never experienced a feeling like it. I had manipulated him every step of the way: he was inside my trap. Would he realise what had happened in the last moments as he fell to his death? Come on, Pullinger! Just a few inches more to get you on the perfect spot. And then:

I dropped my transmitter! It fell quietly onto the grass below my tree!

England has very good trees and your children have plenty of practice getting up and down them. In my country trees are smaller and less inviting, and children of my tribe don't climb them much. They are not very skilled. Nor am I. I went down that tree in a mad panic, hurting myself considerably. If a forensic science team ever examines that tree they will have no trouble finding samples of my skin from which to extract my DNA. I started on the way up again. After all my efforts, I thought, Pullinger was about to give up the chase in disappointment and walk out of the trap unknowing and undamaged!

The Keep came into view again, as I climbed. Where was he? Thank Goodness! He was in the doorway, leaning far out. He must have decided that Polly had been delayed and was scanning the horizon for her approach. I was still in time. I was just bringing the transmitter into line when:

He fell!

Quite naturally. With no help from me. He leaned out too far in the hope of seeing Polly in the distance, his foot slipped, and he fell. Heavily. Hard. He did not move once.

Ten minutes I must have sat in that tree! I was absolutely shattered. Pullinger was dead (although I still had to check it) but all my clever planning had been unnecessary. It was a massive anti-climax. I felt cheated. Eventually I realised that some cleaning up had to be done and I ought to stop behaving like a zombie. To make sure my trap would have worked, I pushed the button on my transmitter. The frame came up with a flash and a whooshing sound and lay quivering in the air outside the wall. It would have worked.

That's one part of the story told. With an extremely flat feeling, I checked that Pullinger was dead, collected my gear, and drove back to Eastcheap. I was seriously tired and even a bath and a bottle of wine did not stop me fretting. What had I really done? Had I killed him? If I should ever stand in a court of law it would be impossible to convict me of murder or even of unlawful killing. He had died in an accident! No doubt about it! And you can't kill people by witchcraft, can you? The most I could be found guilty of was plotting to kill him, and failing. But if I was not guilty of killing him, could I honestly claim my fee? Suppose he had died from some other type of accident. Suppose he had attempted to foil a bag-snatcher and been stabbed to death by the criminal in a way that was nothing to do with me. If my client found out about it would he refuse payment?

Your mind does not work too well when you are tired. In the morning it was all clear. 'Don't agonise over things that will never happen, Nshila. Just take the money and enjoy it. For a while I shall be able to match Mike's spending pattern!'

Chapter Twenty-One

A Full House

The next days were both worrying and boring. Pullinger was not found immediately. His housekeeper was accustomed to abrupt appearances and disappearances and was also rather deaf. She knew he did not like questions and interference, and she might easily have missed his saying, 'I'm going back to London'. Why did she not check where his car was? Because she knew nothing about the cars and would not have known if one was missing. Additionally, she disliked Pullinger and felt no need to act as his minder. So she did absolutely nothing for the first twenty-four hours and only telephoned his office in the late afternoon of the second day. The person she talked to confirmed that Pullinger had not been into the office but said, 'It's not unusual for him to rush off to one of our companies without telling us. I don't think you ought to worry yet'.

On the third day a policeman came to Corner Wood Hall in the hope of interviewing Pullinger about a traffic accident to which he had been a witness. This officer had been involved with missing person cases in the past, most of whom turn up unharmed. Nevertheless he reported the facts to his superior. The latter felt that it was wise to go through the right motions, but did so with little urgency.

During these days I was getting really worried, and

annoyed with myself for imperfect planning. Why was this? Surely I ought to be grateful for the fact that the extra time would make any clues more difficult to read. That's true, but I kept thinking back to the African environment in which a scavenger might have found and shifted the body or even completed the job of eating it. The big predators are killers and not carrion-eaters, but hyenas are a different matter. Call me an idiot and tell me that nothing like that happens in England, but the idea still bugged me. For I needed Pullinger officially dead in order to complete my contract: Pullinger missing was no use to me. I also had the legacy from Mrs McAllister to worry about. She might die at any moment, and if Pullinger was alive when she departed then all the money would go his way. If he pre-deceased her then it would go to Oxfam. Success or failure for one of my objectives might depend on a pathologist's estimated time of death. The pathologist might get it wrong, and I, knowing the right answer, would be unable to correct him.

I cursed myself for being so fixated on bringing about his death that I had never appreciated how little he was valued when alive! For me, his removal was an event that dwarfed the normal business of life. I had subconsciously assumed that it would attract immediate attention. I had not grasped that people who had dealings with Pullinger might react to his absence with quiet relief and a hope that it would continue.

I was saved on the fourth day when Constable Pegworth decided that young Fred Jenson might be telling the truth when he reported a dead body at The Keep at Corner Wood Hall. Fred had a reputation as a skilled liar who would do almost anything to attract attention, so it took time for Pegworth to make a check. He put it off till he had made enquiries about a stolen commercial van and the suspected theft of eggs from a nest of protected birds.

Finally he got to The Keep and found the body. The pathologist reported three days later, and his estimate of the time of death was only two hours wrong. A phone call to Honeyridge revealed that Mrs McAllister was hanging on. 'Nobody thought she would last into this month, but she's a tough old bird'. Well done, Mrs McAllister!

How about Priscilla? As soon as the death was public knowledge I rang Pullmax and represented myself as a solicitor for Mrs Pullinger. 'My client is aware that under the terms of his will she inherits shares in Braderic Domestic that give her effective control of the company. Can you tell me anything about the worth of the company?' After passing me around from one official to another, a voice I knew came on the line. Michael Middleton! Help! He might well recognise my voice. I broke the connection abruptly and got Gillian to ring back a few minutes later, asking for him by name. The answer was great. 'Until recently the company was worth very little, but we have transferred certain items into its ownership and it is now asset-rich.'

'What assets?'

'The most valuable is a hotel in Cheshire. There is also a charter aircraft business that owns three light aircraft and a plot of building land near Hull.'

Bingo! The proceeds ought to do Priscilla some good.

The national papers gave little space to Pullinger. Some serious international news broke at the time, and the accidental death of a tycoon of modest rank was given a single column on an inside page. It was factual, saying that he had fallen from a vantage point in a ruined keep that stood on his estate. Comment followed about his business enterprises, referring to one or two ventures that the city deemed shady.

The reports were sufficient justification for me to post my client an invoice. It referred to 'Services performed up to and including' the date of death. I knew that I could not at present claim any bonus due to an 'ignominious death' but I had not yet given up hope. Maybe details of his worst crimes might yet emerge, and cause somebody or other to categorise him publicly as an evildoer who had got what he deserved.

A different reporting line was taken in *The Garden Gazette*, which was a weekly covering large areas of Kent. The editor there deemed the story worth expanding into a romantic mystery and sent a reporter with a hyper-active imagination.

'Tragic echoes of past romance!' screamed the headline. 'At the majestic ruins of The Keep at Corner Wood Hall a mysterious death recalled the hates and loves of the past. Centuries ago, bowmen on these walls fired arrows at the besieging army: boiling oil was poured from the parapets onto the scaling ladders. In later years the arrow slit was widened to a window and a beautiful girl watched from it for the first glimpse of her lover. A few days ago the present owner, P.B. Pullinger, successful businessman and local worthy, fell from this opening to his death. Why was he there? Did he have some secret assignation? What caused him to fall? Is there some terrible development expected in his business affairs that caused him to take his own life? We understand that the Department of Health and Safety has recently demanded extra safety precautions at The Keep before visitors can be allowed. Was Mr Pullinger choosing the best place for barriers and guard rails? How sad that he should fall to his death while striving to making the place safe.'

The text, most of which was untrue, was powerfully illustrated. A picture of The Keep had been scanned into a digital art program and modified to show different views of the opening. In one of them it was an arrow slit with an arrow protruding from it. In the next it was a much larger opening with the stonework of a window but no glass. There was a silhouette of a woman in the opening. The third showed the present state with the marks of slipping feet and a body hurtling to the ground.

In the bar of the Plantagenet Arms *The Garden Gazette* (The GeeGee in local terminology) was subjected to ribald comment. There was polite grief about the death, but extreme amusement at the inaccuracy of the report. 'The GeeGee has excelled itself this time. It is always good entertainment, but how they have the nerve to call it a newspaper I can't imagine!' That was the general view.

'Circulation. That's the answer,' said Mick Grant. 'You have to get the readership up in order to attract the advertisers. If you get readership, by whatever means, then the advertisers can be persuaded to take space. That's where the money lies.'

Nick Horam objected. 'But printing rubbish won't increase readership. In time, people will decide that there's nothing in the GeeGee worth looking at.'

'Depends how you define rubbish, Nick.' This from Frank Halliday. 'You and I know the piece about The Keep is pure fabrication, but for others it's an exciting story. You don't bother too much these days if a story is true. Look at the masses of people who identify with soap operas and treat them as more real than their own lives.'

'What do you suppose will happen to Corner Wood Hall now?' Janet Hare asked the question. 'Do you think a tragic accident will raise the value or lower it?'

'I don't think that will be a major factor,' replied Vince Gresham. 'What will be really important is whether the estate is sold with or without The Keep. Most buyers will see it as a disadvantage these days. With the government taking so much interest in old buildings, the owner will be afflicted with impossible regulations, whether he makes any use of the place or not. Possession will be a burden.'

253

'But somebody like old Laythorpe might take it on.' This was Nick Horam again. 'His effort failed, but that was a few years back and he did not have unlimited money. As each year goes by people have more and more leisure and want more and more entertainment. Look at these theme parks that are springing up.'

'Are you thinking of Disneyland in Pluckley?' Mick Grant joined in. 'I don't know how that would affect trade here at The Planty. Would we get a share of all the tourists, or would they all stick inside Corner Wood Hall?'

'Probably the hall. You should try for an exclusive catering session for the place.'

'It would depend on the scale of the operation. And that would depend on how much money the proprietor had got, or could screw out of investors. It might be quite a modest theme park, concentrating on history. I think a major Disneyland-type affair would be impossible in our overcrowded county. We don't have the appropriate access for the thousands of vehicles. And think of all the people who would object to the idea!'

'Yes. I can think of a few who know which levers to pull. I don't think we have too much to worry about.'

'Excuse me, but are you talking about the ruin at Corner Wood Hall?' A woman who had been sitting with a companion in a window seat edged into the group round the bar.

'Yes we are. Do you know the place?'

'I certainly do. I researched it years ago for Mr Laythorpe and wrote quite a decent history. Then he ripped all the truth out of it and printed a leaflet that was a load of lurid rubbish. What's happened to the place now?'

'Only a death. The latest owner fell out of a window and killed himself.'

'My goodness! Is that what you are looking at in the paper? By the way, my name is Gwen Charmount. May I have a look?'

There was silence while Gwen read the article. Three times she snorted in disgust.

'What do you think of it?' Nick Horam asked.

'First thing of all, how did the GeeGee get this way? When I lived here it was quite an accurate reporter of local events and had good general features about country matters.'

'We have one-way traffic in this country now.' Vince Gresham spoke up. 'If the GeeGee is going downhill then it's just keeping in step with the food and the railways and the weather and television and state education.'

'You have to be right about downhill. I guess this must be good entertainment for some readers, but it really gets up my nose when things are as wide of the mark as this. I can see hardly anything here in the description of The Keep that is not hopelessly wrong. They can't even get the names of the architectural features right.'

'You write and tell them, then. The GeeGee quite likes printing argumentative stuff. Whoever wrote that piece won't love you, but the editor will.'

'Good idea. Anyway, thanks for filling me in. I'm glad I interrupted you.'

'That's all right. Will you have a drink with us?'

Gwen Charmount and her husband joined the group round the bar and the discussion continued for some time. A great deal was said about Pullinger and his accident, but not much about the history of The Keep.

The following week the main text of Gwen's letter appeared in the GeeGee inside an editorial piece headed 'WAS IT A ROMANTIC EXIT? PROMINENT LOCAL HISTORIAN SAYS NO!'

Readers of our last issue will not have missed the

255

dramatic piece about the accidental death of P.B. Pullinger, who fell from an opening in the walls of The Keep, a ruined castle that stands in his grounds.

Most of us thought that this opening was a window, from which, in earlier days, the lady of the castle might have watched for the return of her husband or lover. We speculated that perhaps Mr Pullinger had some romantic assignment lined up and was leaning out of the opening like the 'blessed damozel' to catch sight of his beloved. Alas, our dream is shattered. Gwen Charmount, a respected local historian, writes thus:

> I researched The Keep at Corner Wood Hall some years ago at the request of the then owner, Mr Laythorpe. Amongst the documents I turned up were some drawings in the county archives of what it looked like in 1505. At that time it had plenty of arrow slits but nothing large enough to be called a window. What it did have was a latrine chute. The opening from which Mr Pullinger fell has been much enlarged over the years and somebody ignorant of the history might well have thought it had been a window. In later and more peaceful times castles did indeed have windows and this would have been a natural mistake. But serious research of the structure shows beyond doubt that this was the latrine chute; a civilised facility, in those days, for discharging human waste into the moat. If there were a stone seat close by, it would not have been occupied by a lady watching for her lover, but by an anxious soldier, desperate for the man before him to hurry up. The poor fellow who suffered this fall may have entered heaven through

the pearly gates but he left this world through
a very sordid channel.

As I have told you before, I subscribe to a press cutting
agency, and The Keep was one of the code words I had
given them to watch for. Their report reached me two
weeks after Pullinger's death, when I had almost given
up hope of earning my bonus. Was this going to be
enough? Disappearing down a latrine chute was certainly
an ignominious exit, but *The Garden Gazette* was a local
paper with limited circulation. Would my client disgorge?
Did one article in a local paper tell enough people about
Pullinger's fate?

I was in two minds. Nobody likes missing out on a
bonus, but I don't like haggling over payment and I don't
like dissatisfied customers. If I asked for the money and
the client protested then I would have the sort of argument
that I find distressing.

Luck came my way. I say that, but what is luck, really?
The engineering definition of 'chance' is 'the absence of
an assignable cause'. That does not mean to say that no
cause exists: merely that nobody can put their finger on
it. Who knows what criterion is used by the minion in
the broadcasting service who picks the 'fillers' that end
a news programme? You know the sort of thing I mean.
The interesting bits of the news end just two minutes
before the scheduled time, and they need something to
say in those last moments. They have a stock of unusual
and amusing items of the 'man bites dog' type or 'Fire
chief rescues pedigree cat'. There has to be a minion who
controls that archive of clips, and he sorts out something
suitable. He knows, for instance, that 'gigantic pothole
swallows London bus' was on air yesterday and that 'last
manned level crossing in Scotland goes electric' was featured
last week. So transport-related things are out and he must

go, perhaps, for 'Magpie steals wedding ring outside church' or 'Charwoman left a million in Managing Director's will'. Somehow or other the story of Pullinger and the window versus latrine chute controversy caught his fancy. The moat was described as rat-infested and they included a beautiful shot of the place. By 'beautiful' I mean beautiful in my eyes. The place looked totally revolting: something swimming across it with a tiny head showing above the water could well have been a rat.

I had a full house. Pullinger dead. The 'ignominious' point made. Priscilla Pullinger a rich woman. Mrs McAllister's legacy safe.

There was a sequel that I had never expected when Pullinger's baby sister turned up. My research had shown no close relatives. Apparently Juliet was much younger, the child of his parents' old age, and had never been close to her brother. She saw the report of his death on the news and made contact with the local police. It took her a while to decide what to do, but in the end she made up her mind that family loyalty required a decent burial with all the proper trimmings. I went to it, intending to avoid being noticed, but only a few people attended and I stuck out a little. So I passed myself off as a secretary in Pullmax to whom Pullinger had once been kind. I rather think that Juliet was conned by the undertakers into buying more than was necessary. The estate had plenty of money, and I imagine the undertakers asked whether she wanted 'the full service'. She probably could not be bothered to investigate what that meant. There was a full team of bearers, all in frock coats and top hats and on the top hats were those little strips of cloth called 'weepers'. It looked so dignified, and I loved the incongruity of such a fine turnout for such a vile human. I gave full marks to Juliet for a brave personal performance. She did the eulogy herself, and made

Pullinger look quite a decent fellow. She obviously remembered the views of Mark Anthony that 'the evil that men do lives after them' and hoped to prevent it. Good try, Juliet. If I had not known the truth I would have been convinced that the world was worse for his death and not better.

At the graveside I listened to the clergyman saying 'In sure and certain hope of a glorious resurrection'.

In this case, I hope not.

Two weeks later, I walked into the office and found six bars of Peppermint Cream on Peter Grace's desk. 'Are your tastes changing, Peter?'

'They certainly are. I wish somebody had told me about these things years ago. I was somehow all against them. I have been missing out in a big way.'

The icing on the cake! Haven't I done well!